Cast (

Beatrice Adela Lestrange Bradley. ...ing *A Small Handbook of Psychoan...* ....gy of crime, she also works as a private detective and frequently is called upon by the police to assist in criminal investigations.

Fenella Lestrange. Mrs. Bradley's great-niece, she is on her way to be married when she stops in the village of Seven Wells for lunch and finds herself involved in strange Mayering rituals.

Jack-in-the-Green. Fenella meets up with the folk lore character on more than one occasion. She will come to know him by another name and will not be displeased.

Sir Bathy Bitton-Bittadon. The local squire and a bit of a lecher but popular with the locals in his own way. He is murdered even before Fenella reaches the village.

Lady Bitton-Bittadon. His younger, second wife and at 41 still a great beauty.

Jeremy Bitton-Bittadon. Sir Bathy's son by his first marriage. He's just back from India. He's fiancially quite well off on his own.

Jem & Liz Shurrock. They run the local pub, *More to Come*, and warn Fenella to avoid Mayering activities.

Sukie Lee. A gypsy, she cooks at the pub and is rumored to be Jem's mistress.

Clytie. The pub's young general maid.

Bob. The pub's general factotum and Clytie's young man.

Hubert and Miriam Cromleigh. Brother and sister, they are Fenella's cousins.

The Kingleys. They take over the running of the *More to Come*.

Detective Inspector Callan. He's officially in charge of the case and answers to **Superintendent Soames.**

The Zodiacs. They see to it that the special local Mayering traditions are carried out. Finding out who hides behind their masks could be important.

Talbot. He's hardly worth mentioning, as Fenella would tell you if asked.

A HEARSE ON MAY-DAY

A Mrs. Bradley mystery

Gladys Mitchell

Rue Morgue Press
Lyons, Colorado

A HEARSE ON MAY-DAY

First published in Great Britain in 1972
First U.S. Edition 2012

Copyright 1972 © by the Executors of the Estate of Gladys Mitchell
New Material Copyright © 2012 by The Rue Morgue Press

978-1-60187-066-7

Rue Morgue Press
87 Lone Tree Lane
Lyons CO 80540

ABOUT GLADYS MITCHELL

Gladys Mitchell's career as a mystery writer began in the late 1920s during the Golden Age of Detection and carried into the 1980s. Critics of the genre called her one of the "Big Three" women mystery writers of the age, the other two being Agatha Chistie and Dorothy L. Sayers. Most of ther books feature Beatrice Adela Lestrange Bradley, a brilliant woman who doesn't suffer fools gladly but is capable of showing great kindness to others, whether it be an aging village woman, reluctant witnesses or the grandson she obviously adores. She is far more understanding of murderers than the police or other fictional detectives of the Golden Age (1913-1947), partly because as a psychiatrist she takes the time to understand their motives. This may explain why many of her murderers escape the gallows or long prison terms. Her moral values are her own, not society's. She considers rape, because of its long-lasting psychologically damage, a far more serious offense than a murder committed in the heat of the moment. Indeed, she has even been driven to commit murder herself, obviously getting away with it. She certainly shows more sympathy than we would to the murderer in, say, *Death at the Opera* whose motive—well, that would be telling.

Educated at several universities and holding a degree in medicine, she operates a clinic and is a consultant to the Home Office. She is the author of several books, including *A Small Handbook of Psychoanalysis*. Specializing in the psychology of crime, she also works as a private detective, though it is not always clear if she collects a fee for those services. "Her detecting methods," as Michele Slung so aptly put it in *Twentieth Century Crime and Mystery Writers*, "combine hoco-pocus and Freud, seasoned with sarcasm and the patience of a predator toying with its intended victim." Mitchell herself admitted that she was not surprised that Mrs. Bradley "annoys people," since "she is never wrong... she has a godlike quality of being much larger than life, and of being so much superior to ordinary people." She is also surprisingly skilled at a number of physical activities, from billiards to knife-throwing, and, on one occasion, when a cellist was unable to perform, Mrs. Bradley stepped in and played flawlessly, "smirking" at the audience's enthralled appreciation "like a satisfied boa-constrictor." She became a Dame of the British Empire in 1955.

As one of the most famous women in England, Mrs. Bradley's reputation almost always precedes her to a crime scene. While at times this puts witnesses on guard—eventually Mrs. Bradley's persuasive powers allow her to break through their reserve—it also prompts others to open up to her, partly because she has an extremely mellifluous voice. However, she is known to frequently cackle in delight, especially at her own brilliance.

Her voice may be the only attractive thing about her. Her reptilian, almost repulsive appearance combined with a bizarre fashion sense would make her a formidable subject for one of those extreme makeover programs so popular on television today. Mitchell based Mrs. Bradley's looks on "two delightful and most intelligent women I knew in my youth." She is frequently compared to a lizard ("dry without being shrivelled") or to a "dreadful bald-headed bird." One character went so far as to liken her to a pterodactyl. Her limbs were considered especially striking. "She possessed nasty, dry, clawlike hands, and her arms, yellow and curiously repulsive, suggested the plucked wing of a fowl." Given her interest in the paranormal, Mrs. Bradley would probably be amused to hear herself described as "witch-like."

Born in the 1870s, Mrs. Bradley is already in her mid-fifties when the series began with *Speedy Death* in 1929. If Mitchell had paid any attention to chronology, Mrs. Bradley would have been nearly 110 when *The Crozier Pharaohs*, the sixty-seventh and last book, appeared in 1984. Golden Age writers, however, felt no compunction to watch the calendar. Just as Ellery Queen (with one notable exception) remained frozen at the age of 35 in the books published from 1940 on, Mrs. Bradley reached her mid-sixties and stayed there. Others of Mitchell's characters would age or not, depending on the demands of the plot. Modern writers of mystery series go to great lengths to develop and age their characters, making it almost a necessity to read their books in order. Golden Age writers were perhaps a bit wiser. For the most part, each of their books could be read independent of the others. The suspension of disbelief is, after all, one of the primary requirements asked of the mystery reader.

Mrs. Bradley's closest personal relationships are with Ferdinand Lestrange, a superb criminal defense attorney as well as her son, and with his wife, Caroline, and small son, Derek (and later two further children, Sebastian and Sally, who, like their parents, age far more rapidly than their grandmother). She had at least one other son from another marriage (she was married and widowed three times in all, though absolutely no information is ever give about one husband), but he emigrates to India and is really never mentioned again. George, her chauffeur, appears in many of her books but she doesn't acquire the Watson needed by every Great Detective until the arrival of her secretary, the attractive Laura Menzies, in the early 1940s.

When she died in 1983, Mitchell may well have been the last of the British Golden Agers still working at her craft. She was an early member of Britain's famed Detection Club. Sponsored by Anthony Berkeley and Helen Simpson, she was inducted by G. K. Chesterton. Founded by Dorothy L. Sayers, it wasn't an easy club to get into. When Mitchell joined their ranks in 1933, there were only thirty-one members. Club members took an oath to play fair with clues, to avoid sinister Chinamen, not to steal each other's plots, and never to eat peas with a knife or put their feet up on the dinner table at club meetings. Mitchell's favorite writers included many fellow members, including Sayers, Agatha Christie, Edmund Crispin "(that delightful boy")", and especially Ngaio Marsh. She had little use for the works of Margery Allingham and Michael Innes. The only American writer she enjoyed was, oddly enough (his books being so very different from hers), Hilary Waugh. Contemporary critics lumped her with Christie and Sayers among England's "big three" women mystery writers but in fact less than a third of her prodigious output was published in the United States during her lifetime, whereas Marsh, Allingham, Josephine Tey, and Georgette Heyer were far better known.

Indeed, Mitchell earned her living not as a writer but as a teacher for most of her life. Following her graduation from the University of London in 1921 (she later earned an external diploma in history from University College, London, in 1926), Mitchell taught at a number of private (called public in England) schools until she retired in 1950. She returned to teaching in 1953 before retiring for good in 1961 at the age of 60, and no doubt this explains why she so often used schools in her books. She taught English, history and games. Her lifelong interest in athletics earned her membership in the British Olympic Association. Her first attempts at fiction in 1923 were rejected. She also wrote a number of books as by Malcolm Torrie and Stephen Hockaby. Born in Crowley, Oxfordshire, April 19, 1901, she never married (any knowledge of romance and sex in my books was purely academic, she explained). She died on July 27, 1983.

Most of our introductions to the books in this vintage reprint series are carved from original sources. With Gladys Mitchell we were privy to a wealth of information gathered by abler hands. We borrowed freely from essays by B.A. Pike, Andrew Osmond, Nicolas Fuller, William A.S. Sargeant, and Jason Hall, the latter of whom maintains a remarkable website devoted to Mitchell (www.gladysmitchell.com. What is good in this essay is due solely to their efforts and any errors belong exclusively to us.

Tom & Enid Schantz

With love, friendship and gratitude to
DUNCAN SPENCE,
who gave me the idea for this story.

A HEARSE ON MAY-DAY

CHAPTER ONE
No Haste to the Wedding

" 'Ride softly up,' said the best young man;
  'I think our bride come slowly on.'
  'Ride up, ride up,' said the second man;
  'I think our bride look pale and wan.' "

Anon. – *The Cruel Brother*

When she was questioned about it afterwards, Fenella Lestrange was forced to admit that there was no very good reason why she should have chosen to break her journey at the village of Seven Wells. It was off her route, she had never heard of it before and she had no reason to suppose that she would be able to get a meal there. All she could say was that she had been guided partly by a whim and partly because she had a superstitious partiality for what, until that particular thirtieth day of April, she had always regarded as a lucky number: that is, the number seven.

She left her great-aunt's Stone House on the edge of the New Forest at ten o'clock on that beautiful Spring morning at the end of April with the firm intention of breaking her journey only in order to have lunch at Cridley. It was about the halfway stage between Wandles Parva, where she had been spending a short holiday, and Douston, where in a week's time she was to be married from the house of some cousins. She expected to arrive at her destination in time for tea or, in any case, in plenty of time to dress for dinner. Her parents were dead, and her pied-à-terre was a London flat which she shared with three other young women, so this accounted for the fact that she could not be married from her own home.

She had never made the journey from the New Forest to Douston Hall by car, and she was looking forward to it. The route she had chosen took her first to Cadnam and from there to Romsey. Here she parked the car and went to look at the abbey. She had always loved its austere beauty and she spent more time in renewing her memories of its transitional Norman architecture, its carved stone crucifixes in the south choir aisle and outside the abbess's door, its beautiful window-mouldings and the remains of the Saxon church below the present flooring, than she had allowed for. In consequence, she was three-quarters of an hour

11

behind schedule when at last she turned out of Romsey and made for the market town of Waymark.

After Waymark she had to swing eastwards to take a secondary road across what the map had indicated was open country. It was not the most direct way to Cridley, which she still hoped to reach in time for lunch, but it enabled her to avoid a couple of towns which had been developed as overspill areas not far from some new factories near a motorway.

Twelve miles out of Waymark, however, she was held up in an infuriating traffic jam in the narrow main street of Evebury, where it happened to be market day and where, to complicate matters still further, a procession of workmen, anticipating May-Day, were holding a protest rally with much shouting of slogans and display of crudely-lettered banners.

It was after she had managed to get clear of Evebury and was still thirty miles from Cridley and the lunch she had planned to have at the *Crown* hotel there, that what she afterwards diagnosed as a fit of madness overtook her. The road she was on seemed to stretch into infinity and there was not even a farm in sight. The time was half-past one and she was desperately hungry. Then she saw a signpost. It had only a single arm. This pointed to the left and read: *Seven Wells 7*. Fenella thought of a village pub and a ploughman's lunch at the bar. The turning she took was narrow and winding, and the miles seemed long ones. The undulating pastureland was occasionally broken by belts of dark trees on the low-crowned hills, and once she passed a manor house whose drive ran almost parallel with the road until it suddenly veered off at right-angles and was lost in woods, although there was a glimpse of the house beyond them.

The road which Fenella was following mounted and dipped more steeply until, at the top of a ridge, it skirted a beech-wood and then, at an unfenced stretch of the hilly chalk, it turned for the last time and wound steeply downwards to a village.

It was a fairly considerable place, but was so quiet that, instead of being a Wednesday, it might have been a Sunday afternoon at the hour of siesta. The whole of the main street showed no sign of life or activity except for a stray cat which ran across in front of the car and a curtain which one of the cottagers drew aside and hastily closed again.

The main street was a long one, and the houses and cottages seemed to have been built at various periods from the fifteenth to the late nineteenth century. There were no new bungalows or raw, brash, new houses, and the setting of the village was pleasant enough, although the general impression was that of a place which had ceased to exist in the Diamond Jubilee year of Queen Victoria. Some of the cottages were thatched, others tiled, and Fenella, driving slowly on the look-out for the village inn, also noticed a row of plain, neat, Georgian dwellings, each with its fanlight over the door and its long, rectangular windows from whose frames the paint was peeling. These houses were indistinguishable from one another except for their curtains. The front doors, with their characteristic Georgian panels, were not even numbered, and the blank façade had something uncanny about it, as though the occupants had gone to sleep before the turn of the century and nothing had caused them to wake up again.

To her great relief, almost at the end of the village street Fenella came upon the inn. Before she reached it she could see, half-hidden behind some cottages, a fourteenth century church. The inn was near it, but was on the opposite side of the street, about two hundred yards further on. With its over-hanging storeys and diamond-paned windows, the inn appeared to date from the early sixteenth century. It was half-timbered and picturesque and its sign-board bore the unusual name MORE TO COME.

"How much or how many more, I wonder?" thought Fenella. "It sounds quite promising, anyway. It's got a car-park at the side and it advertises snacks at the bar."

She drove into the small, unfenced yard, shut off her engine and looked at her watch. It showed seven minutes to two. The seven miles had not been as long as she had thought they were.

There was a door from the car-park into the building. Fenella opened it and found herself in the saloon bar, which was occupied by two or three men in pullovers and sports jackets. She went to the counter, behind which was a good-looking, fresh-complexioned fellow of about forty, and addressed herself to him with a hopeful smile.

"What can I have to eat?" she asked.

"Well, being as it's today and not any other day, anything you fancy, except a cut from the joint and two veg., love," he replied. "Sandwich, sausage roll, meat pie, Scotch egg, cold leg of chicken and salad – you name it and, if we've got it, you shall have it."

Fenella revised her first impression of the village and settled for chicken salad and a glass of sherry.

At twenty-five minutes past two, rested and refreshed, she left the now untenanted bar by the door she had used when she entered the inn, and five minutes later she returned to it. She twisted the handle, but the door, not unexpectedly, was now locked. She hammered on it and it was opened by a bold-eyed woman who looked as though she might have gipsy blood. She stared insolently at Fenella.

"What now? We're closed till six," she said.

"Yes, I know. I've just had lunch here. I can't get my car to start," said the girl. "Could you find somebody to help me?"

"No business of ourn," said the woman, preparing to close the door.

"Well, is there a garage anywhere near?"

"Only if you care to go into Croyton."

"Nowhere in the village?"

"No."

"In that case, may I use your telephone?"

"Not on the phone."

"Well, is there somebody who could drive me to Croyton? You said there's a garage there, didn't you?"

"Half a mo, then, but I don't think there's much chance. It's the Mayerin', you see," said the gipsy, more amiably. She closed the door in Fenella's face. Several minutes passed and Fenella had begun to wonder whether the woman ever intended to come back when the door was opened again, this time by the handsome, jovial landlord.

"In trouble are we?" he asked. "That's too bad, love. Anything I can do?"

"I can't get my car to start. I can't think why. It was perfectly all right on the way down," said the girl.

"Like me to have a look at her?"

"Oh, yes, please, if you would." They went across to the car and the landlord tinkered about for a bit, then straightened himself and shook his head.

"Afraid it's a garage job," he said, "and there's nowhere nearer nor Croyton."

"Oh, well, I suppose there's somebody in the village with a taxi who could take me there and bring back a mechanic?"

"I doubt it. No taxis hereabouts, and all the men be out at work, you see. Not as there's all that many of 'em with cars, even if they were at home. Tell you what! I'll run you in myself when I've had a bit of dinner. Say an hour. That suit you?"

"Well, it's very kind of you," said Fenella, "but I don't want to wait as long as that if I can possibly help it. I've got to be in Douston by six. Perhaps I'd better try telephoning. I suppose there's a phone-box in the village?"

"Outside the post-office. It's the general stores. But I don't think you'll get much satisfaction that way today. Far better do like I say, and hang on a bit until I've finished my dinner."

"Well, I will then, if there's no quicker way, but I think I'll try the telephone first. Anyway, thank you very much."

"You're welcome." He closed the door before she could ask him where to find the post-office, but outside the inn she encountered a long-haired, untidy, whistling youth and put the question to him.

"Can you tell me which way to go to get to the post-office, please?"

The youth suspended his whistling and stared at her.

" 'Tain't no sort of use you goin' there," he said. " 'Tis early closin' day. They'm shut."

"I only want the phone box, not the shop."

"That's out of order." He grinned. "Us done 'er yesterday."

"What a way to spend your time! Suppose somebody had an urgent call to make – a doctor or the hospital?" said Fenella, speaking severely.

"Too bad, wouldn't it be?" He sniggered and then swaggered past her, thumbs in the side-pockets of his deplorable jeans, and she heard him whistling again as he walked away.

She returned to knock again at the back door of the inn. This time it was opened by a girl of about nineteen.

"Yes?" she said. "You want sommink? We're just 'aving our dinner."

"Will you please tell the landlord that I shall be glad to accept his offer to drive me into Croyton?"

"'E's 'aving his dinner," said the girl, in a tone of rebuke. "We're *all* 'aving our dinner."

"I know. Tell him I'll be back in about three-quarters of an hour, will you, please?"

"What name shall I say?"

"Lestrange, but that doesn't matter. He'll know who it is."

"Right you are, then." The door closed again. Fenella went back to her car and tried once more to get it to start. She was unsuccessful. There seemed nothing for it but to while away the time as best she could until the landlord was ready to drive her into Croyton. From there, she reflected (prepared to make the best of matters), she could not only get hold of a mechanic who would come back with her and fix the car, but she could telephone Douston from the garage and let her cousins know that she would be later than she had expected.

She strolled along the village street, found the side-turning which led to the church, stopped to admire the fifteenth century double lych-gate and then walked round the outside of the building and craned her neck to look up at its unusually tall tower before she went inside. Here she wandered around the dim interior. The clerestory windows were so high up that they seemed to leave the lower part of the walls and pillars, as well as the poppy-headed pews, almost in darkness, but she looked at the fine Jacobean pulpit, the fifteenth century bowl of the font, and a couple of late murals – sixteenth century, she thought – on either side of the chancel arch, before she wandered out again.

As she had walked round the churchyard, she had been surprised to see a small crane in operation. It was attended by three men, and it was engaged in lifting the stone lid of a gigantic sarcophagus. This was in the nature of a vault, for the lid was almost level with the ground. The inference which Fenella drew was an obvious one. They were preparing for the interment of someone of importance in a communal grave. She had skirted the tomb and entered the church by the south door. The porch was modern, in terms of ecclesiastical building, but the door itself was the original one, she thought, and retained a sanctuary knocker.

When she returned to the churchyard she discovered that the three workmen had gone, leaving the crane in position and the sarcophagus open to the sky.

Fenella approached it and peered in. It was deep and she fancied that a musty smell came up from it; but that, she thought, might only be her imagination. She could make out shelves and what appeared to be armoured knights lying on them. By the time she had finished her inspection and returned to the lych-gate there were still twenty minutes to dispose of before it seemed reasonable to return to the inn. She wondered where the seven wells were, from which the village took its name, and whether, in fact, they still existed, but the time at her disposal was too short to allow of exploration and there was still nobody about to whom she could put any questions.

She wandered aimlessly back past the inn and noted that at the end of the main street there was a low-crowned hill which seemed to guard the village on that side. It had been fortified in pre-Roman times with banks and ditches, and Fenella wondered whether any archaeological excavations had been made there. She had passed a half-timbered house which advertised itself as a folk-museum, but it was closed and so could supply no information on the subject.

Although it did not seem to be very far away, she still had not time enough to get to the hill-fort and back, so she continued to stroll, thankful that the weather was fine and the afternoon reasonably warm for the time of year. She met only one person on the way back. This was the unsavoury youth who had boasted of wrecking the telephone kiosk. He leered at her as they passed one another and muttered something which, perhaps fortunately, she did not catch. She ignored him and quickened her steps towards the *More to Come*.

The inn had that never-to-come-alive-again appearance common to pubs out of licensing hours, but she took heart, knowing that the landlord would be expecting her, and knocked loudly and confidently on the door she had used before. The gipsy-woman opened it and there floated out the rich aroma of a big country home-baking.

"Will you tell them I'm back, if they're ready to go to Croyton?" said Fenella, taking refuge in the plural form, as she did not know the landlord's name.

"Best you come in and wait," said the gipsy, her sloe-black eyes expressionless in her high-boned, dark-skinned face. "Master been called away while you was gone."

"Oh, dear!" cried Fenella. "And I'm terribly behind time already! I suppose my wretched car won't change its mind and start?" She ran over to it and wrestled feverishly, impassively watched by the gipsy who called across to her at last, in repetition of her previous invitation.

"Best you come in and wait."

"How long do you think he'll be?" asked Fenella, entering the house.

"No tellin', with that one," said the gipsy, closing the door. " 'Tis Mayerin' Eve, you see. Come this way, then." She led Fenella through the saloon bar into a scullery and through a kitchen where the air was hot and the smell of baking more aromatic and pungent than before, to the blocked-up hall door of the inn. Near it there was a well-carpeted staircase which the gipsy indicated. "Up there. Lounge be the first door you'll come to. You'll be well enough there for a bit, so not to fret."

"Thank you. It's a fine old church you have here," said Fenella, in a friendly, conversational tone.

"They do say as the *old* church was built right where this house is," said the gipsy, with a secretive smile which reminded Fenella of one of the stone heads she had seen on a pillar in the church.

"The *old* church? But the church I visited must have been built five or six hundred years ago," she said. "Do you mean there was an even earlier church here?"

"Time passes when you be out of the swim of it," said the woman. She nodded and turned back towards the kitchen. Fenella mounted the steep stair and found the lounge. It overlooked the street and was dark-panelled, had a handsome carved-oak overmantel and a ceiling ornately decorated with plaster-work. The windows were closed and, although there was no trace of dust, the room gave the impression that it was seldom used.

Fenella opened a casement window which looked out on to the village street. She felt the exasperation of helplessness and cursed the idle whim which had caused her to abandon the safe certainty of Cridley, where, at least, there were garages with facilities for dealing with recalcitrant cars, to come to this out of the world village. She also wished that, having come to this cul-de-sac, she had remained at the inn and attempted to persuade the landlord to abandon his own errand in favour of hers.

There was nothing to be gained by staring out of the window. The street was still deserted and the inn, she was now aware, stood opposite a row of dilapidated, unoccupied cottages which looked on the point of crumbling into ruins. Some of their windows were boarded up and one cottage had no front door. She turned to the room and studied the backs of the books in a glass-fronted, flyblown cupboard. They offered little prospect of entertainment until she spotted a copy of *The Swiss Family Robinson*. The bookcase was not locked. She took out the preposterous volume, a love of her very early years, and, seating herself in an ancient but stable armchair at a large table near the window, she settled down to pass the time as best she might until the landlord returned to the inn.

He was back much sooner than, in her jaundiced frame of mind, she had anticipated. He walked into the lounge and announced unconcernedly.

"Struck me I might as well go over to Croyton myself. Save you the trouble, like. Brought a bloke back with me. He's having a look at your car. Care to come down, love?"

"Oh, that *was* good of you!" said Fenella, regretting any hard thoughts she might have entertained towards him. "I'm very much obliged."

"My pleasure. Be my guest, love," he said automatically. He led the way downstairs and out into the yard. The mechanic straightened up as they approached the car.

"Can't do nothing here," he said.

"What do you mean?" asked Fenella, with a sinking heart as she looked at his grimy, implacable face.

"What I mean, you won't get this little bus to start until I gets her put right, and that's a garage job. Have to give you a tow into Croyton and look her over there where we got the wherewithal," said the man.

"But there can't be anything seriously wrong, surely? The car was completely serviced only a few days ago. I'm in an awful hurry to get to Douston. Can't you just patch things up sufficiently for the time being?"

"I could if I wanted your death on my conscience, but I don't, miss. How's about it, gov'nor? Are you willing to tow this little job as far as my garage?"

"Nothing else for it," said the landlord, "but I've got to get back in good time. What do you say, love? Shall us give it a go?"

"Well, if it has to be Croyton, I suppose I've no choice," said Fenella. "How long is the job going to take?" she asked, turning to the mechanic.

"Ah, that's what I can't tell you off-hand, miss. Depends what spares we got in stock, I reckon, if anything needs to be replaced, and well it might. Any road, I'm bound to tell you – warn you, that's to say – as I'm single-handed at the garage – 'cept for the petrol-pump girl – till my boy gets back, and I'll be lucky to see him any time short of midnight. He was sent for over to the manor, and they won't let him go till they're satisfied, it bein' the family hearse as they'll need to get using tomorrer."

"Oh, but, look here, I've told you I have to get to Douston tonight," protested Fenella. "You really *must* get the job done."

The mechanic shrugged his shoulders.

"I'm no magician, miss," he said. "It wouldn't be no good for me to make promises I mightn't be able to keep. If you ask me, I reckon this job's a day and a nighter, as you might say."

"Well, when we get to Croyton, you can drive me to the station, I suppose? I shall have to go by train," said Fenella. "Oh, what a nuisance it all is!"

"Nothing doing with me. There ain't no station at Croyton and I've told you I'm single-handed. I can't drive nobody to no stations today, miss. It's only to oblige the gov'nor here as I've come out this far. There's nobody, I just told you, but a bit of a gal to work the petrol pumps back home, and I'm in a fair lather to get back there and see as everything is all right. Best make your mind up quick. Is it Croyton or not?"

"Oh, well, then, I suppose Croyton it is," said Fenella. "I can telephone my friends from your garage, I suppose? And then I shall have to find somewhere to stay the night."

"That's right, love," said the landlord. "You telephone them as you may be stopping along of us at the *More to Come*. And perhaps there *is* more to come, at that," he added cryptically, with a sly glance and a wink at the mechanic.

"Oh, ah," said the latter, grinning. "Mayerin' Eve. So it is! And Mayerin' Day tomorrer."

"Where *is* the nearest station?" asked Fenella, when they were on their way to Croyton. She was seated beside the landlord, who was driving his own car, and the mechanic was steering hers, which was on tow.

"Cridley," the landlord replied. "There did used to be one at Croyton, but they closed it down."

"If we have to leave my car at the garage – if it can't be repaired tonight – couldn't *you* drive me to Cridley, then? I'd make it well worth your while. I really ought to get to Douston tonight if I possibly can."

"Me take you to Cridley? Couldn't be done, love. I might, at that, if it wasn't Mayerin' Eve, but I can't leave the women to cope tonight, and I open at six. I couldn't take you to Cridley and get back by then, you see. You phone your friends and tell 'em not to expect you. That's the best way out of it, I reckon."

CHAPTER TWO

Rumours of Mayering

"The purely temporary arrangement thus proposed might have been convenient enough to the young lady; but it proved somewhat embarrassing. . . ."
Wilkie Collins – *The Woman in White.*

The seven miles to Seven Wells had seemed long ones because the road was narrow, hilly and winding and because to Fenella it was unfamiliar. The nine miles to Croyton seemed even longer in proportion. It was slow work towing the damaged car and also she was in a fever to get to the garage in the hope – faint, by this time, but still not altogether quenched – that, after all, the repairs could be effected in time for her to reach her cousins' house that night.

The first thing she did upon arrival at the garage was to telephone her cousins. She half hoped that they might offer to come over and fetch her, but when no such suggestion was made from the other end she realised that her faint hope was unreasonable. She was not even at the halfway stage of her journey. By the time her cousins reached Croyton it would be at least eight o'clock, and they would be lucky to get back to Douston by the small hours of the morning.

She returned to the two men to find that her car had been removed to the inspection pit.

"Well?" she said. "Have you found out what's wrong?"

"Can't, until I give her a proper overhaul, miss, and that won't be tonight, not with my boy away. Can't tie myself up with a big repair job while I'm single-handed. Thought I'd told you," said the garage proprietor mildly.

"But you don't know yet that it *is* a big repair job," protested Fenella. "I don't see how it *can* be. As I told you, the car was serviced only a week ago."

"Can't help that, miss. If she won't start, well, she won't start, and that's the be-all and the end-all, as I see it.

The landlord had remained in his own car. He lowered his window and called out:

"Come on now, love. I haven't got all day."

Fenella went to the open window.

"I don't know what's the best thing to do," she said, midway between despair and fury. "I'm sure this man could find out what's wrong if he'd only make a start on the car. He just simply won't be bothered."

"Nothing much you can do about it, then, is there, love?" said the landlord, giving her a kind, fraternal smile. "You just hop in beside me and we'll have you back at my place in no time. Told your folks as you'll be stopping the night along of me, did you?"

"No, of course I didn't," replied Fenella snappishly. "I told them not to worry if I didn't get to them tonight, that's all. I suppose I'd better find a hotel here in Croyton, so that I can be on the spot first thing in the morning."

"Best not try that, love. Wouldn't work. For one thing, there isn't nowhere in Croyton where a lady like yourself would choose to stay, and, even if there was, who's going to take you in without your luggage and that?"

"My luggage is in the boot of my car. Of course it is! You don't think I travel without it, do you?" said Fenella, with a curious and uncomfortable feeling that she was having a bad dream.

"You won't find it there now," he said, looking calmly at her. "I've had my orders. Best you get in beside me and let's be off. Mother'll be getting your room ready, if she have time to spare from the preparations. It's Mayerin' Eve, you see."

"So you told me before. But why did you take my luggage out of the boot? It was an unpardonable liberty! I quite expected the car to be put right this afternoon. There can't be very much wrong with it. I suppose. . . ." She had been about to say, "I suppose this is a put-up job between you and that garage man to make sure of some extra money," but something in the landlord's gaze restrained her. She got in beside him and he let in the clutch.

"You'll let me know how much to pay you for the hire of your car and the towing, of course," she said stiffly, as they drove off.

"Oh, that'll go on the bill, I daresay, love," he replied, in his off-hand, cheerful way. "Won't be much, any old how. You got any money?"

"Well, enough to pay for a night's lodging and the repairs and the rest of it, of course," she answered, not much liking the question.

"Wouldn't matter, anyway." He changed gear and spoke no more until they were approaching the village. Then he said, "It's Mayerin' Eve with us. I told you, didn't I? Means there's always celebrations of a sort. Dates from way back, from the olden times, I reckon, but village always insist we keep it up. Only been here three years, but we've had to learn the ropes."

Fenella decided to make the best of things.

"What do you do?" she asked. "What does the village do, I mean."

"Oh, nothing that would interest a stranger. You'll be in bed and asleep, I daresay, time as anything starts, and best you should be. Anyway, whatever you see or hear, you take no notice. Half the lads'll be dead drunk, any road, but there's nothing to worry about, so long as you keep out of the way. Sober enough, the village, most of the time, but Mayerin' be something a bit special for 'em, with the funeral bakemeats and all. Solemn and spirited, like an Irish wake, is Mayerin' Eve, and glad and joyful is Mayerin' Day, like the dancing after the will be read, if you understand me, love."

"Oh, of course, it's May-Day tomorrow," said Fenella. "That means that this is Walpurgis Night, but that's a German custom, isn't it? I didn't know it was ever observed in England."

"I never heard of it. What's it supposed to mean?"

"Oh, the expulsion of witches, I believe. The villagers fumigate their houses and then burn bundles of twigs and various herbs and make a lot of noise to frighten the witches away."

"Oh, that wouldn't be anything like they do hereabouts."

"What *do* you do, then? I'm interested in folklore, and I've never heard of funeral bakemeats on the eve of May-Day. In fact, I've never heard of Mayering Eve at all."

"It isn't for strangers. Supper you'll need to be taking in your room tonight. Both bars'll be full to bursting, and the lounge, that'll be in use, too and all. Once you're up in your room, you take my advice and stay put, love. Mayerin' Eve is no time for pretty young women to be abroad."

"Good heavens, I can take care of myself," said Fenella, irritated by the last remark. "But do tell me about your Mayering. What happens – or is supposed to happen? Do you have a ritual? If so, it would only be a modern hash-up of a pagan ceremony, you know. What is it like?"

"Well, it isn't nothing like Christmas. I can tell you that much," said the land-lord. "Wonderful how the days draw out this time of the year, isn't it?"

Realising that, so far as he was concerned, the subject of the Mayering was closed, Fenella said no more about it and in less than five minutes they had driven into the inn yard. The landlord took her in to the house by way of the side door again. The saloon bar was empty, for it was not yet opening time, but the gipsy woman was in the kitchen which was still redolent of the grand smell of cooking. The nineteen-year-old girl was assisting at the oven, but she put down a tray of what looked like small meat pies when the landlord ordered her to "brew up for the lady," and put on a kettle. He added that she was to take the tea-tray up to the lounge.

"If you'd like to wash," said the gipsy woman, without looking round from her pastry-making, "take the new-painted door next outside of the lounge. There's a towel put out for you ready. Missus is tidying you out a bedroom, but the sheets has got to be aired. Us put the lady's baggage down in the hall, master. Her can take her washing things out of it and have 'em up along of her in the bathroom until the bedroom's ready. She won't need only them and her night-clothes."

Fenella, who, until her return to the inn, had concluded that the gipsy was the landlord's wife, felt a certain interest in meeting the mistress of the house. This happened just as she was drinking her second cup of tea in the lounge. The door opened and a youngish, full-bosomed, red-haired woman came in, closed the door behind her and said pleasantly.

"Well, now, as soon as you've done I'll take you along to your room. I'm Liz Shurrock, Jem's wife. How d'you do?"

Fenella rose and they shook hands and covertly (as women will) took stock of one another. Fenella noted that Mrs Shurrock had green eyes and a large, good-humoured mouth, artificially darkened eyebrows, false eye-lashes, a low, broad forehead and a slightly freckled nose. There was no doubt that she was attractive. She smiled at the dark-haired, grey-eyed Fenella and said,

"If there's any tea left in that pot, I'll have some." She foraged in a cupboard under the bookcase, produced a cup and saucer, brought them over to the large table and, sitting down, poured herself some tea. "Fact is," she went on, "I've been kept so busy with the catering, and then you coming and wanting a bed-room and all, that I don't think I've sat down all day until now. Even had my dinner while I was running around, as you might say."

"Oh, dear! I'm very sorry to add to your jobs," said Fenella, "but really it was by no wish of mine that I'm having to stay the night. I can't think what happened to my car. It was perfectly all right coming down."

"Oh, you haven't made all that difference to the work, dear. I was prepared for you, in a way. Sukie told me you'd be stopping along of us tonight."

"Sukie?"

"Ah. Her in the kitchen. Helps with the cooking and cleaning. She warned me, soon as you come here, as you'd be needing a bed. She *sees* things, you know. It's the gippo in her."

"How extraordinary! It was only by the merest chance that I came this way. I really intended to go straight through from Evebury to Cridley. Sukie couldn't possibly have known something I didn't know myself." Fenella was much less impressed by Sukie's omniscience than she pretended to be. It was easy enough for Mrs Shurrock to be wise after the event and to claim that her servant had made a prediction which could neither be proved nor disputed.

"Sukie's a gippo," repeated Mrs Shurrock. "Well, if you've finished your tea, let's go. The sooner I get you safely out of the way, the better Jem will be pleased. He's conscientious, is Jem." She set down her empty cup, smoothed her dress and led the way to the door. "The lad will bring your baggage over as soon as I've seen you settled. Some things of yours in the bathroom, aren't there, now? Right, I'll warn Clytie to pick them up, unless you'd care to bring 'em along with you now."

"I've heard Mayering Eve and Mayering Day mentioned several times," said Fenella, following Mrs Shurrock along a narrow, dark corridor rendered hazardous by various short flights of steps, some leading up and others down. "What are they all about? I asked your husband, but he did not explain very much."

"Oh, seeing is believing, and strangers don't need to know nothing about the Mayering, my dear. Just you keep yourself to yourself and stay right out of the way tonight, and there won't be any harm done, I assure you."

They came to what proved to be the last short flight of stairs and Mrs Shurrock switched on a light which disclosed a door. This she opened with a pass-key and led the way into a small, square, stone-floored room which contained a single bed, a small chest of drawers and not much else except for an old-fashioned washhand-stand and a couple of worn rugs which were the only floor-coverings.

"They do say as this used to be the priest's room in the olden days," she said, "but I wouldn't know about that. Well, I hope you'll be comfortable. What time you get your breakfast will depend, but I'll see you get some somehow, Mayering or no Mayering. Supper will be up about eight, if that'll suit. I know this isn't much of a room, but there it is. Think you'll be all right, then?"

"Oh, yes, of course," said Fenella.

"Clytie'll come for you in the morning when it's time for breakfast, but as I can't say when that'll be, I've put some biscuits and a bottle of bitter lemon in the drawer there. Won't be early tea, I don't suppose, on account of the Mayering. Oh, before I forget. Look, there's your key" – she handed it over – "but I got Jem to fix a couple of staples across the door because that doesn't have any bolts. See that piece of wood? Well, fix that across before you get into bed. It's teak and would keep out an army, and the door's solid oak. Nobody won't break *that* down, don't you fret. Your luggage will be here in a minute. See you in the morning, then. If you hear folks traipsing about, it won't be nothing to do with you, so don't you take no notice, and, whatever happens, don't you open that door to nobody. Get very fresh, some of 'em do, when they've had a couple."

Uncertain as to what Mrs Shurrock might consider "getting fresh" to involve, but feeling certain that it had something (on this particular night) to do with the mysterious Mayering, Fenella waited until she was certain that her hostess was out of ear-shot and then tried out the primitive barrier. The length of teak slotted handily into place across the door and she left it there until there came a gentle tapping, to which, forgetting for the moment that her visitor could not accept the invitation, she thoughtlessly said, "Come in."

When she had unbarred the door and opened it, an unknown youth stood there holding two suitcases.

"Oh, thank you," she said. "Just put them over by the wash-stand, please." She tipped him and received perfunctory thanks and a broad grin. He motioned towards the piece of teak.

"Safe bind, safe find," he said. "Not such a bad sort of notion, at that, on Mayerin' Eve. I'm courtin' with Clytie, as so happen, so nothing to fear from me."

"What's your name?" asked Fenella, who hoped that his remark was good-naturedly bucolic and not as impudent as it sounded.

"Bob, miss," he replied.

"Well, Bob, I wish somebody would tell me what this Mayering Eve thing is all about. I seem to hear of nothing else. What happens, and why does it happen?"

"Why, don't you know, miss?" He sounded genuinely surprised.

"If I did, I shouldn't be asking."

"If you don't know, then maybe you're just as well off. But if you don't know about Mayerin' Eve, what call have you got to be stoppin' here the night?"

"Well, it isn't your business to ask me that, but my car broke down. That's why I'm obliged to stay here."

"Broke down?" He laughed. "That's a good 'un! A likely sort of tale *that* be!" Still laughing, he went away. Fenella, for the first time, felt perturbed rather than exasperated. A likely sort of tale? Something which had been at the back of her mind, but never quite pushed out of sight, came into the foreground and stayed there. She knew very little about machinery and what an engine did and precisely why it did it. These were matters with which she had never seriously concerned herself. However, it certainly seemed strange that a car which had been running as sweetly as a limpid stream up to the time she had switched off its engine in the inn yard, should have refused to start, or even to give so much as a belch, a grunt or an imitation of a dying duck, less than an hour later.

Reason attempted to come to her aid. There could be no purpose, no point, in anybody meddling with the car. Nobody could possibly want or need to keep her in the village for the night. Not only was she a complete stranger, but it was obviously inconvenient for the innkeepers to put her up for the night. Even if this had not been the case, they had nothing to gain except a pound or two for their trouble and the laundering of her bed-linen and the food she ate. Then she remembered the ill-conditioned youth whom she had asked to direct her to the post-office. It was well within the scope of such types to damage a car, she supposed, if only for the doubtful satisfaction of making thorough nuisances of themselves. He had thought that to put the only public telephone out of order was a good joke, so what more likely than that it had amused him to tamper with her car?

She was engaged with these thoughts while she unpacked a bag and was wishing that she had the youth in her clutches with nobody standing by to see fair play, when there came another tap at the door. This time it was her supper, brought by the girl Clytie.

"Sorry it's not all that hot," said Clytie. "Fact is, it's a fair old way from that kitchen up to here." The supper consisted of two of the small meat pies and some baked beans from a tin. To follow there was a slice of fruit cake and an orange.

" 'Taint much," said the girl, "but we be kind of put about today on account of. . . ."

"Don't tell me," said Fenella, wearily, "that it is because of the Mayering!"

"Oh, so you knows about it, do you?"

"No, I *don't* know about it. All I know is that I've heard of nothing else ever since I've been here. What's so mysterious about it, anyway?"

"Oh, well, seeing you don't know, I better not tell you. Missus told me to remind you to batten fast that there door. There won't be coffee tonight and us haven't got no sherry wine to spare, so I've brought along a half-bottle of the best light. Will that do ee?"

"Oh, yes, I suppose so, but what about a glass?"

"All bespoke. We're open." She put down the tray on the bed, produced a half-pint bottle of beer from the sagging pocket of her overall, opened it, dumped it on the floor and departed. Fenella, who had no intention of remaining immured in the bedroom, found her way back to the bathroom, rinsed out the tall mug which she had found on her wash-hand stand and which appeared to do duty as a tooth-glass, returned to the bedroom and sat on the bed to eat her meal. When she had finished it she put the tray outside the door and went to the window. Sunset was still an hour and a half away. In the village street there were now a few passers-by. Most of them were men. They were making, she supposed, for the inn, whose entrance, judging by the length of the corridor she had traversed, was some distance further up the street from her present quarters. She decided to go for a stroll in order to pass some of the time. On the way back, she thought, she might as well abstract *The Swiss Family Robinson* from the lounge in order to have something to read before she went to sleep.

She took the key from the inside of the door, locked up from the outside and, finding herself in the dark, remembered the electric light which Mrs Shurrock had switched on. She found it and lighted the short flight of stairs outside the bedroom door. Then she noticed that they turned on themselves, so that the flight continued downwards.

CHAPTER THREE
Chance Encounter

" 'Then may I go with you, my pretty maid?
May I go with you, my pretty maid?"
'You must do as you please, kind sir,' she said,
'Sir,' she said, 'sir,' she said,
'You must do as you please, kind sir,' she said."

Folk Song (slightly altered)

It occurred to Fenella that the staircase might lead to an exit from the house which would absolve her from being obliged to walk through one of the bars to reach the street, as the main entrance to the inn had been blocked off.

The steps proved to be of stone and they wound somewhat dizzily around a central pillar. Fenella remembered that Mrs Shurrock had mentioned a priest's room. This stair, then, might once have been a way down from a parvise into the church. Childish enough to be pleased with the narrow, winding stairs, but feeling her way with a cautious hand on the newel post as the first turn of the spiral took her out of the orbit of the electric light, Fenella ventured downwards.

As she had anticipated, the staircase was quite short, for the priest's room would have been built, in all probability, above the south porch of the church. She came out into a dimly-lighted space which smelt of mouldering hay. She looked hopefully about her, but there was no sign of a Norman pillar or of anything else by which the place might be recognised as part of the nave of an early ecclesiastical building. There was, however, a door which, she assumed, opened on to the street.

She decided to try it and was advancing across the wooden flooring when she saw the iron ring of the trapdoor. Remembering that she was in what might have been the nave or possibly the chancel of an early church, she realised that the trapdoor must open on to a way down to the crypt.

Steps and cellars had always fascinated Fenella. In the dim but sufficient light she bent down and took a firm grip on the iron ring. It was smooth, very cold and entirely free from rust, a factor which somewhat surprised her. What surprised her still more was that the trapdoor did not stick when she raised it. Finding it heavy, however, she let it fall away and her heart jumped apprehensively at the noise it made as it crashed back on to the floor, narrowly missing her feet as she leapt out of the way.

She remembered that she must be a long way from the habitable rooms of the inn and that the staff were so busy with their preparations that it was unlikely that any extraneous noise would perturb them, so she steadied herself and stepped to the side of the hole which the opening in the floor now disclosed.

"If only I had an electric torch!" she thought. She could see that a stout ladder reached almost to the top of the hole and she was strongly tempted to take the chance of climbing down into the crypt, but the darkness below restrained her. She actually tested the first couple of rungs, arguing that it might be lighter at the foot of the ladder; that there must be some form of ventilation, and that this probably meant a window, or at least some sort of opening on to the outer air which would ease the absolute blackness. However, she failed to convince herself, and scrambled back to the surface.

Here, having closed the trapdoor again with a louder bang than she intended, she began a tentative exploration of the church, if that was what it had been. If Sukie could be believed, (and she was unlikely to have made up such a tale unless there was a tradition in the village about it), a Norman or even a Saxon church had existed on the site of the inn and had been allowed to fall into decay.

There must be an explanation of this, and it was not far to seek. The village, like others she knew, must have been abandoned at the time of the Black Death, and when it came to life again the old church was ruinous and so a new one had to be built. What she had seen of the church she had already visited bore out this view. The lych-gate and the tower, the windows and the chancel screen, the pillars and the interior of the roof gave sufficient indication of a building be-longing to the very late fourteenth or early fifteenth century. Such a building, in a remote village outside the fashionable areas of its time, could even date from the *second* half of the fifteenth century, she reflected, as, skirting the trapdoor, she walked towards the door which she thought must lead out to the street.

It was bolted both top and bottom, but the bolts, like the door itself, were comparatively modern. They slid back noisily but with well-oiled ease, and she found, as she had expected, that she was in the main street of the village some fifty yards or more from the car-park entrance to the inn. The sun, however, was getting low and the end-of-April air was uncomfortably chilly. Fenella closed the door, bolted it, and decided that she might as well put on a coat before venturing abroad.

Her desire for fresh air, she realised perfectly well, was really only half of what she had in mind. Honesty compelled her to admit to herself that, simply because she had been advised to remain in her room, she was fully determined to be out of it. She had no real desire to wander about the village.

The electric light outside her door was still on, and as she put her key in the lock she heard footsteps coming along the corridor. Almost in a panic, although she despised herself for this, she slipped inside her doorway and closed the door as quietly as she could. A moment later there was the sound of somebody just outside, followed by a tap on the panels. It was Clytie, who, it appeared, had come with a message and to collect Fenella's supper-tray. She had picked this up from the floor and had it in her hands as Fenella opened the door. She spoke up at once.

"Good thing you thought to leave the light for me, so as to show me where you'd dumped the tray," she said blithely, "else I might have put my number-nine foot in it, mightn't I, then?"

"Yes, I suppose you might," said Fenella. "Are there many people in the bar? I mean, is the inn very busy?"

"Fillin' up very nice, that is. Only to be expected on. . . ."

"Mayering Eve," said Fenella, finishing the sentence for her. "I'm getting a bit tired of Mayering Eve, do you know."

"Did you want another drink, miss? That's what I was knockin' on the door to find out."

"Oh, no, thanks. I had thought of going out for a breath of air, that's all."

"Best you wouldn't. There's riff-raff about as soon as it starts to get dusk-fall." She balanced the tray and, jerking her head towards the newel staircase, she added, "And best not start rannygoozlin' about down there. Might break your neck on them stairs, and, anyway, master might not take it kindly, not on Mayerin' Eve."

The advice, more especially as it had been given by a girl much younger than herself, irritated Fenella. She waited until Clytie had gone, then she put on her hip-length car coat, put a pound note and some loose silver into her pocket, hid her handbag under the bedclothes to save the trouble of taking it with her, locked her room, dropped the key (fortunately an ordinary small one on a short piece of string) into another pocket, groped her way down the stone staircase and was soon in the street. She looked over to where, black, sinister and desolate against the declining sun, she could make out the humped, strange outline of the prehistoric fort, and wondered whether, after she had made the people at the post-office telephone the garage first thing in the morning, there would be time to explore the encampment before the mechanic brought back her car.

Scarcely had she left the inn when she heard swift footsteps behind her. They sounded purposeful and she thought of Clytie's no-doubt friendly advice, the remark Mrs Shurrock had made with reference to the villagers "getting fresh" and the landlord's even more definite warning that Mayering Eve was no time for pretty young women to be abroad.

With all this in mind, Fenella hastened her steps and realised immediately that she was being pursued, for the footsteps behind her broke into a canter and seconds later a man had caught up with her and clutched the sleeve of her coat.

"All right! Don't be affronted, much less scared," said he. His voice was young, cultivated and pleasant. "It's only me." Fenella endeavoured to free herself, but, at this, he put both arms round her, holding her own arms firmly to her sides, and went on: "You can scream, of course, if you like, but nobody pays any attention to a screaming girl on Mayering Eve. It's all part of the fun and games. Look here, now! You jolly well go straight back to the pub and bolt your bedroom door. I don't know what the hell you're doing here, but I was in the bar just now and that girl Clytie mentioned you, so I nipped out and hung around, just in case you should decide to do anything foolish."

"Such as what?" asked Fenella, as, realising, apparently, that she was not proposing to make a bolt for it, he freed her arms from his embrace although he kept tight hold of her sleeve.

"Such as going up to that hill-fort," he replied. "I saw that you were heading towards it. Go tomorrow, if you're interested, but not tonight nor at this time in the evening. I don't mean to frighten you, but you do as I say."

"I wasn't going as far as that this evening," said Fenella. "But, anyway, why shouldn't I?"

"High jinks," said the man, "of a kind you wouldn't like and which, feeling about you as I do – I spotted you when I was having a snack and a drink in the saloon bar of the pub at lunch-time—"

"Look," said Fenella, interrupting him, "if this is part of the idiotic Mayering, of which I've been hearing every second minute since, very foolishly, I decided to break my journey here, I'm simply neither interested nor amused. And if it's an attempt at a pick-up, the same attitude applies. So now will you *please* let me go?"

"Foolishly decided to break your journey? Oh, no, not *foolishly*," said the man. "If it isn't an embarassing question, though, why exactly did you?" He let go of her sleeve. This, and his tone of voice, relieved Fenella's immediate anxiety that he really did intend to molest her in the tradition (apparently) of the "idiotic Mayering" to which she had referred, and she contrived to lighten her voice.

"I don't know," she said. "It seemed a good thought at the time, but, of course, I had no idea, when I stopped for a snack lunch. . . ."

"Chicken salad and a glass of sherry. . . ."

". . . . that my car was going to break down. I'm trying to kill time until it's put right, but it's all extremely exasperating and annoying."

"What went wrong with the car?"

"That," said Fenella, perplexed (and also surprised at herself for confiding her troubles to a complete stranger), "is just what *I'd* like to know. It was perfectly all right – recently serviced and going perfectly well – until I tried, after lunch, to get it to start, and then it just simply wouldn't."

"Really? Well, bad luck for you, but not for me."

"Please! None of that!" said Fenella, feeling agitated again, and angry with herself for being frightened.

"I beg pardon. All the same, you know, I'm a very superstitious man. What's more, I believe these things are *meant*. There's a purpose behind them. A divine purpose? – well, that depends on how you've been brought up to look upon these things. Perhaps your car was acting like thingamy's horse – or was it donkey? – or a faithful hound or something. You know – it probably spotted an angel or a precipice or some frightful accident looming – and saved you in spite of yourself. Had you thought of that?"

"Oh, please, don't be idiotic. I'm not in the mood for nonsense," said Fenella. "And now I'd like to continue my walk – alone."

"Well, the goblins'll get you if you don't watch out! Much better let me come with you. It's Mayering Eve, you know."

"Oh, for goodness' sake!"

"Well, go back to the inn, then. No, really, I mean it. Be good, and do as you're asked, for once."

"Kindly mind your own business, and let me mind mine."

"That's all very well, but I know this village and you don't."

"As though that makes any difference! Anyway, I came out for a short stroll, and that's what I'm going to have. *Good-night!*" said Fenella shortly.

"Oh, well," he said, "when lovely woman stoops to folly! I suppose I've already done enough (in any civilised community) to get myself arrested for molesting you, but this place, on this particular night, *isn't* civilised. I don't mean the local lads and lasses. May-Day and the night before have been their *laisser-faire* from time immemorial, although I wouldn't want you to suffer any annoyance worse than that which I've just offered you. But *other things* go on, and I heard a rumour that there's likely to be a shortage of osteological specimens in the near future. I'd hate to see you among the otamys in Surgeons' Hall."

"I don't know what you're talking about! Please go back to the pub and finish your pint, or whatever it was. You talk as though the village goes in for Babylonian orgies, but I'm a city girl and don't fall for those sort of idiotic suggestions, so please take yourself off."

"The difference is that the Babylonian were dissolute, and probably knew they were. The villagers do everything in the name of righteousness, and that can be very dangerous," said the young man, re-establishing his hold. "They happen to be pagans suckled in a creed outworn, that's the trouble!"

"For an educated person, you are not exactly behaving like a gentleman," said Fenella furiously. "Will you *please* let go of me!"

"With – I won't say pleasure – with complete acquiescence, if you'll allow me to escort you as far as you decide to go, and then take you back to the pub. Apart from anything else – and what I said just now about the village is perfectly true on this particular night – I feel I could bear for us to become better acquainted."

"Well, I don't agree with you, so now will you leave me alone!"

"Very well. But there is nothing to prevent me from following you to see that you come to no harm."

"I don't need your escort, thank you, either beside me or walking behind me. Look. . . ." her tone changed. . . . "please do go away. You may mean well, but your behaviour strikes me as being not so very different from that of the villagers you were just now talking about."

The man freed her, but kept step with her as she walked (at a brisk pace which she had not planned to employ) along the road which led to the hill.

"I ought to tell you," said he conversationally, "that really I am a respectable semi-professional man and all that, and definitely *not* lupine, I assure you. *Please* let me tag along. I'd feel very much happier if you would. Of course, if you've any real objection to my presence, I suppose I shall have to remove it, but. . . ."

"I have *every* objection," said Fenella.

"Oh, very well, then. I hope we shall meet again when you are in softer mood. So long, and don't say I didn't warn you. Goodnight." He turned back and Fenella strolled aimlessly towards the hill, but the pointless walk soon palled and the air was chilly in spite of her warm coat. After about a quarter of an hour, during which she was twice whistled at by young men on their way to the inn and once growled at by a dog, she returned to what she now thought of as her secret entrance and, after shooting the bolts and avoiding the iron ring of the trapdoor in the floor, she mounted again to her room. By her watch it was still only twenty minutes past eight, far too early to think of going to bed. She had nothing to read, but she remembered *The Swiss Family Robinson* which she had replaced in the bookcase in the lounge, and decided that it would be far better than nothing with which to while away the next couple of hours and get her thoughts, which had been thrown into confusion by the encounter, sorted out again.

She traversed the long corridor with its tricky up and down flights of steps, mounted the steep front staircase and, not stopping to pause, opened the door of the lounge and walked in.

CHAPTER FOUR

The Signs of the Zodiac

"The material with which I have to deal is so elusive, the whole subject is wrapped in such obscurity and hampered by so much prejudice, that I can find few really qualified persons who care to approach these investigations seriously."
E. and H. Heron – *The Story of Y and Manor House*

As soon as she was across the threshold, Fenella realised that it had been an error on her part to go to the lounge on that particular evening, but not an error whose consequences she might have anticipated. The persons seated at the table, which had been opened out to the full extent of its two leaves and now was circular, were not a collection of local froth-blowers, the over-spill from the bar, but a sober and silent company whose only claim to notice (but it was a powerful one) lay in their utter absorption in a game of cards they were playing, plus the fact that each member was got up in what appeared to be fancy dress.

Realising that they were unaware of her entrance, she stood for a moment or two in contemplation of them. They were all black-gowned, but only two of them wore the same shape or pattern of head-dress. Their faces were masked. Some were intended to represent animals or fish, others had a human semblance. One bore on his head the likeness of a canvas bucket, another the model of a pair of scales. Two of those who happened to be sideways-on to Fenella wore human face-masks with fair wigs, one close-cropped, the other with long, yellow tresses. A broad band, possibly stiffened with wire or whale-bone, joined the crowns of their flaxen heads.

After the first moments of fascinated surprise, Fenella had no difficulty in recognising that these fantastically-costumed creatures represented the signs of the zodiac. The only lighting in the room was by candles, one of which had been placed at the left-hand side of each player. This left most of the room in darkness and made the figures of the mummers (or whatever they were) picturesque, remarkable and frightening. The shifting shadows, as little eddies of air made the candles flicker, were flung huge, dark and dancing on the walls and window-curtains, and the effect, as great black hands manipulated the shadow-game of cards which was being played, was that of a child's nightmare.

Secure in the fact that the bulk of the fairly large room was in darkness, Fenella remained where she was, partly because she was fascinated by the strange, unexpected company and their proceedings, partly because to betray her presence was, of necessity, to be obliged to explain it and, considering that she had been told not to enter the room – it seemed for a very good reason – this, she thought, might be embarrassing.

She felt fairly certain that the party consisted of both men and women, although, in the flickering candlelight and because of the all-enveloping nature of the black robes and the concealment given by the masks, she could not be sure that she was right about this. The signs of the zodiac, she noticed, were not only represented in the wearers' headgear, but were marked out in white on the black cloth which covered the table. From where she stood she could see that the designs on the cloth corresponded with the caps of the wearers, and although her view of the tablecloth was limited, being partly obscured by the shadows cast by the players' voluminous sleeves as they manipulated the cards with which they were playing their silent game, it seemed reasonably clear that each one of the party was seated opposite his own sign on the table.

In front of her she recognised Sagittarius. She could not mistake the arrow which appeared to be stuck through the top of his head. On his left was Capricorn, with his goat's mask from which depended a ridiculous, ragged beard. She was less certain of the figures further away from her, although she had already recognised Libra and (she supposed) Gemini and, as the figure on the right of Sagittarius was undoubtedly Scorpio, she took it that the signs were following their established order of months and days.

As the candlelight eddied and flickered, she gradually picked out and recognised more of the fortune-telling symbols. She noticed Leo's magnificent mask and terrible mane; the curled horns of Aries; the splendid fish – a salmon, she guessed – which decorated the head of Pisces; the ferocious bull-mask and wicked, forward-thrusting horns of Taurus.

The game was being played with cards, but, apart from the unusual fact that there were twelve players, for everybody held a hand, (Gemini having one between them), Fenella had never seen the kind of designs which were on the pack. Moreover, far more than the usual deck of fifty-two cards was being used, for, although she was unable to take a reliable count, it seemed to her that each player must be in possession of at least ten cards, of which none was discarded, but, as a point was won or lost, the cards simply changed hands and, in extraordinary silence except for a very faint and occasional rustling, the strange game went on as though it would never come to an end.

It was Fenella herself who finished it. A tickle in her throat made her give an involuntary cough. Immediately all the playing-cards were slammed face-downwards on to the table and Scorpio leapt to the switch and put on the electric light.

"An interloper!" he exclaimed harshly. The others hastily blew and pinched out their candles, pushed back their chairs and stood up, those with their backs to the door swinging round to face Fenella. She was considerably startled by the hostility in the eyes which glared at her through the masks.

"I'm awfully sorry," she said. "I didn't realise the room was occupied. I left a book here. I came along to fetch it. I didn't like to interrupt when I saw that you were – that you were busy."

"She's broken the magic number. She makes us thirteen," said Pisces, the fish listing heavily and a woman's cultured voice coming slightly muffled through the mask.

"She ain't sat down, though, nor yet she hasn't ate nor drunk," said Aquarius, and Fenella noticed the array of bottles and the dishes of food on the broad window-ledge and on the mantel-piece.

"Best give 'er the book, whatever it is, and let 'er go," said Sagittarius.

"Did we ought to swear her?" asked Taurus.

"Depends," said Leo. "What d'you reckon we be up to?" he demanded of Fenella. "Answer, now, as at the Judgment Day."

"I imagine it's something to do with Mayering Eve," she said, "but, as I haven't the faintest idea what Mayering Eve is all about, I've no notion at all of what you're up to, and I'm extremely sorry I. . . ."

"Oh, well, I reckon as 'ow the maiden meant no 'arm," said Capricorn. "You *be* a maiden and not a married ooman, I take it?" he added, turning towards her.

"Oh, well, yes. I mean, I'm not married," said Fenella, with what she hoped was a propitiatory smile. "I'll just take my book, then, shall I? I can see where it is. It's on the bottom shelf of the bookcase."

"You hold on a bit," said the short-haired half of Gemini. "I reckon us ought to look into this a bit more close, friends. Who might you be, anyway?"

"Look," said his other half, "if anyone's goin' to question the young lady, it did ought to be one of us oomen, and not you clumsy great men. Frightenin' the girl, you be, and her a stranger in our midst."

"Yes, and what's she doin' in our midst?" demanded Taurus. "Let 'er give an account of 'erself – and it better be a good un."

"May I sit down?" asked Fenella. Since her early childhood masks had always disturbed her and she was disturbed and rather frightened now. However, determined not to show what she was feeling, without waiting for an answer she took an armchair which had been pushed against the wall to make room for the extended table and seated herself in what she hoped was a composed and nonchalant manner. "Now, then, what do you want me to say?" she asked. "I've apologised for gate-crashing your meeting. It was unintentional and, in any case, this is the only lounge in the place, and I am a guest in the hotel."

"And how come that about?" demanded Libra. "This here ain't an 'otel. It's just a pub. Do you mean as Jem Shurrock has tooken you to be his lodger?" At this, Aries gave a youthful, furtive snigger and with sudden recollection Fenella glanced at him.

"Only for tonight. My car broke down. I shall be on my way tomorrow," she said, in reply to the question. Libra, judging by his voice, was a very old man, and she spoke soothingly.

"I suppose it's all right," said the peace-making Aquarius. "Us don't know the maiden and her don't know us. I reckon no harm done, friends. So be as she keep out of our way from now onwards, I take it we say no more about it. Time march on and there's plenty of work ahead of us before the young folks starts their Mayerin', which, as we all knows to our cost, be liable to get goin' in the earliest hours of the mornin'. While we goes on a-quizzin' of this here maiden, there's precious minutes goin' beggin'. Us 'aven't even *begun* the proper discussion of the evenin', and the cards 'aven't 'elped us none, so far as I can make out."

"Only because of this interlopin' interruption," snarled Scorpio. "The card fell right for Squire, then, didn't un? Not as I holds with 'aving a funeral on a May-Day. Still, can't be 'elped, and it's opened the grave all right."

"Not altogether "is card didn't. Ask me, they never wasn't goin' to come out, not the cards wasn't, not if we'd played till Doomsday," said the female half of Gemini. "And, like our brother say, the time do be gettin' on, and you all knows what come to be settled. Not a whole one left, when tonight's business be over, and us need three more, at the least, to make all safe for posteriety. Five, if us can manage it."

"Hold your tongue, you foolish woman!" commanded Leo sternly. "Who made *you* a ruler and a judge?"

"I'm as good as you are, any day, Brother," retorted the woman, "and *I* say let's get on with it. Them as sides with me, "ands up and keep 'em up while we 'as 'em counted and checked."

"Look, this ain't a vote to strike or not to strike," said the plaintive female voice of Virgo. "I be the Maiden, and I says we should ought to let this other maiden go, and then get on with our business."

"If maiden 'er be. Didn't seem so very sure of it, to my way of thinkin'," said Cancer, in disagreeable tones. "Howsomever, what about knockin' off for some eats and a bit of a booze up? Seems a pity all them vittles settin' there doin' no good to no one all this time, and as we've made a stoppage, though unforeseen. . . ."

"Fair enough. Let's all knock off and 'ave a nosh-up," said the youngest voice which Fenella had heard so far. It came from Aries, and again she fancied she knew who he was. For some reason, this gave her confidence and restored her courage. After all, these people were only harmless villagers, she remembered. She stood up and faced them.

"Well, I'd better say goodnight. I – I hope you enjoy your party," she said, in the most friendly and impersonal tone she could manage to adopt, "and I'm still very sorry for the interruption."

"We did ought to swear her," said Taurus, "before us let her go away from here."

"Don't talk so foolish," said Sagittarius. "Only parson, bein' the Church, or squire (and he's dead), bein' the Bench, can do any good by swearin' folks, Brother. Wench wouldn't reckon to keep no word she might swear to us, any-way, and why the devil should she? Us ain't authorised to swear folks to their own undoin'."

"Really, you know," said Fenella, "there wouldn't be any point if you did swear me. I mean, there's nothing I could talk to anyone about. I've seen you in your fancy dresses, and very original and amusing I think they are, and if there's a procession tomorrow I do hope I'll still be here in time to see it. Apart from that, all I know is that you've been having a friendly game of cards. I'm sure it was friendly. I mean, I didn't see anybody trump anybody's ace, or revoke, or argue, or anything. Apart from that, well, I just do hope you enjoy your supper, and I wish you a very happy May-Day. And now, please, may I take my book? I'm sure you don't want me to keep you any longer from your feast."

It was a longish speech, and, under the circumstances, she felt, a rather bold one. The youthful Aries seemed to be in agreement with the first of these opinions and commented briefly and bitterly on the length of her oration.

"Women's tongues!" he said disgustedly. "Let's have done and get shut of
her. My tongue's fair hangin' out, with all the fug in 'ere, and them candles
smokin' and stinkin', and all of us, "specially they women, spillin' all this yap
about sommat as never ought to 'ave 'appened if things 'ad been organised like
what I said they'd ought to be. Come on, now! Who's for the nosh and the
booze?"

"Not so fast, young Brother," said Leo. "You pipe down and let your elders
have the say." He turned to Fenella. "Before you takes your book – if so be
that's *really* what you come bustin' in for, and not to spy on us worshipful company of brothers and sisters – you'll answer some questions as I be about to put
to ee. Now, then: answer me boldly."

"Very well," said Fenella, her heart beginning to beat a little faster, "but please
don't ask me again whether I'm a virgin. It's insulting – and it's certainly none
of your business. Anyhow, to save you trouble, I may tell you that I'm going to
be married next week."

"Fair enough," said Virgo, giggling. "By custom in this village, you don't fare
to be a virgin then, I reckon. Any road, one of us virgins be enough in this room
at one and the same time, I reckon."

"Who be *you* miscallin' out of 'er virtue, then, Sister?" demanded the female
half of Gemini, in a belligerent tone.

"Pardon, I'm sure," said Virgo, in a mincing voice. "Allus ready to give anybody the benefit of the doubt, that's me. Broadminded, if you sees what I mean."

"Now, see here, you two," broke in Leo, "us don't want nothing of that. Kindly
bear time and place in mind. Time presses, and place been sanctified against
you all knows what. There's business to be done and, so far, cards haven't helped
us to come to no conclusions. Squire's death may be providential in many ways,
but substitution is ticklish work, as you should all know if you uses a bit of
commonsense."

"Well, us never been faced with this sittiation before," said Aquarius. "No
wonder women's nerves can't stand the strain of it."

"Didn't you tell us as how your grandfather was one of them as helped to cast
the cards?" asked Capricorn.

"Ah, but they was luckier nor us, I reckon," the old man replied. "All they
asked of the cards was *which*, and not *who*. There was the scarlet fever about
awful bad when old squire was a young man, so, you see, it was nobbut a question of seein' how the cards fell out for one and another, and who should be
buried and who should be translated. Of course, I be talkin' of *old* squire, not
him as is to be buried tomorrer—"

"Have done, Brother," said Leo. "While you be maunderin', business is bein'
'eld up. And you," he added, turning on Fenella with something not far short of
ferocity, "you take your domn' book or whatever it was you come for, and not a

word of anything you seen or heard in this room! Ancient customs don't concern painted Jezebels."

"Oh, now, really!" protested Fenella, facing him; but the eyes which stared into hers from the lion's mask were so charged with hatred, suspicion and, strangely and frighteningly, by what seemed to her to be lust, that she left the rest of her protest unuttered, picked up her book and ran to the door.

CHAPTER FIVE
Mayering Eve

"By the noise of dead men's bones
In charnel-houses rattling."
Michael Drayton – *The Court of Fairy*

At the foot of the lounge staircase she found Mrs Shurrock. It seemed clear that the landlord's wife had been lying in wait for her.

"You've never been into the lounge when you were specially asked not to?" the red-haired woman demanded. "I didn't think it of you, poking and prying into something as doesn't concern you."

"I object to your tone," said Fenella, "and even more to your choice of words. Far from poking and prying, as you call it, I merely went into the lounge to get a book I had been reading. I had no idea that the room had been let to a secret society. I thought it was only acting as an overspill to the bar."

"Took you long enough to get your book and come out again, didn't it?"

Fenella, feeling that she was being put in the wrong, carried the war into the enemy's camp.

"I consider it quite ridiculous," she said, "to let out a room which happens to be the only lounge for the guests whom you have staying in the house. Who are these people, anyway?"

"The village elders, that's who they be."

"Elders? When one of them is a gormless boy who, with his mates, put the only public telephone out of order? And that's another thing: if he and his friends tampered with my car while it was in your car-park," Fenella went on, "I shall hold your husband responsible."

"That's not the law, as an educated young lady like yourself should know," retorted Mrs Shurrock. Her belligerent tone changed. "Look," she said, "I know you never meant no harm, and I believe you when you say you only went to fetch a book, but this is Mayering Eve, when strange deeds that date back the Dear knows how long ago do be carried on in this village. Best you see and hear nothing. That way, no bones get broken. Now you do me a favour and get back to your room afore Jem knows you've been out of it. And keep that bar across the door. We don't want no trouble tonight."

"Well, I think all these restrictions are quite ridiculous," said Fenella, feeling suddenly inadequate and lonely.

"That seem to be your only word on the subject. Nothing ridiculous about it," retorted Mrs Shurrock. "I'm warning you for your own good. In another couple of hours village'll be getting red-hot, and us wouldn't want to see you in any kind of trouble. Not as I wanted you here in the first place, because I never, and so I tell you. You be off to your room now, afore Jem catches you out of it. Bar that there door, and be not afraid with any amazement, as the Good Book says."

"Well, really!" exclaimed Fenella, helplessly.

"Yes, really," said Mrs Shurrock. "Jem and me have only been in this village three years, but that's long enough to know as no maiden be safe, except under lock and key, at the Mayering of Seven Wells, and so I'm warning you. Different for such as believes in it, but you're not one of 'em, a young lady brought up careful, like you."

"Surely this is a respectable inn?"

"The rest of the year it is, but the Mayering is something special. What do you reckon the Mayering mean, then? Have you any idea? Maybe your book-learning tell you."

"It derives from the goddess Maia, who gave her name to the month of May," said Fenella, desperate to keep her end up in this strange argument and suddenly realising that Mrs Shurrock's apparent anger was really a mask for fear.

"Not in olden times in England it never. Mayering mean the feast of the maidens – in other words, the day when, with good luck (or, as some thinks, with bad luck) they don't fare to be maidens no longer. High jinks," concluded Mrs Shurrock with relish, "is what this village get up to in the early hours of Mayering Day, but Mayering Eve, that's different."

Irritated, but, in an angry sort of way, intrigued by all the warnings she had received, including that from the unknown man, Fenella returned to her room. A childish feeling of defiance made her reluctant, at first, to bar the door as she had been instructed to do, but she recognised this attitude for what it was, and slotted the stout wooden barrier into place before she settled down to her book.

As she read the absurd story her habitual good-humour returned and at about half-past ten the sounds of turning-out time in the pub – voices, laughter, and swearing – which came up from the street below her window, made her think it was about time to go to bed. She wanted to be up in very good time in the morning.

"And to hell with Mayering Eve," she said aloud. "Talk about Cold Comfort Farm! Anyway, I don't believe that ridiculous business in the lounge had anything to do with folk-lore." These words were scarcely uttered when there came a tap at the door. "Yes? Who is it?" she asked, her heart beating a little faster as she thought of Mrs Shurrock's warnings.

"It's Clytie, miss. I've brought you a drop of hot water. Bathroom's out of bounds tonight, the missus says. If you wants a bath it'll 'ave to wait till mornin.'"

Fenella opened the door. Clytie had disappeared but had left behind an old-fashioned receptacle shaped rather like a gardener's watering-can but with a much shorter, broader spout and a half-lid which opened on a hinge. There was a small towel thrust underneath the handle, and Fenella recognised it as the one she had already used in the bathroom. She had her sponge-bag with her, but there was no provision for cleaning her teeth and she had used the tooth-mug for her beer at supper.

While she made do as best she could with the can of hot water after she had barred the door again, she debated whether it would be worth while to go to the bathroom in defiance of Mrs Shurrock's embargo and investigate the possibility of brushing her teeth. There was also another problem, but a solution to this had been provided, she discovered, by the installation of a large, bucket-like chamber-pot which she found on the mat at the further side of the bed.

This decided her. She had no particular wish to traverse the long, stair-broken corridor again, or to repair to the bathroom which was almost next-door to the forbidden lounge. The only course left was to go to bed. She had been between the sheets less than ten minutes, and was still very far from going to sleep, when she heard the first sounds outside her door. She sat up in bed and listened, half-expecting, because of Mrs Shurrock's hints coupled with the precautions the land-lord had taken by providing the bar to the door, that an attempt would be made to enter her room.

This was not the case. There was not so much as a tap at the door. All the same, the people, whoever they were, were anything but silent. There was the sound of bucolic voices in conversation and the clumping of countrymen's heavy boots on the stone floor. Fenella had no doubt of where the visitors were going. They passed her door and she felt certain that they were descending the stone stairs at the bottom of which was the area with the trap-door in the floor.

Curiosity traditionally killed the cat, but Fenella's mind, far from being on cats, was on goats, scorpions, lions, rams, and all the other signs of the zodiac which she had seen and recognised in the lounge, and she was persuaded that here might be her chance to find out more about the mummers whose meeting she had unwittingly invaded, unless, of course, the footsteps were merely those of the landlord and his friends going into the cellar for more beer.

She slipped out of bed, dressed with unusual speed, unbarred the door, went to the head of the stone staircase and listened. There was only one sound to be heard. She could distinguish none of the words, but a deep male voice was intoning what sounded like an invocation or a prayer. Fenella, herself praying in pagan fashion that she might not slip while she was descending the blacked-out spiral stair, put her hand on the newel-post and crept cautiously downwards, secure in the knowledge that her rubber-soled shoes were noiseless.

The thirteen people she had encountered in the forbidden zone of the lounge were standing in a circle round the open trap-door and three of them were carrying flaring, smoking torches. Fenella crept along the line of the wall to a dark corner where she knew she would be invisible, and just as she gained her vantage point, the intoning ceased and the speaker, who happened to be Leo, assuming what appeared to be his natural voice, said loudly,

"And now the bidding. Thrice three times, and you all mind as you be word perfect, not to shame the dead. Now – takin' your time from me, as we re'earsed it. One, two, three."

Fenella had a good verbal memory, but, even had it been less receptive and retentive, she could hardly have failed to learn the doggerel which followed. It was spoken in unison and was repeated the nine times which the leader had stipulated.

"Sagittarius be archer and shoot at the sun;
Capricorn butt bachelors and cause 'em to run;
Aquarius 'e stand wi' 'is bucket o' water,
Pisces come swimmin' a christened babe arter.
Aries 'ave killed off the bleatin' old wether,
Taurus come snortin' to bring cows together;
Gemini twins be a man and an ooman;
Cancer walk side'ards, can't see 'im a-comin'.
Leo be king o' the dark jungly plain;
Virgo be matchless till Spring come again.
Libra hold fair and a true judgment give;
Scorpio be pi'son and stung men can't live.
"Ere us comes Mayerin' all in a round,
Three times and nine times to dance on this ground.
Pick out a whole man and bury un deep,
Peace be upon 'is bones, sound may 'e sleep."

The promised dance was a disappointment. The three torch-bearers twirled round three times, the others nine times, three twirls to the right, three to the left and three to the right again. There was no music, but at the end of each turn the company stamped three times, the sound of the men's heavy boots echoing around the vault beneath their feet.

The next part of the ritual was interesting and macabre. Lighted by Aquarius, who was one of the three torch-bearers, Pisces, Aries and Taurus began to climb down the ladder which led to the crypt. Those left in the circle, which they re-formed so that the gaps were filled up, began a solemn dirge consisting of the words:

"Home, get thee home,
No more to roam.
Thee we will lay to rest,
Dear soul, the Dear know best.
Sleep till the Judgment Day.
Lord, take this soul away."

A shout from below acted as a signal to the next four mummers. The second torch-bearer, who happened to be Leo himself, led Cancer and the Gemini twins (who had to unhook the contraption which joined them together) into the depths, the dirge was repeated, and then the last of the zodiacs climbed down and Fenella could hear the weird chanting come booming up from below.

She longed to find out what was going on, but felt that she had dared enough and that, in any case, to follow the others into the crypt would lead to certain discovery. The attitude of five of the company had been sufficiently menacing when she had gate-crashed their meeting in the lounge to convince her that her presence among them in the crypt would be anything but welcome, and the last thing she wanted was to invite trouble. Horrid memories of a film in which a branch of the Ku Klux Klan had discovered a woman spy in their midst came back, unsought, to her mind, and, although she did not lack courage, at the recollection of the too-realistic picture she shrank back into her dark corner and decided to leave well alone.

She had not long to wait for the next part of the performance. The first torch-bearer, followed by his three satellites, reappeared, and these were soon joined by the others. The circle around the open trap-door was re-formed and the long doggerel verse and the unaccompanied dance (if such it could be called) were repeated, but there was a significant and part-ludicrous, part-terrifying addition to the ritual. Apart from the torch-bearers, who still held nothing but their flaring, stinking, smoking illuminations, each member of the party seemed to be carrying either a large bone or a collection of smaller ones. Scorpio, who came last, held a pelvic girdle under his left arm and carried a human skull in his left hand, and Fenella realised that the rest of the bones were also human. The crypt must have been in use as a charnel house, she decided. She had heard of the same thing in a remote parish in Suffolk where the church crypt had been closed because visitors stole the skulls as souvenirs.

When the circle was complete, the trapdoor was ceremoniously lowered and the bizarre company left the inn by the door which Fenella herself had used earlier in the evening. She waited until they had closed the door behind them and then, agog to see the end of the queer business, she stumbled up the black spiral of the stone staircase, regained her room and pulled on a dark overcoat.

Then she groped her way down the stairs and back to the big door, opened it and slipped out into the street, pulling the door to behind her. The torches were plainly visible in the distance and were heading towards the hill-fort which she had noticed earlier, and against which the strange young man had warned her. Curiosity, stronger than fear, drove her on.

Keeping close to the walls of the ruinous cottages opposite the *More to Come* and glad, once again, that (unlike the villagers' clobbering boots) her shoes made no sound on the metalled road, Fenella thought that she would have no difficulty in following the mummers without being detected, for there was neither moon nor street lighting.

The company of thirteen soon left the village behind them, for the inn was almost on its borders. The village street became a country road and a little way along this the cortège halted to beat out their torches. Then the clumping of their footsteps was the only guide Fenella had until she lost the sounds as the party presumably came to another halt. She froze back against a hedge and waited for them to resume their pilgrimage.

She strained her eyes in the darkness and thought she could make out a huddled group on the other side of the road. She was closer to them than she had thought, her quick, light, townswoman's steps having gained on their steady country-folk's tramping. She could hear scraps of conversation.

"Can't ee find 'em, then? 'Urry up! Gettin' close to midnight and the lads and lasses rarin' to go a-Mayerin'."

"Take this 'ere bone, then, and let me 'ave a feel round. Must be just about 'ere somewheres. Allus leaves 'em in much the same bush every year."

" 'Old on. 'Ere's a spade, I do declare."

"Ah, and 'ere's another."

"Two'll do, if us can't light on a third."

"Don't talk daft. Lucky number is three, make no error. Search around. Can't be that far away."

"All I meant, time's runnin' out. Got to bury un afore midnight, else it's May-Day. Can't 'ave no buryin's on a May-Day. 'Twouldn't be lucky for crops."

"What about Squire, then? Don't 'e count for a buryin'?"

"Us left the meetin' too late, that's what us done," said the previous voice, leaving the question unanswered.

"All on account o' that dratted maiden comin' in and interferin', that's for why," said the other speaker querulously.

"I wouldn't 'arf mind 'avin' she for my May Queen, any road. Proper luscious, I reckon 'er ud be," said a lascivious voice, following the remark with a rich chuckle.

"Ontameable," said an older, heavier voice. "Who wants a May Queen what's ontameable? Come on, now, lads. Shoulder they spades and let's get at it."

"Ah, 'ere be third. Come on, then," said another voice.

Suddenly the top of the hill, out of which was carved the primitive fort, seemed to burst into flame. The group disintegrated and, by the sounds, its members had broken into a shambling run. Fenella followed. By the lurid light of what must be, she knew, a gigantic bonfire on the top of the hill, she could see so many figures up there that it seemed to her that the whole village must have turned out and that, among them, she would be in a safe and strategic position to be able to find out what was going to be done with the bones from the crypt.

Some kind of ceremonial burial seemed indicated by the scraps of conversation she had overheard, but nothing in her reading had prepared her for what actually took place. She was breathing heavily as she breasted the crest of the hill. She slipped in behind some vociferous young women who were chanting, together with the rest of the company,

> " 'Ere come the Dear One, a soul to the good.
> Take what you want and make payment in blood."

As Fenella screened herself behind them, she was able to see by the light of the bonfire that a large rectangular hole had been dug about ten yards away from where she was standing. It was at least three times the width of a single grave and appeared to be about three feet deep, she thought. The reason for its width was soon evident.

First the band who had brought the bones from the crypt put them in a heap on the ground. Then from someone in the crowd on the other side of the bonfire they obtained a cockerel. This the Twins held by the legs over the heap of bones while Leo slaughtered it by cutting off its head. There was an eerie silence from the assembly while this was done. The blood from the slain bird dripped on to the dead man's bones, and the weird signs of the zodiac chanted again, but this time the words were different and undoubtedly hinted at a pagan origin.

> "Crops for your blood,
> Blood for our good,
> Soul, take your rest,
> And give the Dear best.
> Us buries you deep,
> Not long for to sleep,
> And when Judgment Day come,
> The Lord take ee home."

Fenella tried to shake off the nightmare effect which all this primitive ceremonial was having upon her by quoting to herself, "This is the silliest stuff that ever I heard," but she knew that this was a lie. Blood, fire, the mournful chanting, the weird costumes of the celebrants, the midnight hour, the hilltop setting above the banks and ditches raised and hewn out by who knows what sweated labour or exactly how long ago, combined to fill her with a horrid kind of superstitious awe which she could not shake off or rationalise.

She saw why the hole had been made so wide. Libra, the absurd pair of scales on his head-dress waggling in the light of the bonfire, jumped down into it and the bones were handed to him by the others in what seemed to be a ritual order, finishing up with the skull, so that, by the time everything was in place, there lay in the wide grave a skeleton which, if not quite complete, was so nearly so that even the rib-cage was indicated by a number of small thin bones spread out above the pelvic girdle and almost touching the breast-bone.

Before the ceremony was completed, however, from somewhere in the crowd came the incongruous sound of an alarm-clock going off. The women in front of Fenella groaned softly and one of them whispered to another, " 'Tis May-Day! They ain't got it done up to time. That'll bring bad luck, you see if it don't!"

At the sound of the alarm-clock the whole crowd of villagers was galvanised into movement. Some began streaming down the hill towards the village. Others – the young ones – began to play a game of tag, the boys running after the screaming, laughing girls and chasing them away from the glow of the bonfire towards the woods which lay on the other side of the hill. May-Day had come to Seven Wells, and Fenella escaped into the darkness, dreading that some bucolic youth might fancy her fair game in the screaming, shouting free-for-all which seemed to be going on all over the hillside.

Fortunately, owing to her late appearance on the scene, she was on the edge of the crowd, and the young men she was anxious to avoid were all moving away from her and away from the village. Thankfully she added herself to a knot of sober men and women who were hurrying downhill on the track along which the bones had been carried as though they, too, wanted no part in the future proceedings, and so, in the wake of this quiet and respectable company, her heavy coat rendering her inconspicuous in the darkness, she made her way back to the *More to Come*, slipped in by the big door and mindful of the trapdoor – she had forgotten that she had seen it closed down – she crept up the spiral stone stair to her room, flung off her clothes and, having previously barred the door as she had been instructed to do, she fell into bed, suddenly conscious of extreme exhaustion.

Her only regret was that she had not stayed to see the end of the ritual burying, but she comforted herself with the thought that nothing remained for the zodiac figures to do except to heap earth upon the blood-bedabbled skeleton and stamp the ground flat. She did wonder, however, whether there would have been a last bit of doggerel chanted over the finished grave, and what her greataunt, Dame Beatrice Lestrange Bradley, consultant psychiatrist to the Home Office, would have made of the bizarre goings-on.

"One thing she would have noticed," thought Fenella. "I wonder whether it was by intention or by accident that they buried a hermaphrodite? Those legs, and possibly the arms, were those of a man, and I'm not sure about the breast-bone, but I know they added a woman's pelvis. I remember the pictures I wasn't supposed to look at in the medical book at home when I was ten."

Nobody disturbed her rest, neither did she have bad dreams. She woke at seven to find that the morning was clear and sunny. At half-past there came a tap at the door.

"Managed you some early tea arter all," said Clytie, cheerfully, "and bath-room be vacant and breakfast at eight-thirty, and master bin over to Croyton about your car, and that'll be ready soon as you've 'ad your dinner. Be you goin' out to see the finish o' the Mayerin'? Started at dawn, that did, arter Mayerin' Night in the woods, and goin' on nice, that is."

"People spent the night in the woods at *this* time of year?"

"Oh, there's ways of keepin' warm," said Clytie, with a lascivious little giggle," and a goodly old flourish of christenin's round about the turn of the year."

CHAPTER SIX
Mayering Morn

"Everything was conducted with great decorum and broke up in good time."
James Woodforde – *Diary of a Country Parson*

"Clytie," said Fenella, "what *really* goes on in the village on Mayering Eve?"

"I just told you," replied the young servant, with a reminiscent grin.

"Oh, I know all about the woods and the lovers, and I suppose, when dawn comes, you all gather nosegays and green branches and the hawthorn and go round the village putting garlands on the doors."

"Ah, or a bunch o' nettles to them as nobody likes, as it might be the cheats and tell-tales and the skinflints and them as is knowed to 'ave ill-wished others."

"Yes, I know about the nettles, too, and it can be worse things than nettles, can't it? I've read a lot about village May-Day customs. Some of them are the same all over Europe. I mean, what does Seven Springs do which is different and rather special? What does the village get up to on Mayering Eve?" She was interested to hear what the young servant would have to say, if anything, about the hilltop ceremonies.

"Why, nothing," said Clytie, giving a wary glance over her shoulder. "Why should it?"

"I had an idea there might be some sort of local ceremony – something other villages don't do."

"Best not ask they sort of questions. If I knew I wouldn't tell 'ee, but truth is I *don't* know and I don't fare to be any the worse for *not* knowin'. Ancient customs don't bother I none. I looks forrard to the Mayerin' same as others, but what go on below ground ain't no business o' mine, nor yours neether, miss, if you won't take no offence bein' told so."

"I'm not offended, Clytie, I'm merely curious. My car was meddled with yesterday, wasn't it? I'm interested to know why."

"P'raps Sukie put a spell on it," said Clytie, with another giggle, "and p'raps master 'ad a go at it. You never know. Or p'raps there was others as wanted you stoppin' along of us."

"I wish you'd tell me what you know. That car didn't put *itself* wrong. Some-body tampered with it while I was having my lunch. I'm certain of that. Why should anybody want to put it out of action so that I had to stay here the night?"

"Oh, I don't reckon it was nothing of that. It were only 'avin' you on. If anybody touched it, it would be they lads. Up to their tricks as usual they was, I reckon, "specially that Ted Pitsey. Dunno what *'e* got up to last night. Not a sign of 'im s'mornin'. T'others don't mean no 'arm. They just get fed up with the peace and quiet. Nothing for 'em in village, you see, so they makes their own fun, and a right old nuisance that can be. This time, though, I wouldn't wonder if they was *directed*, if you take my meanin', miss."

"Directed? By whom?" Fenella looked somewhat startled.

"Could be master; could be the Elders. I *did* 'ear tell. . . ." she giggled again . . . "as you was an unseemly spectator of their meetin' yesterday."

"Of their – oh, you mean the zodiac people in fancy dress who met in the lounge? Yes, accidentally, I did go into the room. But who told you anything about it?" There could only have been one person, and that was the sniggering youth.

"Oh, that get around," said Clytie. "Can't say you wasn't warned, can you, now? I likes you, miss, so I do, and I wouldn't want no 'arm to come to you nohow. Egg and bacon do for your breakfast?"

"Yes, I shall enjoy that."

"Right-o, then. Pity about Squire, bain't it?"

"I've no idea. Who is Squire?" Memories, none of them very clear, came back to Fenella from the meeting in the lounge.

"Sir Bathy. Died on us Saturday. Farin' to be buried s'arternoon. Some says as he was done for. There was inquest, but nobody seem to know the rights and wrongs."

"Do you mean they think he was murdered?"

"Well, that's what they do be sayin', the police and that. I wouldn't fare to know. Any road, that'll have to do the well-wishin', I suppose, be that alive or dead, 'cos Mr Jeremy is in foreign parts and won't be in time to get back for the funeral, but it ain't the same as if Squire was a livin' soul, is it now? You seen the 'ouse, I reckon, when you went out yesterday."

"Oh, well, I passed a large park with a long gravel drive as I came along here and I could just see a big house through the trees. Would that be it?"

"Ah, I daresay. P'raps and p'raps not. Oh, well, I better get on, I suppose. Got plenty to do before I goes off to see the finish o' the Mayerin'."

Fenella asked no more questions. She drank her tea, bathed and dressed and then went along to the saloon bar, but Mrs Shurrock, drying and polishing glasses and pewter tankards, directed her to the lounge. Any animosity which the landlord's wife might have felt towards her guest on the previous evening had entirely disappeared. She was smiling and friendly again.

"Got our garland all right. Bigger and better than last year," she said, "and thankful to see it on door, I can tell you! Did Clytie tell you your car will be all ready for you, soon as you've had your lunch? You'll find the lounge all cleared up and aired out, and we'll bring you your breakfast in there, and your lunch as well. I'm real sorry you were put about yesterday, but the Mayering, well, that's how it go, and nought to be done about it, heathenish though that be."

"I thought of going and having a look at the hill-fort this morning," said Fenella.

"Ah, you do that. A lively old bonfire they had up there last night, so I hear tell. And don't you miss the well-wishing. A very old custom that is, and worth a look, if you haven't never seen it before."

"I don't even know where the well is," said Fenella.

"Seven of 'em, like the name of the village. Down at the other end of the road they be. Anybody will show you. Funeral will have to go widdershins round 'em, I don't doubt. Dead or alive, Squire'll have to face up to his work, seeing as Mr Jeremy can't get back in time."

"Couldn't he fly?"

"Not from the top of some Indian mountain, which is where he's gone climbing. Don't suppose he's even got the news yet awhile. Very sudden it was, the Squire's death, and not expected for another twenty years, so the maiden ladies did prophesy."

"Who are the maiden ladies?"

"Them that acts as keepers of the wells. 'Tis another old custom, that's all. Do you go off and get your breakfast. That's all ready dished up in the kitchen, and Clytie'll bring it to the lounge. Tea you've had, so coffee I've made, but tea again you can have, if you'd prefer it."

Fenella settled for coffee. She enjoyed her breakfast and when she had finished it she returned to her room for a coat before she went out for her walk. As the door she had used on the previous evening would save the up-and-down trek through the house and also forty yards or so of road-walking, she elected to go down the stone stair outside her bedroom door, telling herself that she was not in the least afraid to go that way again.

The trapdoor was still closed, and it was easy to be brave at that time of day.

There was the iron ring in the lid and Fenella yielded to the temptation this offered. It was heavy work, but she was both strong and determined. When she had opened up, she went back to the foot of the stair and listened, but there was no sound from above, so she returned to the black hole and very cautiously groped her way down the ladder, feeling for each rung as she went. It was an eerie experience and when, after a short descent, she found her exploring foot on firm ground, she wondered why she had made the attempt, for it was so dark in the crypt that there was nothing to be seen and she had a superstitious feeling that if she proceeded further she might commit some sort of sacrilege by treading on a dead man's bones.

She remained where she was, but as soon as she had both feet on the floor of the crypt, she turned round and tried to accustom her eyes to the thick darkness. After about two minutes she gave up the attempt.

"Black as the pit, from pole to pole," she murmured to herself. "Next time I'd better bring a torch or at least a box of matches." She listened again, to make certain that nobody was up above, and then climbed back towards the gleam of daylight which came from the cobwebbed window at the side of the street door. She closed the lid of the trap, but it was so heavy that, once she had raised it a little beyond the perpendicular, she was obliged to let go, and it fell into place with an ear-shattering boom which, she felt sure, must be audible even as far off as the kitchen and the saloon bar. She leapt to the big door, opened it and was in the street almost before the reverberations had died away.

She walked briskly towards the hill-fort and found it deserted. There was a reminder of last night's happenings in the form of the remains of the gigantic bonfire and, near it, evidence of the stamped-down grave. She explored the banking of the primitive castle. It was of an early Iron Age type and looked as though it had never been completed. She made the round of it and then returned to the village, wondering whether there was any chance that she would encounter the young man whose arms had imprisoned her so unceremoniously the evening before. One object which she had in returning to the village was to purchase a small electric torch, if such an thing was to be found. She supposed that the post-office which, as she already knew, was combined with a shop, was the likeliest place to try.

She did not remember having passed the post-office on her way to the *More to Come*, but she found that, some way past the row of Georgian dwellings she had noticed previously, there was a sign with an arrow which pointed down a side-street, and, following this, she found the shop without difficulty.

It was presided over by two middle-aged women who were undoubtedly sisters. One of them appeared to manage the post-office side of the business, the other was in charge of the shop. Fenella, who had already discovered that the telephone kiosk outside the shop had indeed been put out of order, bought some stamps and then asked whether she might use the post-office telephone.

"Oh, dear me!" said the woman who had sold her the stamps. "Out of order again, I suppose, the one outside. Those dreadful hooligans! But I can't allow you behind my counter, I'm afraid. Perhaps you would remit your call through me."

"Yes, of course," said Fenella. "It isn't a particularly private matter." She gave the exchange and number and then the message. "Please tell them that I expect to be with them at about six this evening," she concluded.

The woman carried out this instruction and then added:

"I wonder whether you ought to have telephoned a telegram? I believe so, you know. There must be some sort of regulation, mustn't there?"

"What do I owe you for the call?" asked Fenella bluntly. "You can treat it as a telegram, if you like, but, after all, it isn't my fault if the public telephone is out of order, is it? Perhaps you'd like to connect me with your supervisor."

"Oh, dear me, no. That will be quite unnecessary. It's only that there are so many rules and regulations, you see, that sometimes one hardly knows what to do for the best."

Fenella turned to the other grey-haired woman. This one was sorting over a display of birthday cards, but more in order to appear to have some occupation than because the cards really needed to be re-arranged.

"I don't suppose you can sell me a small electric torch?" said Fenella.

"A torch? Oh, yes, I expect so," said the woman vaguely. "I have them over here. I suppose you won't want a battery to go with it."

"Well, it wouldn't be very much good without a battery, would it?" said Fenella, smiling.

"Oh, I meant a *spare* battery, of course. We shouldn't think of selling you a useless object," said the woman, shocked at such an idea.

"Oh, I'll take a spare battery, then," said Fenella, not that she thought she would need it for the purpose she had in mind. The purchase was made and change given. Fenella said,

"Are you going to the Mayering?"

"The Mayering? Oh, yes. The village expects us," said the sister behind the post-office counter. "We're the Guardians, you see. We don't believe in any of it, but we happen to be the only possible people, so we have to do our bit."

"You're the Guardians of the Well?"

"Oh, you've heard of it, have you?" The woman looked surprised.

"Only by chance. I shouldn't have been staying in the village, except that my car broke down, but I think it was tampered with, like the telephone kiosk, so I had to stay."

"I see. What a pity Sir Bathy had to be buried today. The funeral won't be popular, I'm afraid. The Mayering is the biggest village fête of the year, and people look forward to it and expect to enjoy themselves. This year there won't be any garlands on the lych gate and, of course, the usual dancing in the church-yard is out of the question."

"Good gracious! Does the vicar allow dancing in the churchyard, then, in the ordinary course of events?"

"Well it isn't, strictly speaking, the churchyard, I believe, but, in any case, why not? King David danced before the Lord and before the ark of the cov-enant, didn't he?"

"Yes, but his wife despised him for it, if I remember the story," said Fenella.

"Ah, but Holy Writ does not say that she was right to do so. In fact, the re-verse seems to have been the case, because she was punished by never being allowed to have a child, although – "said the elderly spinster, with a slight smile – "whether that was the Lord's will or David's remains a matter of conjecture."

"This title you have, the Guardians – is it a very ancient one? I am interested in folklore, and I've never heard of this particular custom."

"I don't think anybody knows how far back the custom goes. There is a leg-end that one of the wells – they are not really wells, of course, but springs – gushes out holy water and that King Arthur's father, Uther Pendragon, was healed of his war-wounds by bathing in it. The Guardians originally lived their lives in a hut made of the branches of an ash-tree, but nowadays we use it only on May-Day to keep up the old custom. You will see, when you go there, that there are several ash-trees growing on the slopes which lead down to the waters. The Guardians, by tradition, are two women who must be at least forty years of age and they must be virgins."

"It sounds rather like the Greek vestals," said Fenella. The sisters gravely agreed. "What happens if more than two women qualify?" Fenella went on. The post-office sister shook her head.

"In a village – any village – such a happening is unlikely," she said. "This place is highly moral. We have no unmarried mothers or promiscuous young men, for, of course, marriage is the goal for every girl. Mayering morning, in the small hours, is when the boys and girls pair off, but, of course, they have made their minds up long before that, and they always marry as soon as there is a baby on the way."

"Yes, I suppose so," Fenella agreed. Something impelled her to add, "I'm getting married myself at the end of next week. I was on my way to Douston when my car broke down. This delay is an awful nuisance, because I've heaps of things to do."

"Of course you have," they said, and the shop sister added, "Is it to be a white wedding?"

"Oh, yes – church and fully choral. I didn't want all the fuss, but my cousins insisted."

"Of course they did," said the shop sister. "Everybody who is *entitled* to a white wedding should have one. It is a sign of respectability."

"And is the Mayering respectable?" asked Fenella.

"That," replied the shop sister, "is hardly for us to say. We can only speak to our own part in it."

"Oh, yes. What, exactly, do you do?"

"Why, nothing. We are the remnants of a legend, most of which has been forgotten. Two females have always acted as Guardians on May-Day. We simply remain in the hut which has to be erected freshly every year and we make certain that nobody pollutes the wells, but nobody ever does."

"Not even the kind of hooligans who put the telephone kiosk out of order?"

"They would be dealt with."

"What sort of conduct would pollute the wells if anybody was rash enough to try it? I mean, would throwing rubbish into the water be the kind of thing you mean?"

"We don't mean anything," said the post-office sister. "We have no idea *what* would pollute the water."

"How very odd! How are you to prevent it, then?"

"Well, of course, we should stop children from paddling in it. That kind of thing, I suppose. It is only on May-Day they must not do it. They paddle there every other summer day."

"I see." Fenella glanced at her watch. It indicated that the time was only just after eleven o'clock, and she had been told that she would not be taken to Croyton until after lunch. Even if lunch was at twelve-thirty – and she thought that one o'clock was more likely – she still had an hour or more to dispose of before it was of any use to return to the inn. Suddenly she thought of the folk-museum. There might be something of interest there and, in any case, a visit to it would use up some of the time which threatened to hang heavily on her hands.

"Will the little museum be open today?" she asked.

"Oh, no. It only opens on Sundays. That is the only day Mr Piercey has to spare," she was told. "All the same, if you want to visit it, I daresay Mrs Piercey is at home and will let you have the key – that's if Lady Bitton-Bittadon remembered to hand it back. She was the last person to borrow it, I believe."

"Lady Bitton-Bittadon?"

"Poor Sir Bathy's wife," they said in unison.

"Oh, I see. I suppose the funeral accounts for the fact that the village seems very quiet for May-Day," said Fenella.

"Well, all the men are at work," said the shopkeeper.

"At work? Oh, of course! I wondered why there were so few people about. I was thinking it was Saturday, but it's only Thursday, isn't it?" said Fenella.

"The farm-workers will be let off at twelve today, and the others will take the afternoon off, with or without permission," said the woman confidently. "On this particular Mayering, permission will certainly be given, because the excuse will be Sir Bathy's funeral."

"Oh, yes, I see." Fenella thanked the sisters and asked when they would be taking up their sibylline duties.

"We leave here just before two p.m.," they told her. "It can't be earlier, because of the dinner-hour. People must eat, and funerals always seem to make them hungrier."

The house to which Fenella had been directed was so near the church that she thought she would pay that another visit by way of the lych-gate before she asked about being admitted to the museum. She stopped again to admire the ancient gate. It was of arch-brace and king-post construction and to the king-post somebody had tied a wilting bunch of cowslips, in honour, no doubt, of the Mayering.

She entered the church. It seemed lighter than it had been on the previous afternoon and she noticed that there were *graffiti* on the bases of three of the pillars. On one there was scratched a crude elevation of what she took to be the original church, for the chevron mouldings on the door and window frames were clearly shown, and the squat Norman tower bore no resemblance to the tower of the church in which she stood.

On the second pillar there was lettering. She took the new torch out of her handbag and switched it on. The wording on the pillar was a reference to the Black Death of 1350, from which the village had suffered badly. The third pillar was rather different. Cut deeply into it, under the date MDCCC, were the unexpected and ominous words: *What Makes the Devils Smile?*

"Well, I should think it might be the impropriety of removing people's bones from the crypt of a church and burying them on a pagan hilltop," muttered Fenella. She returned to the churchyard and the lych-gate and then followed the directions the sisters had given her for finding the curator's cottage.

The woman who opened the door to her made no difficulty about letting her have the key.

"Not as you'll find much to interest you, I don't suppose," she said. "A lot of old junk, if you ask me my opinion. Still, squire allus give us a five pound note each Mayerin' for keepin' it dusted and havin' charge o' the key – not as I reckon us'll get any perks this May-Day, for *she* won't think to give us nothing, and Mr Jeremy, as might, well, he won't be comin' to the Mayerin', seein' as he's away in foreign parts and don't even know, most like, as his poor father's lyin' in state and is to be buried today, more's the pity."

"Why do you say that?" asked Fenella, although she felt she had already had the answer from Clytie.

"Spoils the Mayerin'. Stands to reason that will. A funeral's well enough when there's nothen else to hand, but when folks fare to enjoy themselves, why, then, a funeral's out of place, it seem to me."

"I heard a rumour – I suppose it isn't true – that Sir Bathy was murdered."

"Well, there was inquest, and brought in as person or persons unknown, so that mean murder, don't it? But you be a stranger in our midst. What do *you* know about it?"

"As I said, I heard a rumour."

"Rumours is mostly lies, but this one wasn't. Funny thing. Everybody liked squire, which is more nor I can say for 'is lady."

"Isn't she popular in the village?"

"Us never hardly set eyes on her. Fair tooken aback, I was, when she come here to borrow museum key. Squire's second wife. They *do* say as Mr Jeremy went to India to get shut of her for a bit. No love lost there, by all accounts – or else the reverse, so tongues wag. Myself, I wouldn't know the rights and wrongs of it. Of course, her's a good deal younger nor Squire was, though older by ten years than Mr Jeremy, I'd say."

"Mr Jeremy is the son?"

"Ah. I suppose he'd ought to be called *Sir* Jeremy now."

"Oh, it's a baronetcy, is it?"

"I dunno what that is, nor whether Sir Bathy was really entitled, him not bein' in the direct line, as you might say, bein' brother, not son, to old squire. Ah, well, at any rate, grave will have to be opened up for Sir Bathy, and that'll make a bit of a change after the last two or three of the family bein' killed in foreign parts."

Fenella accepted the key to the small medieval building which housed the collection, but soon decided that from her point of view it scarcely repaid a visit except as a means of using up some of the time she had to spare. The exhibits could be matched in any folk-museum in the country and were not even particularly good specimens of their kind. Many of them were old-fashioned kitchen utensils and other domestic appliances. There were some clumsy flat-irons, an array of kitchen knives, ladles and meat-dishes, a primitive mangle, a roasting-jack and, placed incongruously among this collection of ugly but civilised accoutrements, were three eighteenth century man-traps and a collection of policemen's truncheons.

"Well, however the squire was murdered, I hope it wasn't by getting caught in one of those mantraps," thought Fenella. "Horrible, wicked things!"

Apart from the orderliness and freedom from dust of the collection, she noticed that the heavy, clumsy flat-irons were free of rust, that the pewter objects had been lovingly washed and rubbed up and that all the cutlery was not only polished but sharpened. It appeared that the curator and his wife earned their Mayering five pounds a year. She spent about a quarter of an hour over her inspection and, having returned the key, decided to go along to that end of the village furthest from the iron-age fort and find the site of the seven wells.

She had not far to go, and was guided by the sound of music. She did not think she had passed the ash grove and the springs on her way into the village and found that she was right. There was a lane by the side of a blacksmith's forge and she followed this and the sound of the music until she came upon a small common. Here a number of girls were performing a dance, holding gar-lands of paper flowers fastened to the ends of peeled sticks. The dancing was accompanied by an orchestra consisting of two violinists, a drummer and a man who jingled some small bells such as morris men wear on their legs. These, however, were attached to a piece of leather which the man held in both hands. Anything more innocuous and unexciting could hardly be imagined.

There was only a sprinkling of villagers acting as spectators, not nearly as many as Fenella might have expected. She stood and watched the dancing for a few minutes and then moved on to where another knot of idlers was watching the erection of a small shelter woven from branches on a skeleton of tall poles. This, she supposed as she approached it, was to be the hut for the occupation of the two Guardians. As she drew nearer she saw what appeared at first to be a pond set in a deep hollow, but the water flowed away in the form of a broad, shallow brook and, as she reached the edge of the hilly dip, she could see the springs of water coming out of the hillside and the ash-trees growing almost at the water's edge.

Considering all that she had heard about the Mayering, its celebration seemed to be falling very flat. She supposed that the recent death of the Squire of the village, and the funeral which was to be held on this singularly inappropriate day, were the causes of the unenthusiastic nature of the annual May-Day rites. Disappointed, she decided to return to the inn and find out how soon the land-lord was prepared to drive over to Croyton and reunite her with her car.

CHAPTER SEVEN
The Green Man

"If they do these things in the green tree, what shall be done in the dry?"

St Luke – 23:31

To Fenella's delighted surprise, lunch was on the table by a quarter past twelve. She had returned to the inn and was washing her hands when Clytie tapped on the bathroom door, informed her that her meal was ready for her in the lounge and asked whether she would take anything to drink.

"And master says don't be long about it, as he wants to be in Croyton as soon after one o'clock as maybe, along of gettin' back for the funeral," Clytie con-cluded.

"That's marvellous," said Fenella. "I'll have a glass of beer with my lunch, and perhaps you'd also bring the bill, so that I can settle up quickly."

Lunch consisted of two meat pies (re-heated, Fenella supposed, from the pre-vious day's baking) with potatoes, boiled onions in a thick sauce, and cauli-flower. This was followed by a very good sherry trifle and some cheese. The bill was extremely moderate and included a small sum set against the item: *Petrol for one double, two single journeys*, an understatement.

She had finished the meal by twenty minutes to one. She went back to her room, ostensibly to make sure that she had finished her packing, but really because there was one other thing which she was determined to do before she left the inn. Making certain that there was nobody about, she sneaked down the stone stair, raised the lid of the trapdoor and, torch at the ready, once more felt her way down the ladder into the crypt.

As before, it smelt musty but not otherwise unpleasantly, and, by the light of the torch, which she switched on the moment she was at the foot of the ladder, she was able to make a sufficient inspection of the small undercroft to satisfy her curiosity.

The vault was supported by two squat pillars, and the whole of the floor-space, she judged, was not more than about twenty feet by twelve. Of the bones which had lain there, perhaps earlier than the time of the Black Death, only a few scattered fragments remained. There was not even a skull, and Fenella was relieved about that. There was no dead man's sightless grin to encounter.

She shone her torch over the whole of the floor-space to make sure that she knew where to place her feet without treading on the scattered bones, and inspected the walls. She found the remains of the original steps which must have led down from the Norman church, and she could also make out a blocked doorway. There was nothing else of interest, no traces that the crypt had ever been used as a chapel or, indeed, that it had been used for any religious purpose at all.

She wondered how it was ventilated, for, so far as her unknowledgeable eye could see, there was no trace of any opening other than the trapdoor by which she had entered. Having satisfied her curiosity, she began to wonder how the succeeding years' ceremonies on the hill-fort could be carried out if there were no more skeletons to inter, and found herself propounding various macabre theories as to ways in which the pagan ritual – for it was that, in spite of certain Christian embellishments – could still be made viable.

As there was so little to see, and so little satisfaction to be obtained from what she did see, she soon stepped across the sparsely-littered floor to the ladder, climbed it, dropped the trapdoor back into place and returned to her room.

She was only just in time, for she had scarcely regained it when there was a tap on the door and a masculine voice asked whether her luggage was ready for the car. Fenella, whose heart had missed a beat, for she felt certain it was somebody who had heard the bang as she let the heavy trapdoor drop into place, replied by opening the door and assuring the youth Bob, who stood on the threshold, that she was ready to go.

The journey to Croyton seemed very much shorter this time, although the landlord, who presented to her a stony profile during the whole of the way, clearly had shed his usual joviality. She attempted to make conversation at first, but, finding him morosely unresponsive, she gave up and sat silent until they drew up at the garage.

Her car was in the forecourt and the garage owner came up immediately the landlord pulled in and Fenella stepped out.

"All serene, miss," he said. "My boy had her out this morning and she's running as sweet as you'd wish."

"Oh, good. What was the trouble?" asked Fenella.

"Had to strip the engine right down to find *that* out," replied the man. "Take too long to explain and you wouldn't understand. It's all wrote down on the bill. Five pound, if that's all right."

"It will have to be, won't it?" As she handed him the money she saw the landlord drive away. She waited while the garage proprietor receipted the bill and then she added, "I don't know how I'm off for petrol."

"Oh, I topped her up," said the man. "The only drop gone is what my boy used when he give her the run-around this morning."

"Then. . . ."

"It's all on the bill. Not to worry. Good luck, miss, and don't you never leave her unlocked again, not in a car park nor nowhere," said the garage owner impressively.

"Why, had somebody been tampering with the engine? I thought as much," said Fenella, angrily.

"Hard to say, but 'safe bind, safe find' ain't a bad motto," he rejoined. "Had the devil of a job to spot the trouble, we did."

"Oh, well, anyway, thank you very much. I'm very much obliged to you, of course."

"You're welcome, miss. Hope to see you this way again some time."

"I doubt very much whether I shall be coming," said Fenella. She went over to her car, got in and started the engine. She felt as certain as she could be certain of anything that she had locked the car doors (as she always did) before she had gone to lunch at the *More to Come* that first time, but nothing would be gained and precious time would be lost by arguing the point. She let in the clutch and glided on to the road, wondering, as she passed the *More to Come* again on her way to the road she had left so heedlessly on the previous afternoon, whether she would see anything more of the Mayering.

It appeared, however, that the villagers had all gone home for their midday dinners. The main street was as quiet as it had been on her journey down. Out of curiosity and because she now felt that she was not pressed for time, she turned up the lane which led to the common where the seven springs trickled out of the hillside. The hut for the Guardians had been completed. She got out of the car and walked up to it, but it was untenanted. She stood at the edge of the hollow which cradled the waters and wondered which of the seven springs had the reputation for producing holy water. Hearing a sound which did not come from the streams, she turned round to find a tall man standing a few yards behind her.

He was so twined about with leafy branches that little of him was visible except his face, his hands and his shoes. Staring at him, Fenella saw that the branches were woven in and out of a sort of basketwork cage made of green withies. His face was black and so were his hands, but this, she realised, was because he was daubed with soot, the traditional chimney-sweep effect of the traditional Jack-in-the-Green.

As she stood there he approached her and asked,

"Do you want the lucky touch, my dear?" He spoke in a gipsy whine and Fenella retreated a step.

"Not if it means mussing me up. I've no means of washing off soot until I get to Douston," she said. As she spoke, the church clock chimed the three-quarters.

"A quarter to two. That will be the Guardians, my pretty lady," intoned the man. There was the distant sound of what seemed to be a drum and fife band and then came the first of the villagers. Where they had all sprung from Fenella could not imagine, for the village street had been empty as she came through. She glanced to where she had parked her car, but realised that she would never be able to get it past the people who were now thronging the lane.

Wherever the music was coming from, it did not approach any nearer. Apart from the mass of pedestrians, all of whom seemed soberly dressed for a May-Day jamboree, there was nothing in the nature of a procession except for a kind of litter, borne aloft by six stalwart men, on which were enthroned the incongruous figures of the two women from the post office. Fenella recognised them instantly, for, although they had changed their clothes and were now dressed (she supposed) in their best, the only difference in their appearance was that each carried a long white wand garlanded at the top with a green wreath.

The population parted to allow the bearers to bring the litter to the hut of green branches. Here it was ceremonially lowered to within a foot of the grass and four girls detached themselves from the crowd, ran forward and assisted the women to alight. They then curtsied to the women and returned to be lost in the quiet crowd. The sisters went into their hut and that was the last which Fenella saw of them.

The next sound she heard was that of an approaching car. It was not the hearse proper, for it was nothing but an open truck, although it and the undoubted coffin it bore were smothered in flowers. The people, having made way for it, surged forward towards the seven springs, but kept all the time at a respectful distance from the equipage until it halted. Then it seemed to her that the crowd went mad. They made a concerted rush at the hearse and she thought at first that they intended to overturn it. It appeared, however, that there was merely a scuffle to get hold of the flowers. Men, women and youngsters jostled and fought. The flowers were ripped off the truck and two young men, stronger or more agile than the rest, hoisted themselves on to the vehicle and, amidst a clamour of pleading shouts, tore at the wreaths and sprays and flung the flowers to the milling crowd below. As each person grabbed a flower or a leafy spray, he or she tore down to the water and flung it in.

When the lorry was empty except for the coffin itself, the crowd moved quietly away and allowed it to drive on. It followed the course of the brook for about fifty yards, then drove across it at the shallowest spot, rounded the pond, then turned away from it and circled back to the lane. The villagers streamed after it. One or two were limping; some had blood on their faces and on the girls' bare arms as a result of the frenzied struggle to obtain the flowers from the hearse; but all seemed calm again and, as the last of the band disappeared down the lane, Fenella thankfully returned to her car which, fortunately, she had left well away from the water, so that it had not been in the path of the demonstration.

She had removed herself as far as she could from the battleground around the hearse, so she had some little distance to walk to reach the car. In the excitement of the battle for the flowers she had forgotten the black-avised, sooty-handed Jack-in-the-Green and was startled when he appeared from behind the car. He smiled at her and said, in a different voice, and one which she fancied she had heard before:

"Will you have lucky touch now, my dearest dear?"

"Certainly not!" said Fenella, annoyed and somewhat alarmed by his persistence. "And if you don't go away at once I shall run to that hut of branches and ask for help."

"Scared of me, are you? No need to be. I'm harmless. I am black but comely, O ye daughters of Jerusalem. Besides, the Weird Sisters wouldn't thank you for dragging *them* into a man-and-maid fight, you know. That's not part of their job." He waved a black hand towards the pond which the seven springs kept fed. "What's more, I'm probably the only person in the village who knows which of these tiny rills is the healing stream. Take the luck while you can get it, my dear. Are you wed?"

"No, but I'm on my way to be married."

"Then you need all the luck and all the protection you can get." He approached her and before she could do anything to prevent it, he had taken her hand, passed it across his black forehead, and, with a swiftness and strength which disconcerted her, he rubbed her sooty fingers across her brow. "There!" he said. "And now for the verse and then the ceremonial cleansing. . . . No, don't run away, or I shall be obliged to grasp you with these sooty paws, and then you really *will* be in a mess, won't you?"

Fenella gazed wildly about her, but there was nobody to come to the rescue and even if the whole village had been present, she reflected, their bucolic sense of drama and comedy would have prevented their interference with this idiotic horseplay.

"Well, make it quick, then," she said helplessly, feeling strangely at odds with herself because of her mixed feelings of fear, anger and a horrid kind of fascination which she recognised as sexual and resented accordingly. "I have no time to waste."

The man stepped back a pace and recited solemnly:

" 'O what are you seeking, you seven fair maids,
All under the leaves of life?
Come tell, come tell, what seek you
All under the leaves of life?' "

"I can't answer that," said Fenella. "I know the ballad, of course, but I'm an agnostic."

"And you to be married in church?" he asked, in an amused and yet tender tone. "Well, now, to think of that!"

"Oh, that's my relatives' doing," she said. "So far as *I'm* concerned, the marriage ceremony is completely out of date. Wherever I got married, the ritual would be equally bogus, so far as my feelings and opinions are concerned."

"But you will take your vows to love, honour and obey?"

"Of course not. We don't promise to obey any more. That also is completely out of date."

"Is it, then? And yet you are obeying me."

"Only under threats."

"Don't you want to be cleansed in holy water? Come." He stretched out a sooty hand. Fenella avoided it and went with him down the sloping bank until they stood at the edge of the water. "You stay here," he said. "No need for you to get your feet wet." So saying he plunged into the shallow pool and waded across it. When he reached the opposite side he stooped and washed the soot from his hands, pulling a leafy branch from his costume and using it as a scrubbing brush. Then he plunged both hands into the water which, to Fenella's amazement, seemed suddenly to gush from the hillside, splashed his way back to where she was standing, emerged from the pool and passed his wet hands over her brow. "There!" he said. "May the Lord bless you and keep you. Dry that off with a handkerchief, and go on your way rejoicing."

"Thank you for nothing," said Fenella, scrubbing her face with her handkerchief. "And now I really must be on my way."

"And I on mine," he said. "These are not the trappings in which to attend the funeral rites of the lord of the manor, even if he did not die of natural causes."

"Was he . . . is it true that he was murdered?"

"So the coroner's jury said, and who am I to contradict them? Personally, I wouldn't put it past his lady wife. He was a sottish old devil and rumour had it that he kept a woman somewhere or other. But don't repeat any of this, will you?"

"Nobody would be interested – at least, not in the place to which I'm going."

"To be married," he said thoughtfully. "Why didn't I meet you before you got yourself tied up in this very undesirable way?"

"Goodbye," said Fenella. "If you're going to get cleaned up and changed for the funeral, you'd better hurry, hadn't you?"

"Oh, there's no particular panic," said Jack-in-the-Green. "They've got to take the wagon back to the manor house, switch the coffin on to the official hearse, (which is a family heirloom and looks the part), and collect the so-called mourners. Tell me just one thing: where is your wedding to be?"

"A long way from here, thank goodness."

"Cross my palm with a kiss, and I'll wish you luck."

"Don't be silly. If you really want to know, I'm to be married in Douston parish church. My official home, although not my real one, is Douston Hall."

"A fair answer." His voice had changed again. "Well, Squire's been murdered, and poor Tom's a-cold." He took her right hand and brushed his lips across the back of it. "Think of me sometimes," he said, "even *after* you're married."

Fenella reversed the car and drove back to the main street. She was almost at the entrance to the village and was soon clear of the last of the cottages and on the narrow, winding lane down which she had come so lightheartedly on the preceding day in search of a sandwich and a drink. As she drove with due attention to the road and the possibility of meeting oncoming traffic round the bends, she attempted to place Jack-in-the-Green. He had spoken, at the end, in the accents of an educated man and, within the limits (she supposed) of folklore, he had behaved like a gentleman. She could not make up her mind whether he was a genuine supporter of the village Mayering, or whether (as she was inclined to believe) he was a lone wolf who chose to enact the part of Jack-in-the-Green, Green George, the Green Man, or whatever other folk-name he used, merely in order to satisfy or, more likely, to amuse himself. It was tantalising to realise that she had heard his voice before.

She was occupied with these thoughts when she had to slow down and hug the grass verge of the lane in order to make room for a funeral cortège to pass. By the number of expensive cars which followed the hearse, which was of conventional type but carried no flowers, she realised that this must be the procession which was bound for the churchyard at Seven Wells and the Squire's family vault. In the end she pulled up to allow it to go by, and an association of ideas caused her to go back mentally to the trapdoor and its ladder which led to that other vault, the crypt below the *More to Come*. She certainly would have a story to tell when she reached her cousins' house at Douston, she reflected. On second thoughts, she found herself wondering whether she would tell quite all of it.

She came to the end of the lane and turned on to the Cridley Road. In three hours or less she would be back in the sane, polite, completely accountable world of a country house and the preparations for a fashionable if provincial wedding. To her own surprise, the prospect failed to appeal to her. Her thoughts returned to the Green Man. She began to wonder whether he was real or whether, after her strange experiences, she had conjured him up out of her imagination. Then she glanced down at the wheel. She was not wearing gloves, and she noticed a smear of soot across the fingers of her right hand where he had lightly touched it with his lips.

"So the luck has brushed off on to me after all," she thought. "And – good heavens! I know now who he is."

CHAPTER EIGHT
Douston Hall

"Let never a man a wooing wend
That lacketh thingis three;
A routh o' gold, an open heart
And fu' o' courtesye."

Border Ballad – *King Henry*

One thing of which Fenella had entertained no doubts was the warmth of her reception when she arrived at her cousins' house. She was not mistaken. They received her rapturously. Tea was being served by the time she arrived, and she was glad of it after her unusually early lunch, and although they were eager to hear about her mishap with the car they let her have her tea in peace.

The cousins were equally related to her, for they were not husband and wife but brother and sister. The owner of the property, which was a charming old house in a smallish, well-wooded park a couple of miles outside the town, was a middle-aged widower for whom his older sister kept house. They were informal in manner and in outlook, and Fenella had always got on well with both of them. They were related to her on her mother's side and their name was Cromleigh. Her mother had been the youngest of a well-spaced family, and the cousins were the children of her mother's eldest brother, so that Fenella sometimes felt (and they invariably did) as though they were more like uncle and aunt to her than cousins.

She was as eager to relate her adventures as they were to hear them, so as soon as she had finished her tea and had been shown her room, the three of them settled down to a recitation of the tale which began with the story of the détour and then of the hold-up when Fenella found that she could not get away from the inn after lunch on Mayering Eve.

"And you still don't know what went wrong with the car?" asked Hubert Cromleigh. "What does it say on the bill? – or haven't you bothered to read it?"

"No, I haven't. I don't suppose it would mean very much to me, anyway. I simply paid the man what he asked and was thankful to get on the road again. My own idea is that somebody tampered with the car, and the man said I ought to have locked it, but I always do. It's automatic with me to turn the key and then test all four doors before I leave. It wasn't as though I was in any desperate hurry, either, or anything like that."

"Perhaps the hotel needed custom," suggested Miriam Cromleigh, "and were determined to make certain that you stayed for dinner and at least one night."

"I don't think the place is anything more than a big pub," said Fenella. "I don't believe they usually put people up. The bedroom they gave me was miles from anywhere, and I didn't see signs of any other accommodation for guests. There wasn't even a dining-room. I started off with a snack lunch in the saloon bar, and after that I had my dinner – such as it was – in my room and this morning's breakfast in the so-called lounge. I lunched there again before I came away."

She gave them an account of her invasion of the lounge while it was in possession of the signs of the zodiac, and followed it with the tale of the rest of her strange experiences. The only incident she left out was her meeting with the young man on Mayering Eve and her May-Day encounter with the same man as Jack-in-the-Green. Why she felt unwilling to refer to these she did not know at the time, although it became plain enough to her later on.

"Well," said Miriam, when they had listened with interest and appreciation to the extraordinary story, "now I'm afraid it's our turn for some news." She glanced at her brother.

"Better not to beat about the bush," he said. "The fact is, Fenella, my dear, that we have to postpone your wedding."

"Postpone it?" she said. "Why? What has happened?"

"What has happened is that Talbot has contracted to go abroad on his firm's business and does not expect to be back for another fortnight," said Miriam grimly.

"So *that's* why he hasn't written, the coward!" Fenella exclaimed. "What a thing to do, to go off like that at the last minute! Oh, Miriam! And you've made all the arrangements! I'm terribly sorry! What a wretch he is! He's his own master, though. He wasn't *compelled* to go, was he?"

"Of course he wasn't! But no need to be sorry for me, my dear. It's quite the other way about. We can't imagine anything more frustrating than having one's marriage postponed. Now, look, Fenella, we want you to stay on here, and notify your own friends of the postponement. We've let everybody else know.

What do you think? It's quite ridiculous for you to go all the way back to your flat and then come here again for the wedding."

"But it's such an upset for you."

"Nonsense. We've been looking forward to your visit and are delighted to have it extended," said Hubert.

"Although, of course, we're sorry about the reason," said Miriam. "It's sickening for you to have the thing put off when you were all keyed up to go through with it."

Fenella looked at her, suddenly enlightened.

"Why do you put it like that?" she asked, with a deep flush of embarrassed comprehension crimsoning her neck and cheeks.

"I must apologise for Miriam," said her brother, laughing. "John Blunt – Joanna Blunt in this case – is dreadfully apt to call a spade a damned shovel. Pass off her ill-considered remarks in tactful silence, my dear Fenella, for, believe me, they will not abide your question."

"But I *must* question them," said Fenella wildly. "I must ask her to explain what she means."

"What I mean," said Miriam, "as you have a perfect right to know, is that I have never been in favour of this marriage. It was a put-up job, in the first place, by your father and Talbot's mother. I don't suppose you knew it, but, in their young days, they were in love with one another. I don't know what happened, but the marriage didn't take place and each of them married somebody else. However, they kept in touch and the two families were on friendly terms, and when you and Talbot were both youngsters there was this thing that you and he should marry. Of course, there was no suggestion that pressure should be brought to bear on either of you. That would be unthinkable in this day and age. They simply saw to it that conditions were right, that's all, and I suppose propinquity and common interest did the rest. You're not in love with Talbot, you know."

"Really, Miriam!" protested Hubert. "How can you decide a thing like that? Fenella knows her own business best."

"I didn't decide it. It's self-evident, isn't it, Fenella?" said Miriam. "I'm an old maid and a happy one, and I've seen too many of my friends' marriages go astray to be content to let this one go on without a word of protest. Mind you, Hubert, I wouldn't have taken it upon myself to interfere and I was quite prepared to see it through if Fenella wanted it that way, but I consider that Talbot's conduct lets Fenella out, if she's looking for a way of escape, and I think she is."

"Well," said Fenella, still flushed and feeling, at this forthright setting out of what she recognised as her real feelings, much inclined to weep, "I must say that if Talbot thinks a business deal more important than the date of his wedding, I don't think he'll make a very considerate husband. If you don't mind, I think I'll go and unpack. Has a new date been suggested? I mean, people will want to know. . . ."

"No," said Miriam, almost violently. "I have written and told people that Talbot is indisposed – a useful word which commits me to nothing – and that the wedding is postponed *sine die*." She looked anxiously at Fenella, who rose from her chair and went hurriedly out of the room.

"You know, Miriam," said Hubert mildly, "sometimes I really think you take too much on yourself."

"I take more on myself than you know about," said Miriam. "I have never had a high opinion of Talbot. He is selfish and conceited. I knew that, if he went running off to Europe like this, the marriage would never take place. I took it upon myself to tell him so. Besides, if you ask me, Fenella has met somebody else."

"Really, my dear Miriam! How on earth do you deduce that?"

"Oh, I know Fenella pretty well," said his sister complacently. "I just hope it isn't the landlord of that pub where she stayed last night, because he seems to be married already, but I don't think that's who it is. It is likelier to be somebody she has met in London. She is loyal enough and foolish enough to believe that she was in honour bound to Talbot, but this jaunt of his will have given her second thoughts, as she indicated just now. I think she will stay with us until Talbot returns next week, and then she will give him a piece of her mind and hand back the engagement ring. You see if she doesn't!"

"Well, really!" said Hubert, helplessly.

Talbot's letter was beside Fenella's plate when she came down to breakfast on the following morning. She recognised the writing on the envelope, as she could scarcely fail to do, and tucked the letter unopened into her handbag, preferring to read it in the privacy of her room.

"Dear Fenella," it ran, "you are probably a bit sore with me for going off like this and dishing our wedding date, but your cousins seemed prepared to put off the honoured guests for a week or so, and I know you are only inviting one or two of your London friends. Believe me, dear, this deal was too important for me to pass up on it, and the firm were particularly keen that one of the partners should go, and it was decided that I was the best man for the job, which, of course, is a tremendous compliment. Everything is going beautifully smoothly, so I should think we need only postpone the wedding for about a fortnight. The best man is acting as my second in command at the office while I'm away, so he'll still be available, and so will the bridesmaids, as they are my sisters, so it will be all the same in the long run, and your cousin says he is willing to give you away at any time which suits you. Not to fret, dear, at the short postponement. See you soon. Love, Talbot."

Fenella tore the letter into very small pieces. Then she took out a writing pad and replied:

"Dear Talbot, please don't bother about marrying me. I should hate to come *at any time* between you and your business interests. I don't love you and never have. Why don't you team up with a computer and have a jumbo jet as best man? Regards, (as I must find some way of ending this note), Fenella."

She did not trouble to read through what she had written, but thrust the letter into an envelope, took it down to Miriam, who was in the garden cutting flowers for the house, and said,

"I've torn up Talbot's letter and now I don't know where to address this one."

"Oh, I've got the address in my bureau somewhere," said Miriam. "Don't forget you'll need extra stamps for abroad. You'd better let Salmon take it down to the village and send it at air-mail rates. Thank goodness this has happened. Your breakdown in the car may be the best thing that ever came about for you."

"Well, yes, I think it was," said Fenella soberly. "I've had time to think things over, and the letter has clinched matters. I'm *never* going to marry him, Miriam."

"Thank goodness for that. Here, hold these, will you, while I snip a few more. I like flowers about the place."

Fenella took the flowers and when she and Miriam had carried them into the house and arranged them in vases, she said,

"I think I'll drive into Douston myself and post my letter. Can I shop for you while I'm there?"

"Why don't you write the rest of your letters while you're about it? – the putting-off ones, I mean. Then they will be done and done with, and we can all settle down and enjoy your stay. I'll tell you what, Fenella! Why don't you add a bit to the letter you'll have to write to your great-aunt? She was coming up for the wedding, so why not ask her to come in any case? We always enjoy her company, and as I expect she's put off all her engagements for the days she was staying here for the wedding, it won't cause her to have to change her plans, will it?"

"I'd love her to come," said Fenella. "May I phone her? That's such a good idea, and very kind of you, Miriam."

"Nonsense, my dear! Glad to see dear old Beatrice at any time. Don't know how she manages to keep so busy at her age. Remarkable old lady. She, for one, won't be sorry about this business, you know. I've talked to her on the phone about it and she absolutely agrees with me."

"Really? She always seemed interested in the thought of my getting married."

"Oh, well, we all thought the thing was in the bag, and that you'd made up your mind to go through with it, you see. It wasn't for us to be jeremiahs about the wedding, was it, now? But, O Lord, my dear, I'm so thankful it's all off!"

Dame Beatrice Adela Lestrange Bradley was the great-aunt with whom Fenella had been spending a few days before she began her journey to Douston. Dame Beatrice was surprisingly old, incredibly energetic and was liked by all her relatives except by Fenella's other great-aunt, the Lady Selina Lestrange, who considered her frivolous.

She was listening to a discourse on Rugby football from her secretary's son, Hamish Gavin, when she was called to the telephone, and excused herself to him with a promise to return later and hear more.

"It is Mademoiselle Fenella, madame," said her maid, handing over the receiver. Dame Beatrice said to the mouthpiece of the telephone,

"Good morning. Fenella, my dear. So you arrived safely at Douston Hall?"

"Yes, darling, but yesterday, not the day before. Great-aunt, I've broken my engagement. Will you come quickly and hold my hand?"

"Of course, dear child. I will order the car at once and lunch on the way."

"Well, don't take the turning to Seven Wells, that's all."

Dame Beatrice did not turn aside to the surprising village of Seven wells, neither did George, her chauffeur, take the quieter but lengthier route which Fenella had followed across country. The big car, keeping strictly to main roads, whirled through the long miles and Dame Beatrice, correctly if somewhat individually gowned for dinner, was able to leer amiably across at her great-niece without having kept her hostess's table waiting.

Fenella accompanied her to her room when the meal was over, ostensibly to help her to finish her unpacking, but actually to confide in her in private. That her great-niece was anything but unhappy about the breaking-off of the engagement was soon made clear.

"I never did like Talbot as much as I ought to have done if I was going to marry him," said Fenella, "and now he's proved himself such a hound. . . ."

"He is aptly named," said Dame Beatrice, with her eldritch cackle. "Well, dear child, I, for one, am not at all sorry that you've changed your mind. Who is his supplanter? Anyone known to the family?" She gazed blandly at Fenella's blushes.

"There isn't anybody. How could there be?" said the girl, avoiding her elderly relative's sharp black eyes.

"You spend a night on the road when you were expected to spend it here. You immediately break your engagement. You send post-haste for me. These things are signs and portents. Recline on the bed, whilst I occupy this excellent armchair, and tell me all."

"It's a long story, and it certainly doesn't have the ending you seem to suggest," said Fenella feebly, remembering (with shame) how reluctant she had been to wash the black smudge off her hand on the evening of her arrival at Douston Hall.

"Fire away. I am all ears and you have my undivided attention. Begin at the beginning. The last I saw of your car was on Wednesday morning as you drove off in the direction of Cadnam."

"Do you mean you want every detail, however slight?"

"If you please. I prefer my stories to be told in the round, and this one promises to be full of interest."

"You can say that again, darling," observed Fenella emphatically. "Well, it all went according to plan until I went mad and left my perfectly straightforward road to pick up a snack lunch in a village called Seven Wells. I got the lunch all right, but then the car broke down, and that's how I came to spend a night at the inn. It's a pub, actually, and the people in it are the landlord and his wife – their name is Shurrock – a gipsy cook called Sukie, a general maid named Clytie – she's only a girl, of course – and a youth who acts as general factotum. I saw almost nothing of him and I've no idea what his name is. Oh, yes, I have, though. It's Bob – not that it matters."

"What happened to your car?"

"I wish I knew. Before lunch it worked and after lunch it didn't work. My own idea is that village louts tampered with it while I was in the pub, but I couldn't prove anything. The landlord was very helpful. He got on to a garage and a man came along, but he had to tow behind the landlord's car and that's how it all came about, because the man couldn't get the repairs done until after lunch on the following morning."

She described the rest of her adventures, including her conversation with the post-office shop-keepers, and repeated the rumour she had heard that the local Squire had been murdered. This involved mentioning her meeting with Jack-in-the-Green.

"Most interesting," said Dame Beatrice. "I wonder what was the original function of the zodiac people? I have never heard of anything in folk-lore quite like them."

"They were a bit frightening, in a way, and that business of collecting the fragments of a skeleton and taking it by torch-light to be buried in that pagan place was rather horrible."

"But the people at the inn appeared to be normal enough, did they?"

"Oh, yes, but they must have known about the bones in the cellar and all the mumbo-jumbo concerning them, mustn't they?"

"I wonder why they gave you that particular room?"

"To get me out of the way, I suppose."

"But that is the last thing it appears to have accomplished."

"I know, but I was warned to bar myself in. If I had, I wouldn't have had a clue about the goings-on."

"Well, it is all extremely interesting and attractive. What happened when you left the inn?"

"Nothing much. I thought I might take a look at the seven wells – they're hillside springs, of course, and one of them is supposed to produce holy water."

"Oh, dear me! And this Green Man you mentioned persuaded you to drink from it, and after that you perceived that Talbot is indeed the hound for which he is named? Remarkable and fascinating." She fixed her witch-like eyes on Fenella's and added: "Your village interests me strangely."

"Well, it interested *me*, but, all the same, I never want to go there again – and I *didn't* drink the water."

"Tell me more about this Green Man. He does not seem to belong to the rest of the village ceremonies."

"Oh, he was quite different. Except for a rather pathetic dance carried out by some girls with ribboned garlands, he was the only authentic bit of folkery in the place, so far as I could make out."

"You say that, after a bit, in spite of the greenery and his black face, you recognised him. That means you had already met him somewhere."

"Well, yes, I had," said Fenella. "I'd met him on the previous evening. He followed me and warned me against roaming about in the neighbourhood of the Iron Age fort. I thought it was like his cheek, and I got rid of him as soon as I could."

"What manner of man was he then?"

"Oh, just an ordinary kind. Rather impudent, I thought, and wanted to be very bossy and interfering. He said he'd been at the pub when I first went into the bar, but I didn't notice him."

"Had he anything to say about himself?"

"He said he was a semi-professional man, that's all."

"How was he dressed that evening?"

"Oh, a tweed jacket and a pullover and rather unpressed-looking trousers."

"Seven Wells? I seem to remember the name. Isn't there a school near by?" asked Dame Beatrice, after a pause."

"I suppose there's a village school somewhere near the church, but I don't remember seeing it. You mean Jack-in-the-Green might be a schoolmaster?"

"I was not thinking of a village school. I have a feeling that the Worshipful Company of Shoemakers, or some such, founded a school in the neighbourhood of Seven Wells in about the year 1550 for the sons of poor men. If so, it will have become a public school by now and its scholars will be the sons of anything but poor men. I wonder whether our dear Hubert possesses a copy of the public schools' Year Book? Let us cast the rest of these lendings into outer darkness and go downstairs and find out."

Not surprisingly, since he had no children, Hubert could not produce the volume in question. While he was suggesting useless alternatives, Dame Beatrice scribbled in her pocket diary and showed the message to Miriam, who smiled and nodded agreement that she would be prepared to house another guest.

Douston was a comparatively small place, but it possessed a public library to which George was deputed to drive his employer fairly early on the following morning. In the reference department Dame Beatrice found what she wanted. She rang up the school near Seven Wells. It was called, as she had remembered, Saint Crispin's, since its founders had been the Worshipful Company of Shoemakers. She obtained connection with the headmaster.

"I don't know whether you remember me," she said, "but four or five years ago I addressed the Headmasters' Conference, and then you very kindly asked me to visit your school."

"Of course! Delighted to hear from you, Dame Beatrice. Is there anything I can do?"

"Have you a Jack-in-the-Green on your staff? I seem to recollect holding a conversation with a very young man who told me that in his spare time he was researching into the folklore of the district."

"Oh, you mean Pardieu, I expect. Fellow who puts on the school plays and knows *The Golden Bough* by heart. Do you wish to speak to him?"

"If you will be so good."

A few minutes later, young Nicholas Pardieu, Fenella's Green Man, had accepted the kind invitation of Mr and Miss Cromleigh to spend Saturday and Sunday at Douston, where Dame Beatrice Lestrange Bradley was anxious to canvass his views on the fertility rites implicit in the presentation of Easter eggs and chocolate Easter rabbits.

CHAPTER NINE
Unusual Honeymoon

"Bring hether the Pincke and purple Cullambine,
With Gellyflowres;
Bring Coronations, and Sops-in wine
Worn of Paramoures."

Edmund Spenser – *A Ditty*

"But this is incredible," said Fenella. "Not only that you should be that man I met and also that black-faced gipsy, but that you should know my great-aunt, I mean."

"Oh, but I don't, really, not until now. She came to the school – once, and I spoke to her. My headmaster brought her to give a talk to the boys," said Jack-in-the-Green. "I was determined to find you, of course, but I never expected such luck as this. I don't know how Dame Beatrice swung it, but I've been given leave of absence until Tuesday night. Look here, may I call you Fenella? And will you call me Nicholas – Nick, if you prefer it, although I think the other sounds better from an affianced wife to her prospective husband. More respectful, if you see what I mean."

"I haven't the slightest idea *what* you mean. I don't know what you're talking about. I came here to get married. I told you so, when you were all blacked up and wearing that ridiculous greenery."

"Well, that's all right. I'm in favour of your marriage."

"To a man named Talbot. . . ."

"No, no – to a man named Nicholas. Don't you remember? Look, let's go for a walk and get properly acquainted. I'm told that a charming river flows through this little town. As you know, I am enamoured of water. Beside the Seven Wells we met, and beside the Waters of Comfort will I plight thee my troth. You don't know how lucky you are. I bring the rain that the earth may be replenished; I water the flocks and herds; I am the May King; I am the tree-spirit; I grant easy delivery to women in childbirth and I bring sustenance to the sick; I am the god of growth to crops and beasts; I am the Grass King and I make the flax to grow. In Silesia I visit the house wherein I find my queen, and with her I open the dance. What have you to say to all that? Will you open the dance with me?"

"I'm dumbfounded. And now stop talking nonsense. Besides, we didn't meet – not for the first time, I mean – by the seven springs. I know now that you're the man who stopped me on Mayering Eve and told me not to go to the hill-fort that night. I did go, though, much later on, when they had the bonfire and all the rest of it."

"Yes, I know," said Nicholas. "It was because of that, and because of something I said to you at the seven springs, that Dame Beatrice got your cousins to invite me here. Well, she may have had another reason, but it wouldn't become me to mention that at the moment. Anyway, you seem to have reported your adventures to her pretty fully. . . ."

"She's like that," said Fenella defensively. "One finds oneself telling her things. She's a trained psychiatrist, of course, so that may be the reason."

"No doubt. All the same, you were glad to share your experiences with somebody on whom you knew you could lean, weren't you? I mean, you seem to have told her a great many details which you didn't give your cousins, fond of them though you are."

"That's quite true. You see, there were points about my adventures, as you call them, that I don't understand and don't like. Then, when you hinted that Sir Bathy had been murdered . . . and you weren't the first person to tell me about it, either. It seems there was an inquest and—"

"I know. That's what Dame Beatrice mostly wanted to talk to me about. There *was* an inquest and the verdict was murder by person or persons unknown. It's all a great mystery, because the old chap was popular in the village and, so far as is known, nobody can gain anything by his death. The property is entailed and of no particular value, and there is a son to inherit it. Now look, darling Fenella, how soon will you marry me? I've got a special licence, if it interests you."

"Marry you? – But I've only just broken off my engagement to Talbot."

"That's what makes everything so beautifully straightforward and simple."

"I'm never going to marry."

"That's what *you* think."

"Don't pick a quarrel with me. Let's change the subject. Why did you try to stop me in the road on Mayering Eve?"

"I did stop you. If you chose to be wilful afterwards, that wasn't my fault."

"I saw them bury a skeleton, you know, on that hill. Why do they do it?"

"I've no idea. Some bastard fertility rite, I imagine. The blood from the cock seems to indicate that. The cock represents what was once a living man, and the skeleton the same man when he's dead, I think."

"They've used up all the skeletons which were in the cellar at the *More to Come*."

"How do you know that?"

"I bought an electric torch and went down to take a look. Nothing is left but a small bone or two. What will they do next year, I wonder?"

"Goodness knows. It won't matter to us, anyway."

"It won't matter to *me*. I shall be in London."

"It's a long way to look ahead, but will you bet that's where you'll be? I wouldn't risk it, if I were you."

"No," said Fenella, "I won't bet on it. I would have betted that I was going to marry Talbot, but I'm not, you see."

"Poor fellow! Still, his loss is my gain, isn't it?"

"I've something to tell you, Miriam," said Fenella, a week later. "I'm going to marry Nicholas."

"At once, I hope, then I can re-issue all the invitations and there won't have been time for people to make other engagements, so I expect all our friends can come. Thank God Talbot's impossible relations are out of it, and Nicholas says he doesn't want to invite anybody except his best man, so *that's* all right. I see that Nicholas has got his appointment, but I suppose he'll have to stay at Saint Crispin's until the end of the term."

"Oh, yes, of course he must work out his notice, but isn't it grand about Glenbury? It's a much bigger school than Saint Crispin's."

"He is to be a housemaster, isn't he? Quite a plum for a man of his age."

"He says our marriage will come in handy. It seems that the headmaster likes his housemasters to have wives. It will be lovely to have a ready-made home, too. It wouldn't have been much fun for me during the next few weeks, though, with him at school and me in London, and I don't know of any hotel that's near enough to Seven Wells for us to be able to meet occasionally, so I've written to the *More to Come* to see whether the Shurrocks can put me up from Mondays to Fridays. I'm afraid I took it for granted that you'd have us here for Saturdays and Sundays, Miriam, whenever Nicholas is not on weekend duty."

"I should hope you did take it for granted! We'll be delighted to have you."

The wedding took place at the parish church of All Saints (Early Perpendicular and as vast as a small cathedral) with due pomp and ceremony, and the newly-married couple spent Saturday night in the best of the guest-rooms at Douston

Hall and left after dinner on Sunday evening to deliver Nicholas to Saint Crispin's School and Fenella to the comforts of the *More to Come*. Earlier – directly after lunch – on the same day, Dame Beatrice returned to her own home, the Stone House at Wandles Parva on the edge of the New Forest, and Miriam and Hubert, having bidden the guests *au revoir*, resumed their kindly and peaceful existence.

Three days later Dame Beatrice received a letter from her great-niece. An extract from it was as follows: "I can't tell you how happy I am. Of course, when I met Nicholas again, after the springs, I knew I was fated, but I was afraid it was going to be one of those yearning, unhappy, unfulfilled sort of fates, like those of heroines in romantic stories of the past. How on *earth* did you guess? Sometimes I think you must be a witch! And I *know* you got him this plummy appointment.

"Talking of witches, a most strange, unaccountable thing has happened. Perhaps you remember that when I stayed the night here, only just over a fortnight ago, there were five people living in the house. Well, now there are seven. So what, sez you? Well, I'll tell you. Every one of them is different from those who were here before. Instead of Mr Shurrock there's a manager whose name I don't know; instead of the gipsy Sukie there's a chef (a man) and there's another kitchen-maid in place of Clytie; there's a proper reception desk with a woman in charge of it, and a numbered board for the keys of the rooms and a register to sign; there's a chambermaid, a waiter for the new dining-room – a conversion from the saloon bar – and a barmaid who lives out and comes in for the opening hours.

"I made some remark about all this to the woman at the reception desk yesterday when I asked whether there were any letters for me, and was met by a *very* blank stare and an 'Oh, really, madam?' which seemed to make further inquiries impossible. There was no suggestion of the Shurrocks' going when I was here before, but, of course, all the circumstances then were unusual and I stayed only the one night, so there was no reason why they should say anything, especially as I don't suppose they ever expected me to stay there again – certainly not so soon – but, all the same, it seems extremely odd that the servants have gone as well.

"Nobody but myself is staying in the house as a guest, but there seem to be five bedrooms prepared. They open off that long corridor with all the up-and-down steps which I had to traverse to get to the priest's room, and I've got one of them and am informed that the priest's room is no longer used except as a storeroom.

"Nicholas is producing a weird and wonderful pageant at the school, and I've been lugged in to help with the costumes, so I see much more of him during the week than I ever expected to do, and it's all perfectly heavenly and the boys are absolutely charming, but I feel there's something very fishy about this new set-up at the *More to Come*."

Dame Beatrice had a number of other letters which came by the same post as Fenella's. Laura Gavin, her secretary, always sorted the letters out and made three piles of them. Dame Beatrice's personal correspondence came first, then such letters as were personal in that they came from her London clinic with its cypher on the flap of the envelope, and thirdly there was the rest of the mail. This consisted of begging letters, advertisements, and invitations to open bazaars or to lecture to learned societies. Laura invariably carried these off after breakfast and read and vetted them before passing on the few with which she was not competent to deal.

On this particular morning there was among Dame Beatrice's personal letters an envelope on which she recognised the handwriting of Assistant Commissioner Robert Gavin, Laura's husband. Laura was naturally intrigued, and hoped that, when it had been perused, Dame Beatrice would disclose some, if not all, of its contents. She was not disappointed.

"Well," said Dame Beatrice, as she re-inserted the last of the personal letters in its envelope, "two interesting communications by one post are more than we have a right to expect. This one—" she handed Laura the letter from Gavin – "you will like to read for yourself. The other is from the great-niece who was staying here and left us to go to Douston Hall to be married. I will outline its salient points when you have absorbed what our dear Robert has to say. The letters have some slight connection with one another and, taken together, they open up a wide field of interesting speculation."

Laura read her husband's letter and handed it back.

"Shall you go?" she asked.

"Most certainly. It will be a professional visit, as our dear Robert is at some pains to point out, and should be an intriguing experience. I wonder why Lady Bitton-Bittadon is so anxious to have me stay in the house?"

"I suppose there's no doubt that this Sir Bathy Bitton-Bittadon has been murdered? If so, she may well feel very nervous."

"No doubt at all. Robert has enclosed a short report of the inquest, which I shall study."

"Do you want to take a Doctor Watson with you?"

"I would not dream of equating your undoubted intelligence with that of Sherlock Holmes' faithful but somewhat obtuse amanuensis. However, as I shall be going disguised as a psychiatrist and not as an amateur detective, I think it will be better if I do not take you with me, especially as I can scarcely plant an extra guest on the household."

"When will you go?"

"Tomorrow. The sooner I get there the better, I think. Robert is sending one of his own men down, so I shall not be without support."

"What did you mean about your great-niece's letter having some connection with this one?"

"The murdered squire lived just outside the village where Fenella spent the night when her car broke down after she left us to join her cousins in Douston, that is all. She writes to say that she is staying at the same inn, as it is nearest to her husband's school. She goes on to tell me that in the space of about a fortnight the management and the whole staff at the inn has changed. Not one of the inmates whom she met on her previous visit is the same. She regards this as strange, and so do I."

"I suppose the other people sold it, or else the brewers have put another manager in charge."

"The inn may have changed hands, but one would think that some, if not all, of the staff would have stayed. Seven Wells is only a village, and in a village there are not so many chances of employment that people lightly change their work. Besides, there were some slightly bizarre features about that particular inn which I find extremely interesting. I shall certainly pay it a visit while I am staying with Lady Bitton-Bittadon. I really cannot think why she wants me. When I wrote to dear Robert I fully intended to put up at the *More to Come* if they could accommodate me. However, it seems that Lady Bitton-Bittadon is determined to have me at the manor house."

"Wants to keep an eye on you, perhaps. *Could* look a bit suspicious," said Laura cynically.

"Well, at any rate, the local superintendent of police and Robert's London detective-inspector have been warned of my imminent arrival and are to give me their full co-operation."

"Yes," said Laura, eyeing her employer, "I bet they are! And if Fenella hadn't got herself mixed up in something fishy, you wouldn't be going within a hundred miles of Seven Wells, would you?"

Fenella was finding the *More to Come* changed in other ways, apart from the disappearance of the Shurrocks, Sukie, Clytie and Bob. At the end of the journey from Douston to Seven Wells, after she had dropped off her new-wedded lord at Saint Crispin's school, where he was to finish the term before taking up his appointment after the summer vacation, she had driven to the *More to Come* where she had written to engage a room, fully expecting to find the inn in its former condition and herself entering it, as before, by way of the side door to the saloon bar.

All that was altered. During her comparatively short absence, the car-park had been covered smoothly with asphalt and a neat notice on the side door read: *Entrance at front*. She walked out into the street, found the front door, which previously had been barred, standing wide open, and entered a neat, square hall with two small, swinging, glass signs above doors which faced one another. One said *Bar*, the other *Dining Room*. The only feature which Fenella recognised was the front staircase, at the foot of which was a notice: *Visitors' Lounge. T.V.*

Another notice, adjacent to it and supplemented by the painting of a large golden hand with pointing forefinger, said: *Reception.*

As she had told Dame Beatrice in her letter, there was no sign of the Shurrocks, Clytie, Sukie or the boy who had helped with Fenella's luggage on her previous visit. A golden-haired woman was in charge of the reception desk and a uniformed porter who collected her baggage when she had registered her name, address and nationality, led the way up the front stairs past the lounge and the bathroom which Fenella had used on her previous visit, and up another flight of stairs and along a corridor. Here he unlocked a bedroom door, handed Fenella the key, dumped her suitcase on to the stand designed to receive it, thanked her for the tip she handed him and departed, closing the door behind him.

The furnishing of the room was new, adequate and functional. There were hand and bath towels and an armchair as well as a dressing-table stool. The taps ran hot and cold water, there were writing paper and envelopes in one small top drawer, shoe-cleaning impregnated paper in another, and there was a neat list of meal-times under the glass top of the dressing-table.

"This could be simply anywhere," said Fenella aloud. She went to the window and looked out. Her room was at the end of the corridor and she realised that it could not be "simply anywhere" after all. The window was at the side of the inn which faced away from the village. The prospect before her was of a country road and the menacing hill-fort on which the hermaphrodite skeleton had been buried not much more than two weeks before.

There was a bathroom on the opposite side of the corridor. Fenella bathed, dressed and went down to dinner. The dining-room was what had been the saloon bar, but she scarcely recognised it. A waiter showed her to a small table and she had scarcely seated herself in the chair which he sedulously drew out for her when she saw her husband advancing towards her. This was completely unexpected.

"Hullo again," he said, seating himself. "Hillson offered to take prep. for me tonight, so I came along. Are you pleased to see me, or had you made other arrangements? This is a dashed unsatisfactory sort of peculiar honeymoon, anyway."

The waiter handed them menus and a tall, dark man, wearing a flower in his buttonhole, approached with the wine-list.

"I hope you will be very comfortable with us, Mrs Pardieu," he said. "I am the manager. I think you met my wife at the reception desk when you checked in."

"There seem to be a good many changes since I was here last time," said Fenella.

"Really? When was that? I didn't know that the old-style *More to Come* took guests."

"Neither did it," said Nicholas, breaking in with an abruptness which surprised and startled Fenella. "My wife hit upon this place for a meal when her car

broke down one time. I'm afraid the best they could do for her then was a snack
in the saloon bar and a dock glass of sherry or something or other. Now, then,
let's see what we are going to eat. You can leave the wine-list and we'll order
when we've chosen our meal."

"Oh, very good, sir," said the manager, completely changing his voice and
attitude.

"Why didn't you want him to know that I'd actually stayed a night here?"
asked Fenella, when the man had gone.

"I don't really know," said Nicholas. "A sort of instinct prompted me. I'm
superstitious about this village and its peculiar little ways, and I could wish you
weren't staying here. Wouldn't some place in Cridley have been better?"

"Rather a long way from your school, darling, and – well – I admit the village
is a bit frightening in some ways, but I liked the Shurrocks and Clytie and I
thought they'd be quite pleased to have me again. Of course I had no idea they
wouldn't be here."

"But surely when they answered your letter. . . ."

"It was only a printed card to say that a single room was available and it was
initialled, not signed, so I didn't think anything about it except to feel that the
More to Come had gone up in the world to have printed cards."

"So it has, I must say. Wish I were staying here with you."

"Well, it won't be so very long now before we get our own place, and we do
get three week-ends out of four at Douston, don't forget."

"God bless Hubert and Miriam. At least we can honeymoon while we're with
them. Shall I write you a bucolic *Epithalamion*, like Spenser's, only more so?"

"No. Tell me what this is all about – if I can remember it. I think I can. I heard
it nine times altogether and in this very house.

> *Sagittarius be archer and shoot at the sun;*
> *Capricorn butt bachelors and cause 'em to run;*
> *Aquarius 'e stand wi' 'is bucket o' water,*
> *Pisces come swimmin' a christened babe arter.*
> *Aries 'ave killed off the bleatin' old wether . . ."*

Nicholas interrupted her.

"It's a fertility rhyme, darling. Who repeated it to you?"

"Nobody. The zodiac people chanted it down in the old church under the
priest's room and in the crypt when they were bringing up those bones they
buried on the hilltop."

"Old Bitton-Bittadon repeated it to me once when he was in his cups, the old
lecher."

"Was he really?"

"A lecher? Oh, yes, and usually as drunk as a lord as well. Still, bibulous old backwoodsman as he was, he wasn't a bad old boy, and certainly wasn't the sort who made enemies."

"He certainly seems to have made *one*."

"Yes, indeed. 'Aries have killed off the bleating old wether.' And, talking of christened babes, the son, Jeremy Bitton-Bittadon, came home from his travels long, long before anybody could have expected him."

CHAPTER TEN
The Charnel House

". . . and now there is nothing left of him but his bones."
Frederick Marryat – *The White Wolf of the Hartz Mountains*

Her brief courtship and her plan to marry another man in place of Talbot, coupled with her first experience of being truly in love, had left Fenella mentally breathless, spiritually uplifted and physically in such a state of exuberant health that she rose blithely in the mornings and passed her days in a kind of dreaming haze of surprised happiness, her only longing being for the next meeting with the beloved.

The village no longer seemed strange or unfriendly. In fact, during her walks abroad, she met with so many smiles and pleasant greetings that, after a few days, she found it almost impossible to recall her first impressions of the place.

She did not like to ask point-blank what had happened to the Shurrocks and their servants, or for an account which would explain the complete metamorphosis of the *More to Come*. Her room was comfortable, the food was good and Nicholas contrived to get away from the school every afternoon during games periods. At these times he drove over to spend a precious couple of hours with her and twice a week, when he was off duty, he dined with her at the inn and on Saturdays and Sundays they were together at Douston Hall.

Twice she made a pilgrimage to the hill-fort at the end of the village and came back baffled. She could no longer believe that she had been a witness to what she thought she had seen there on Mayering Eve. Nevertheless, she could not ignore the blackened ground where the bonfire had been, or the stamped earth which now covered the strange grave. It was after the second of these walks that she had an unlikely and terrifying dream and that the dream had an equally strange and terrifying aftermath.

Before that happened, however, she had another experience which left her uneasy and somewhat perturbed. Nicholas had dined with her at the inn and she had accompanied him a couple of miles on his way back to the school. He was driving his own car. She had left hers at the *More to Come* and had planned to return to the inn on foot.

It was a beautiful evening, and was unusually calm, a circumstance which, when she thought it over, struck her as having been sinister. As it happened, the school lay in the opposite direction to the hill-fort, and so, on her walk back, she decided to turn aside for another look at the seven springs from which the village of Seven Wells took its name, and which now had romantic associations for her. This time, of course, there was no Jack-in-the-Green to accost her. In fact, except for a courting couple who were jammed against the trunk of one of the grey-boled ash trees, the common appeared to be deserted.

She wandered round the edge of the water away from the absorbed couple, then climbed the bank and saw, approaching her from the direction of the village main street, a man whose walk and figure seemed familiar. He was exactly like Jem Shurrock, the former landlord of the *More to Come*. The time was a quarter to nine, the sun was setting and the walking man had his back to it. It was not until she was almost up to him that she realised that the long shadows had deceived her. The man was about Jem Shurrock's height and build, but there the likeness ended.

In country fashion he gave her a civil "Good evening', and was passing on when Fenella, acting on impulse, (as she often did), halted and said,

"I've been trying to locate a Mr and Mrs Shurrock. They used to keep the *More to Come* public house, but nobody there seems to know what's happened to them."

The man's attitude changed with considerable abruptness. He stared at her and said brusquely,

"Them as asks no questions won't get told no lies. Best you be off back to where you come from and not to be meddlin' any more in things as don't consarn ee."

"Thank you for your advice," said Fenella. She gave him a curt nod and passed on her way. She thought she had recognised his voice as that of Leo, but it was difficult to be sure. However, the encounter had an unpleasant effect on her. All her earlier impressions of the village and its inhabitants crowded back on her. "How thankful I shall be," she murmured to herself, "when the summer holidays come, and Nicholas and I can be shut of this place for ever!"

She returned to the inn more than ever convinced that there was a mystery connected with the disappearance of the Shurrocks and their staff. She supposed that some kind of scandal must have blown up which had necessitated their abrupt departure. It was idle to speculate upon what might have happened, but, all the same, she found herself doing it. Something must have occurred to drive them away at such short notice, unless they had failed to comply with the brewers' explicit instructions about something or other, and had been summarily dismissed as a consequence.

All the same, although that might account for Jem Shurrock and his wife, it hardly seemed to account for Sukie, Clytie and the young fellow Bob who had helped with the odd jobs, unless, of course, the staff had all resigned out of loyalty to the landlord. In the case of Sukie, whom Fenella, at first, had thought was the landlord's wife, this might be the explanation, but Fenella was much less sure of it in the case of the two adolescents, unless they had received some inducement from the Shurrocks to go with them to take on other employment. As for the man she had met on the common, there was no doubt that he had recognised her, and that his earlier suspicion and dislike of her, when he had been one of the masked and gowned figures in the lounge on Mayering Eve, had been renewed at meeting her again, and intensified by her remark about the Shurrocks. That he knew the reason for their disappearance she felt certain.

Fenella had a good ear for voices. She felt that, because of this, she now could be pretty certain of the identity and ordinary appearance of two of the signs of the zodiac, Leo and the horried young Aries. She had no suspicion at the time that this knowledge was likely to prove useful in the future, but continued her walk back to the inn in less good spirits than when she had turned aside to revisit the seven springs.

She thought afterwards that her slightly unpleasant encounter with Leo might have been the cause of her sinister dream, but the dream did not follow until she had been to the hill-fort again, so the connection was not a direct one. Her objective, on this further occasion, was not the fort itself, but the country-side beyond it. She breakfasted early that morning, and having on the previous day asked for a packed lunch she set off in her car, drove past and partly round the hill and then left the Croyton road, of which she had far from happy memories, and turned into a winding lane which seemed to encircle the village.

It was an unfenced road and there had been no sign-post to indicate where it led. She began to wonder whether it led only to a farmhouse, but, about three miles further on, it merged into a slightly wider road which came into it from the left, and this she pursued until it crossed a tiny river. This was hardly more than a brook, to which the country road had descended before it mounted again to reach a hamlet. This was a tiny place, and on the further side of it a narrow lane turned off to the left. Following an idle fancy, on the verge of this lane Fenella pulled up and left the car, proposing to walk up the tracks, which looked inviting, and take her *al fresco* meal at a convenient spot on the hillside up which the little road climbed.

She soon realised that she could not have brought the car much further, for the lane petered out into a narrow grass-grown footpath. It wound upwards on an easy gradient which encouraged walking, and half a mile further on it passed through a wood. A long way off, between the trees, she could see a small manor house and she paused to look at it before she continued to climb the hill.

As no drive appeared to lead up to the house, she concluded that she was inspecting it from the back or from one side. It was built, so far as she could make out from such a distance, in Tudor style, although, owing to the tall trees which were in almost full leaf, she could not see the characteristic Tudor chimneys at all clearly. What she did see clearly was a tall man who suddenly dropped out of a tree almost on to her toes. He scrambled to his feet and seized her petrified arm.

"Don't tell anyone you've seen me," he said urgently. Fenella shook him off. She was considerably alarmed. He must be either a maniac or an escaped convict, she thought. She was not certain which would have been her preference, had she been called upon to choose. Fortunately the man gave a hunted glance round about him, ejaculated, "Here they come," and, vaulting the wall which separated the public path from the manor park, he began to run towards the house. Fenella wasted no time. She also began to run, not towards the house, which, in any case, was walled off from her, but up the hill. It was heavy going and she was soon winded. She dropped into a walk, then stopped to look back. Nobody was following her, and she was soon clear of the trees and out on the grassy, pleasant hillside. The sun was shining, there were cowslips among the grasses and from where she stood she had a clear view of the Tudor manor house. It looked quiet and completely innocuous. She wondered whether perhaps it was a private nursing-home for the mentally afflicted, and whether the man was a patient there.

As though this thought had conjured up spirits from the vasty deep, as she turned to follow the hill-track up and over the brow of the rise she was aware of a small, thin, female figure, attended by a sturdy, thick-set male one, coming down the slope towards her.

"Oh, great-aunt!" she cried. "And George! Oh, I *am* glad to see you!" She started forward and embraced Dame Beatrice with fervour. "Is that a madhouse down there?"

"It may warrant that somewhat unsympathetic appellation," replied Dame Beatrice, when she was released from Fenella's hysterical clasp, "but it is not so designated officially. That is the residence of the late Sir Bathy Bitton-Bittadon. He was once the squire of your village of Seven Wells, but is now defunct and, as the old song says, laid in grave, as you know."

"But I thought the manor house was on the road I took when I first came to Seven Wells," exclaimed Fenella.

"All roads lead to Rome, child. But why do you betray symptoms of alarm? Has anything happened to cause you distress?"

Fenella explained that she thought she had lately encountered a lunatic and that this had frightened her.

"It was so sudden and unexpected, you see," she concluded. "He just dropped out of an oak tree at my feet. It was horribly disconcerting."

"Ah, had you been looking for squirrels you would not have been taken unawares. In Robin Hood country, always look for squirrels, and then you will avoid having outlaws dropping, with or without evil intentions, upon your nature-loving head," said Dame Beatrice, who seemed in high spirits.

"Well, I'm glad you're here, anyway. I hated the thought of having to go back that way alone," said her great-niece.

"Why would you need to return by that route?"

"Because I've left my car at the end of the lane. I've brought a packed lunch, and I liked the look of the lane, so I followed it and decided to have a picnic at the top of this hill. But, really, Aunt Adela, what are *you* doing here?"

"I am merely taking my morning constitutional, but I have been obliged to promise the police that I will take George with me when I walk abroad."

"Good heavens, why? Are you doing something dangerous?"

"Well," said Dame Beatrice, "from what you yourself have told me, it seems that they collect *skeletons* hereabouts." She leered at Fenella as she spoke, and cackled ghoulishly. "I am investigating the murder of Sir Bathy, you know," she added in an off-hand tone. "Are you thinking of walking much further?"

"No, I'm going back to the car, if you and George will come with me. I can drive you to the hotel where you're staying, can't I? You must have walked an awfully long way, so perhaps you'll be glad of a lift."

"That is extremely kind of you, dear child." She waved a skinny yellow claw at the trees below the brow of the hill. "That is the place. That ancient house."

"Where my madman jumped over the wall? But that's not where the funeral came from, is it? I made sure it came from the other direction. It entered the village the same way as I did – that first time, you know – before my wedding," said Fenella.

"I expect it made a tour of the village before the body was placed in the family mausoleum."

"Then who lives in the *other* manor house, the one I passed as I drove to the village that first time?"

"I have no idea, but I do not think it can be in this parish. I also passed it on my way down. It must be four or five miles from here." She glanced at her watch. "I must be getting along. I promised to lunch with the family."

"If you're staying in the house," said Fenella, as they walked downhill towards her car, "you must know this man who dropped out of the tree. Something about him suggested that he wasn't an indoor servant or a groom, but he was very peculiar, I thought, and asked me not to tell anybody I'd seen him. He then said, 'Here they come' – meaning you and George, I suppose – and vaulted over the wall."

As the path, lower down the hillside, entered the wood, Fenella pointed out the spot where the disconcerting episode of the man dropping out of the tree had taken place.

"I think he must be Sir Jeremy, who is home from India and has inherited the estate," said Dame Beatrice.

Fenella, having deposited her passengers at the front of the gabled Tudor house, drove to the hill fort and had her lonely picnic on the side farthest from the village, well away from the burnt grass where the bonfire had been lit and where the hermaphrodite skeleton had been buried. After lunch she drove aimlessly around until it was time to pick up Nicholas at the school gate. There he told her that he had to be back by six to take prep. in place of a colleague who had been taken to hospital with a suspect appendix. They drove to Croyton, where Nicholas knew of a place for tea which was unlikely to be infested by his schoolboys, and at table Fenella told him of the meeting with her great-aunt and the singular episode of the man in the tree. On the way back she stopped for petrol at the garage where they had repaired her car. The proprietor himself attended to her and, on impulse, she asked him whether he knew where the Shurrocks had gone.

"I'm staying there again," she said, "but the place has been opened up a good deal, and there are new people managing it and an entirely new staff."

"Jem Shurrock gone?" said the man. "First I've heard of it. Got the offer of something better, I suppose. Wasn't much of a place, what I saw of it when I went over to look at your bus. Going all right again, is she?"

"Oh, yes, thank you. Didn't you know Mr Shurrock, then, before he called on you about my car? I had the impression that you and he were acquainted."

"Oh, he had his own bus serviced here and called in for petrol and that, but I'd never been to the pub before," said the man.

"But you seemed to know all about the Mayering."

"Only by hearsay, and not from Jem Shurrock. There we are, then. I've put you in two quid's worth. We do it that way now, 'stead of four gallons. It's easier reckoned up."

"You know," said Nicholas, on their way back to his school, "I shouldn't broadcast it that you know too much about the Mayering. You might let out something you're not supposed to know."

"What on earth do you mean?"

"Well, you seem to have seen things the village might not want you to see, that's all. As for your great-aunt's flippant remark about skeletons, well, there are some very queer customs carried out in villages up and down the land, you know. I could tell you some tales as the result of my own researches, things you'd scarcely believe even if a bishop told you about them. Not for nothing did the sea-wolves leave their barbaric imprint all over the eastern counties, and their ghosts to be-devil the spots where they raped and burnt and robbed."

"Well! What a note to leave me on!" said Fenella. "Enough to give a nervous person nightmare."

"You are not my idea of a nervous person, so you jolly well stay out of trouble," said Nicholas, "if only to please your husband."

In the middle of the night Fenella woke, shivering and sweating. She got out of bed and walked about the room to make certain of shaking off sleep and the terrible nightmare it had brought her. What she had actually been dreaming

about she scarcely knew. There was nothing tangible, so far as she could remember, nothing but senseless, unnamed, atavistic terror. It was a long time
before she could nerve herself to go back to bed. When she did, she remained
awake for more than an hour, but when she did sleep there were no more bad
dreams.

In the morning she woke with the impression that her terrors had had something to do with the signs of the zodiac and with the crypt from which the bones
had been removed by the masked and gowned mummers.

"I'd better reassure myself," she thought. "I know there aren't any more skeletons down there – well, not a whole one, anyway, not even a skull. And what's
so frightening about a skeleton, anyway?"

After breakfast she returned to her room, changed her shoes and put on a
coat, then, making certain that the coast was clear, she went to the entrance hall,
which could not be seen from the reception desk, and took the long corridor to
the door of the room in which she had slept on her previous visit. The door was
open and she glanced in, but the small chamber was no longer furnished as a
temporary bedroom. It was empty except for some rolls of wallpaper, an array
of paint-pots, a long trestle table and a couple of step-ladders.

She walked to the head of the stone stair and felt her way down its spiral.
There was the same dim lighting from the same cobwebbed window when she
reached the foot of the stair, and there was the same trapdoor between the stair
and the outer door. The trapdoor was closed, but she raised it without too much
difficulty, and there again was the ladder. Fenella had not forgotten her torch.
She had it in her coat pocket while she descended the ladder, and as soon as she
felt both feet on firm ground she turned her back on the ladder, fished out the
torch and switched it on.

Laid out neatly on the floor of the crypt were five skeletons. There were no
hermaphrodites among them. So far as her limited knowledge could advise her,
two were male, three female, and all, so far as she could tell, were complete.

Some previously forgotten fragment of her nightmare came back to Fenella's
mind, although she tried to keep it out. It had been concerned, she remembered,
in some horrible fashion with Jem Shurrock and his wife, and with the gipsy
Sukie. She remembered nothing in her dream about Clytie or Bob, the odd-job
young man who had handled her suitcases, but five persons had vanished from
the inn, and five skeletons lay in its cellar where, she could have sworn, they
had only recently come. Fenella's head began to swim. How she managed to
climb the ladder and close down the trapdoor she never knew. Of one thing she
was certain. Not even to be near Nicholas could she spend another night at the
More to Come.

CHAPTER ELEVEN
Witch's Sabbath

"A-hunting she goes;
A crackt horne she blowes;
A which the hounds fall a-bounding;
While th' Moone in her sphere
Peepes trembling for feare,
And night's afraid of the sounding."

Robert Herrick – *The Hagg*

Upon receiving Fenella's frantic telephone call on the following morning Dame Beatrice acted promptly.

"Are you at the inn?" she asked.

"No, I couldn't telephone from there, and, in any case, I wouldn't have dared. I'm with Miriam and Hubert at Douston. I've let Nicholas know that I didn't feel I could spend another night at the *More to Come*."

"You have done wisely to leave, I think. Has anybody there any knowledge of what you have seen in the cellar?"

"I don't think so. I pulled myself together when I got back to my room, then I went to the reception desk and checked out. As I'm only booked from day to day it was quite easy, and I don't believe they were all that sorry to see the back of me. Unwisely, in the opinion of Nicholas, I let out, a day or two ago, that I had been there in the Shurrocks' time. He covered up for me very quickly, but I expect somebody in the village has recognised me and given it away that I spent Mayering Night at the pub."

"I will come along to Douston at once. I have made little progress at the manor house and shall be glad to talk things over with you. It will be interesting to compare notes, because I think your mystery impinges on mine and by this time I have no doubt that a connection exists between them."

"Miriam invites you to stay the night, great-aunt. You will, won't you? Anyway, I don't see how you can get back to the manor house after dinner unless you want to travel in the dark and knock your people up in the small hours."

Dame Beatrice had received the telephone message at ten in the morning of the day which followed Fenella's flight from Seven Wells. She explained to her hostess, Sir Bathy's widow, that she had received an urgent summons from a relative, and would be back at the manor house in a couple of days' time. She lunched in Cridley and, her chauffeur scorning the by-roads in which Fenella delighted, arrived at Douston Hall in time for tea.

"I am reminded," she said, "of a passage in a light novel by Ian Hay which I read many years ago. The hero was taking tea with an elderly Scottish lady and remarked upon what good bread and butter she always kept. May I pass on the compliment, my dear Miriam?"

"Thanks," said Miriam, "but Hubert always cuts it when we have visitors. He won't leave it to the maids."

"Cutting bread and butter is the only thing I do really well, Aunt Adela," said Hubert. "And now do put an end to our extreme curiosity and tell us exactly what you've been up to in Seven Wells. When you left us after Fenella's wedding, we understood that you intended to spend a peaceful summer at the Stone House and that you and that delightful Mrs Gavin were working on your memoirs."

"I had so intended, but I found myself fascinated by Fenella's adventures in the village of Seven Wells and persuaded myself (and others) that possibly something might be gained by a psychological approach to the case of Sir Bathy Bitton-Bittadon, who was recently murdered."

"But Fenella's experiences had nothing to do with the murder, surely?"

"That is one point which I hope to elucidate. My hostess, Lady Bitton-Bittadon, has suggested a motive for her husband's murder, but really it is such a fantastic one that I feel she must know something which she has not yet made clear to me. The police are baffled because there seems no possible reason why anybody should have thought to gain anything by Sir Bathy's demise. So far as is known, the poor man had no enemies, his past life appears (as they say) to have been an open book (although the pages seem to have been somewhat spotted by alcohol and possibly other self-indulgencies) and nobody had a financial interest in his death."

"What about the heir? Fenella tells us that she has heard a rumour to the effect that father and son did not get on together."

"For one thing, he cannot be the actual murderer, since he seems to have been in India at the time of his father's death. For another, owing to the fact that he won an enormous sum on the football pools the year before last, and has also obtained another large amount of money recently when he received the first prize of fifty thousand pounds on a premium bond, Sir Jeremy is so well off, in fact, that his father's property has ceased to interest him. He is not, so to speak, in the direct line of succession, anyhow, for it seems that Sir Bathy was a younger son, and inherited on the death of his brother. He had been lord of the manor for less than ten years when he was killed, and Sir Jeremy has no sentimental associations with the property."

"Yes, I see," said Hubert. "But what has the wife to say which you find so incredible?"

"She has shown me a motive for Sir Bathy's murder, but, as I said, it is a fantastic one and, at the present stage of the enquiry, I do not think the police would entertain it. I am keeping it to myself, therefore, and am seeking to identify the actual murderer, although, when you have heard the whole story, you will understand why it may take a very long time before the crime can be brought home to any particular person or persons."

"How was Sir Bathy killed?" asked Miriam.

"He was stabbed in the back. The body was found just inside the low wall which encloses the manor house park on the side of it which abuts on to a public footpath."

"Not . . .?" said Fenella.

"Yes," said Dame Beatrice. "The public footpath to which I refer is the one you took when you met me on the hillside the other day."

"Well, that sounds as though a servant or some member of the household is implicated," said Hubert.

"It is not as simple as that. The murder did not take place at the manor house. The body had been thrown over the wall – or so the police think. Fenella will remember that it is only about four feet high along there."

"Why do the police think it was thrown over the wall?" asked Hubert.

"First, because there are no bloodstains where it was found. Second, because the head had received heavy post-mortem bruising, consistent with its having struck the trunk of a tree."

"But they don't know where the murder took place?"

"So far, no, they do not. I have my own theory, again thanks to Fenella, but I have not yet put it to the test."

"But where?" asked Fenella.

"Until I am certain, it might be better if I did not tell you. In this particular case I think I may venture a slight (although usual) misquotation, and say that a little knowledge may be a dangerous thing."

"Then aren't *you* in danger?" asked her great-niece anxiously.

"I suppose I am, but I am accustomed to take precautions and the moment I feel that my personal safety is threatened I shall disclose all my theories – however fantastic they may seem – to the police."

"Oh, well, that's some comfort, I suppose."

"I hope so," said Dame Beatrice easily. "And now, my dear Miriam, since we all seem to have finished tea, I wonder whether you will forgive me if I go with Fenella to her room for a short, but, I trust, fruitful exchange of ideas?"

Fenella had been given the room she had occupied during the week before her marriage. Dame Beatrice took the armchair while her great-niece lolled on the bed, and opened the questioning by saying,

"What were your first impressions of the *More to Come*?"

"Before my car broke down?"

"Exactly."

"Oh, completely favourable. It had a car park and it offered snacks at the bar and they gave me some very respectable sherry and a chicken salad. I thought extremely well of the place."

"And the people there?"

"I thought the landlord was a bit familiar with his everlasting 'love', but one gets used to that sort of thing these days. Apart from that, he was cheerful and agreeable and later, of course, a big help when my car wouldn't go. Mrs Shurrock seemed friendly until I gate-crashed the secret meeting in the lounge, but she came back all right again later on. The woman Sukie was sullen and suspicious just at first, but I didn't see much of her – hardly anything, in fact. I didn't see much of the lad Bob, either. He seemed rather cheeky, but I don't think he meant to be offensive. Clytie, the little servant, was quite a dear. Tell me, darling, do you think . . .? I mean, *I* can't help thinking, after that frightful dream I had. . . ."

"That they are all dead? If that is so, it seems a large undertaking. (I am so sorry! I did not intend to make a somewhat tasteless pun!) We must hope for another explanation."

"Darling, as I've got myself mixed up in all this, do tell me what Lady Bitton-Bittadon's fantastic theories are."

"Her idea, for what it's worth – and there may be something in it, I suppose, now that you've seen those skeletons – is that some person or persons must have been determined to get that sarcophagus opened. Tell me again exactly what you saw when you looked at it."

"Well, before I went into the church I saw three workmen with a small crane mounted near the tomb, and by the time I came out again into the churchyard the top of the grave had been removed, the men had gone and the crane was still there. Nobody was about, so I indulged my curiosity and went to the edge of the cavity and took a peep. It was a very big hole and there were steps going down into it. Some of it had been excavated beyond the limits of the stone slab which formed the lid, so there was a kind of short, quite broad passage to which the steps led down, and the bodies were laid out on shelves like those in the catacombs."

"Ah, yes, that gives me a picture. Well, I think, you know, that we shall have to obtain permission to lift that slab again. It is possible – in fact I think it is highly probable – that while the sarcophagus was left open on Mayering Eve the skeletons you saw in the crypt this last time were removed from it and are those of Sir Bathy's ancestors."

"You mean somebody robbed the family vault and put the skeletons into the crypt so as to prepare for future Mayerings?"

"It seems to me a logical supposition."

"Well, of course, it had been opened up ready for Sir Bathy's May-Day funeral, and I'm bound to admit that on Mayering Eve, so far as I could make out, anybody could have done anything anywhere in the village and got away with it. There's just one thing, though."

"Ah, you've realised that, have you? It doesn't necessarily follow, you know. But I interrupted you."

"I was only going to say that, from all I saw and heard, the people interested in getting hold of some more skeletons were those frightful signs of the zodiac."

"Well?"

"Well, they couldn't have been responsible for robbing the tomb that night. They were far too fully occupied with that burial up at the hill-fort."

"Yes, I understand that. They may not have been the only interested parties, of course. From what you have told me, it seems that a ritual interment within the circumference of the hill-fort was an annual event in which the whole village was interested."

"Do you *really* mean to tell me that anybody – simply anybody at all – could have been Sir Bathy's murderer, and that he was killed just to get the tomb opened and five skeletons stolen?"

"I did not think so when Lady Bitton-Bittadon suggested it, but, at the present stage of our knowledge, I am forced to that conclusion."

"Who (apart from the zodiac people – I'd believe *anything* of that frightful boy and one or two of the others) would have dared to do such a thing for such a reason?"

"Superstition lingers on, and it seems to be beyond the power of orthodox religious belief to remove or eradicate it."

"And I suppose you mean to have the tomb re-opened. The vicar won't like that much, will he?"

"Time will show. Tomorrow I shall share my thoughts with the C.I.D. inspector who has now taken over the case, and we shall see what we shall see. If the vicar can be persuaded that the tomb has been robbed, I think we may assume that he will be as anxious as anyone else to discover who the sacrilegious parishioners are. I wonder, in fact, what the poor man thinks of the whole of the village Mayering, for one assumes that he is cognisant of what goes on."

"Well, Dame Beatrice," said the gentlemanly detective-inspector from London, "if you'll tackle the vicar, the superintendent and I will take a look at the *More to Come*. Know anything about it, sir?"

Superintendent Soames liked his younger colleague's attitude and after a preliminary period of reserve and doubt had accepted co-operation with more goodwill than he had ever supposed he would show towards one who, at first, he had regarded as his supplanter.

"We've never had any actual *trouble*," he replied. "Always kept to the licensing hours, and the law about nobody under eighteen, and no betting-slips, and all that kind of thing. It's true the landlord who gave up a week or two back came to the village with the reputation that he kept two wives, but some of these villagers will believe anything, particularly if there's something spicy or disgraceful attached to it." (The superintendent's station was at Cridley, thirty miles away). "You can't believe all you hear, and Seven Wells is a funny kind of place. Dead from the neck up and festering from the neck down, if you really want my opinion."

This powerful imagery intrigued Dame Beatrice.

"Can you produce chapter and verse?" she asked.

"Well, take this Mayering Eve business," said the superintendent. "We know all about it, of course. There used to be a whole heap of bodies down in the cellar of the *More to Come*. Seems it started when plague struck the village more than six hundred years ago. There was nobody to do the buryings at the rate the people died off, so they chucked the bodies down what was the church crypt before the new church was built, and then, I suppose, when the plague was over, they decided on Christian burial.

"Well, it seems the village priest of the time wasn't too sure they'd all died in the odour of sanctity, as I believe they call it, because the records – I believe they're still scratched on the wall of the space underneath the bell-chamber in the church – show that his predecessor must have been one of the first to go. He took the disease from a sick man to whom he'd given the last rites, which seems ruddy bad luck for him on the face of it. Well, such was the state of the country at the time, with people of all ranks and conditions dying like flies, that no successor was appointed until this new man came along in a year or two, and his argument was that no priest meant no shriving, and so he refused to have those poor unlucky corpses interred in consecrated ground.

"Well, the next best place, the villagers seemed to reckon, was up on the hill. They hadn't a clue, I don't suppose, that it was a fort and not a temple. Well, of course, that accounted for the victims of the plague, but they couldn't bury all of 'em at once, I don't suppose, being that there must have been several dozen of 'em, according to the records, so the thing turned into an annual ceremony, the people seemingly liking it that way."

"But the supply must have given out at some time or other," argued the detective-inspector.

"Not if you follow the course of history, Mr Callon," said the superintendent, "which has always been a bit of a hobby of mine when I've got the time. The ceremony no doubt lapsed for a bit, but villagers have long memories and when a man was hanged (we'll say) and the church wasn't too particular what happened to the body (because they didn't draw and quarter them in those days; they wasn't near so barbarous as what they became in later times) the village claimed it and chucked it down in the charnel house which, after the dedication of the new church, was no longer, I take it, regarded as holy ground, and there it waited its turn for a hill-top burial."

"There couldn't have been that many people hanged, even in those days," objected Callon.

"Maybe not. But then come other plagues – lesser ones, but the plague was always about – and then come the Wars of the Roses and, later on again, the fight between Queen Mary's lot and them that rooted for Lady Jane Grey. Then come the Armada corpses. They weren't *all* washed up in the West Country, not by a very long chalk, and there's a record of them, too, and the village reclaiming 'em from the beaches along by Tymshore, not so very far, as the crow flies, from Seven Wells. Then there was the Civil War, when, again, the village must have put in a plea for to bury the dead.

"After that, I daresay things quietened down for a bit, because this part of the country wasn't touched by Monmouth's rebellion, out of which they might have looked for a pretty fair haul, what with them who died at Sedgemoor and them that Judge Jeffries made away with, but the tradition had been established, you see, and the story is that, for sixty miles around, a malefactor never hung in chains from a gibbet for more than a couple of days. The last lot which finished up as offerings at the Mayering were air-raid victims, I dare say, dug out of the rubble and carted away to the crypt before anybody could do much enquiring about them. When the locals are the demolition and heavy-duty squad, and some of the R.D.C. are also Brethren of the Zodiac, you can see what sort of a fiddle could go on with the corpses, and they, poor sods, couldn't care less where they were put, I don't suppose, do you, Mr Callon? After all, I reckon a pagan grave is better than none at all, and the villagers have always believed that a burial up on the hill-top brought luck to the crops."

"Well!" exclaimed Callon. "I've never heard such a story! And to crown it, Dame Beatrice believes that these skeletons, the ones Mrs Pardieu claims to have seen, were filched from Sir Bathy's tomb before they buried him!"

"One thinks of witches and other night fears," said Dame Beatrice. "Well, if you are bound for the inn, I will get along to the vicarage. I think I had better begin by representing myself to the vicar as a collector of religious *graffiti*. That should engage his interest, as his church seems rich in them."

"More historical than religious, ma'am," said the superintendent, "but one of them don't seem to be either. *'What makes the devils smile?'* Maybe the ruins as Cromwell knocked about a bit, the ugly warthog!"

"And you a man of the eastern counties!" said Dame Beatrice, cackling. "What shocking disloyalty!"

"Devon born, ma'am. All king's men down there!" said the superintendent.

CHAPTER TWELVE
Unconsecrated Ground

"It is a rough truth, ma'am, that the world is composed of fools, and that the exceptions are knaves."

George Meredith – *The Egoist*

"But I have no jurisdiction over the Bitton-Bittadon sarcophagus," said the vicar. "It rests with the family to decide whether it shall be re-opened or not."

"It appears to be in the churchyard."

"It is not in consecrated ground. Have you been to look at it, Dame Beatrice?"

"No, I hoped that, if you could spare the time, we might inspect it together."

"We can do so, by all means, but, by an ancient deed, it is on demesne land and outside the provenance of the church. No funeral service is ever performed at the grave-side. If the family ever wished me to hold prayers in the church I should always be happy to do so. However, Sir Bathy was not a communicant and his interment took place without the rites of the church."

"You do not ask, I notice, vicar, my reason for wishing the tomb to be re-opened."

"No doubt you wish to ascertain whether the body of Sir Bathy is still *in situ.* Oh, I know what goes on on Mayering Eve, and on Mayering Night, too, for the matter of that. There is no particular harm in any of it, so far as I can see. I know they sacrifice a cock, but the killing is immediate and, one supposes, painless, so no question of cruelty is involved. As to the skeletons, one can only assume that they have come, at some previous time, to receive the recognised observances and, in any case, so long as the law does not interfere, there is nothing I can do. To my mind, these people are as innocent as the savages who offer human sacrifices to ensure a plenteous harvest. The superstition is the same and the ritual less repugnant."

"Your broadminded approach astonishes and delights me."

"Oh, the villagers are not to blame. Traditions, you know, die hard. As to your desire to re-open the communal grave of the Bitton-Bittadons, well, I am convinced that you will find the body of Sir Bathy sheathed in panoply of iron and lying in its appointed place upon its appointed shelf."

"I agree with you, but I should be interested to know on what you base your opinion."

"On the same premises as you do yours, Dame Beatrice. Sir Bathy is still in the flesh. He is not yet reduced to the decent cleanliness of bare bones."

"No, but doubtless some of his forbears are."

"Yes. I now see why you want the grave opened up. You suspect that tomb-robbers have been at work, and as the resurrection men (so-called) belong to the past, you think the skeletons have been removed to the cellars of the *More to Come* ready for next year's ceremonies. Have you anything more than surmise to go on, I wonder?"

"Let us call it an inspired hunch," said Dame Beatrice, who found some of the vicar's views so unorthodox that she decided not to mention that Fenella had actually seen the five newly-installed skeletons in the crypt at the inn.

"I know something about your career and your inspired hunches," said the vicar, smiling for the first time during the interview. "They are hardly intuitive, but always appear to be founded on hard fact. You mentioned that you are interested in our *graffiti*. I will get an electric torch so that we may examine them in detail."

"What did you make of the vicar, ma'am?" asked the superintendent when he called at the manor house on the following morning.

"He seems refreshingly broadminded," Dame Beatrice replied.

"He's like they say the curate said about his egg, good in parts," said the superintendent. "Of course, he was a doctor in some outlandish part of Bengal when he was a young man and before he went in for the church. I daresay he saw a few native customs there which make the doings here on Mayering Eve look like a Sunday School play for the tots. Everything is just a question of comparison. There's no such thing as the Absolute."

"What you tell me about him certainly helps to explain his somewhat unorthodox views. He does not seem in the least concerned that the Bitton-Bittadon family are buried in what is called unhallowed ground," said Dame Beatrice.

"Ah, that's a bit of a funny tale, that is, ma'am. The grave is inside the churchyard wall, but it seems that in the eighteenth century it was decided the churchyard needed enlarging and the only enlargement available was land belonging to the squire. Well, as gentlemen did in those days, he'd founded a sort of local hell-fire club and professed himself in every way a heathen and worse. His gang used to hold meetings up at the old hill-fort and pray to the old gods (whoever they might have been in the squire's opinion, for, by all I can read up about him, he was anything but an educated man) and he agreed, being a good-natured sort of cuss in his way, (and very liberal-handed to the villagers at harvest times) to give the parson the ground he wanted except for the piece he meant to keep for his own grave. The parson of that time seems to have agreed and to have signed the papers, and nobody's ever taken any more notice, so far as I'm aware. There's no law against burying folks wherever they've a mind to be buried, so long as the death is reported and the death certificate signed, I believe."

"Most interesting. And none of the family, even in Victorian times, has ever attempted to make the piece of land over to the Church?"

"They say that, in his will, the old chap swore he'd come and haunt the one that did. We're great believers in ghosts around these parts, ma'am. There's all sorts of tales of headless horses drawing a phantom coach with a headless driver, and a ghost that runs at you backwards, and the usual black dog, and all the rest of it."

"Ghosts hardly seem to be a race of original thinkers, or villagers either, do they? How did your enquiries go at the *More to Come*?"

"I can't think we gained much, ma'am. The story, on the face of it, seems likely enough. On the Sunday after the Mayering on the Thursday, the Shurrocks were due for their annual fortnight's holiday, and the present manager was put in as a *locum* by the brewers."

"The Shurrocks did not own the inn, then?"

"Lessees, not exactly owners, ma'am, but, of course, the pub had to be kept open and it seems the Shurrocks themselves didn't know of anybody to take over, so, as was their custom during the other years they'd been here, they asked the brewers to help them out, and the brewers sent along these people whose name is Kingley."

"Had they ever acted in the same capacity before?"

"At other houses run by these particular brewers, yes, ma'am, but not at the *More to Come*. They always seem to have given satisfaction and had been promised the next nomination as soon as there was a vacancy, but, up to then, they'd been unlucky. However, it seems that Shurrock wrote to Kingley (who, of course, he'd met on the Friday just to introduce him to the business and one or two of the regulars) by the first post Monday morning, telling him that none of them were coming back and that if he wanted the lease, and the brewers would let him have it, to go ahead. Seems the brewers were all set on opening up the place and making it residential, but Shurrock told Kingley he wanted no part of it and that there had been a bit of a toss-up with the brewers about the proposed alterations. We've been on to the brewers, but *they* say there was no argument."

"The Kingleys, from what my great-niece tells me, have wasted no time in carrying out the brewers' instructions," said Dame Beatrice.

"Oh, a lot of the work had already been done in odd spots and from time to time, you know. Then, it seems, Shurrock took the chance the holiday gave him to quit, leaving no forwarding address. Seems to me a bit queer, but that's the story, and the brewers received his resignation all right."

"But they do not know where he has gone?"

"Don't much care, either, according to Kingley. Shurrock didn't leave owing any rent, or any other bad debts, and they're just as glad to see the back of him, seeing how discontented he said in his letter he'd been, with the village so dead and alive."

"Oh, well, if he resigned, that clears up one mystery, I suppose. It still seems an unusual way for him to have acted, though. My great-niece represented him as a jovial, sociable man, certainly not a malcontent."

"Yes, ma'am. More than a suggestion of a moonlight flit about it, but it doesn't seem to have been that way at all."

"From the way my great-niece described them, the Shurrocks do not seem to have been the sort of people to go off in what one can only describe as a hole-and-corner fashion, certainly. There must be a factor in the situation which has not come to light."

"I couldn't agree more, ma'am. Oh, well, now to tackle Sir Jeremy and see what he thinks about opening up the family grave. As the vicar has no objections, it's up to the manor house now. Do you think Lady Bitton-Bittadon—?"

Dame Beatrice found her hostess arranging flowers.

"Jeremy?" said Lady Bitton-Bittadon. "Goodness knows where he is. He spends a great deal of time in the park studying the spot where his father's body was found. What good he thinks he is doing I've no idea, but he always was a vague, ineffective sort of boy, and climbing mountains doesn't seem to have altered him."

"Vagueness and ineffectiveness seem strange characteristics for an intrepid mountaineer," said Dame Beatrice. Her own impressions of the new holder of the baronetcy were rather different from those which Lady Bitton-Bittadon appeared to have formed. The young man, upon being introduced to her and informed of the reason for her visit, had been polite but cool; as soon as he and Dame Beatrice had been left together – and this had been at the young man's own curt request, made in a tone neither vague nor ineffectual – he had said abruptly,

"What's it all about? Why are you really here?"

Dame Beatrice told him.

"Absence of motive for my father's death? Yes, I see, and, of course, I agree. There's no possible motive, so far as one can make out. That leaves one with the uncomfortable feeling that there's a maniac about. That's really where you come in, I suppose, although, to my mind, this whole village is one vast loony-bin."

"I am interested to hear you say that. Have you lived here very long?"

"Well, we've owned the place only for a few years, but I was here a good deal in my late uncle's time, the brother from whom my father, as the nearest male heir, inherited the property, so I may claim to know something about the neighbourhood. Well, look, I understand that you've been invited to stay here while enquiries are going on, and I really do hope you will. She hasn't any friends much – the lady mother, you know – and although she puts a good face on things I know my father's death, totally unexpected and, as you've realised, quite pointless as it seems it was, has made her very nervous. I might tell you that I'm carrying out my own enquiries. It's no good leaving everything to the police. If I get in your way you must let me know, of course. Anyway, I hope you'll take *carte blanche* and let's hope that, between the lot of us, we can find the chap or chaps who did for the old gov'nor. I don't know that anybody is all that upset to see the back of him – he was too much of a drunkard for anybody to bother overmuch about whether he was with us or not, you know – but fair's fair. I mean, we may owe God a death, but a death with neither rhyme, reason, accident or illness to account for it, is a bit much, don't you think?"

After that preliminary interview, Dame Beatrice had seen very little of the young man except at mealtimes. She did not mention to him that soon after her arrival at the manor house she knew that he had dropped out of a tree almost on top of her great-niece; in fact, so far, she had not mentioned Fenella either to him or to Lady Bitton-Bittadon. The police paid what seemed to have become routine visits to the house. They were still looking for the murder weapon and questioning the household, including the servants, in an attempt to find out whether anybody had remembered any item of information which might help to solve the mystery of Sir Bathy's death. Apart from that, they continued to make enquiries in and around his old haunts and the house in which he had lived before he inherited the manor, but, until the day on which Dame Beatrice obtained Jeremy's permission to re-open the grave, nothing had resulted. She herself had made up her mind that if the re-opening of the family vault provided no further help in the elucidation of the mystery, she would take up her residence at the *More to Come* in case there was anything to be learned there which Fenella did not already know. She was also aware that Lady Bitton-Bittadon's enthusiastic welcome was beginning to wear rather thin.

This became increasingly apparent when Dame Beatrice, following the superintendent's request, approached her with the first suggestion that the family tomb should be re-opened.

"I know that it is Sir Jeremy's permission we have to seek, as the land in which the sarcophagus rests is now his property," she said, "but the police felt that I should speak first to you. Would you have any personal objection?"

"I suppose not, if Jeremy agrees to such unnecessary desecration of my husband's resting-place. It is for him to decide, as you say. I cannot see what purpose it will serve." Lady Bitton-Bittadone spoke with cold disapprobation and eyed Dame Beatrice with an open unfriendliness which she had not hitherto shown, although Dame Beatrice was well aware that it existed.

"It will certainly serve a purpose," she said, "otherwise we should not have considered it. You agree, then, that we should speak to Sir Jeremy about it?"

"As you wish. It is out of my hands. I should have thought that the medical evidence given at the inquest was more than sufficient, without taking up the body and opening the whole wretched business again."

Dame Beatrice did not disclose that the police had no intention of taking up the body. Armed with the grudging consent she had received from the widow, she sought out the son.

"Open the grave? Whatever for?" he asked. "Isn't the village ghoulish enough already? I know what goes on at the Mayering, you know, but my old man isn't a skeleton yet, not by a very long chalk, so they won't want him dug up for several years yet. They're a lot of necrophiles, you know, but their only interest is in bones."

"Most interesting. Well, Sir Jeremy, may we have a definite answer?"

"To what? Oh, about opening up the family mausoleum. Yes, go ahead by all means, so long as you don't want me to be present when you do it. I'm not keen on dead men's bodies."

"I think you should be present, sir, if you don't mind," said Callan quietly. He had asked to be present at the interview.

"I don't see any point in my being there," argued Sir Jeremy. "I wasn't present when the funeral took place. I shouldn't have any idea whether anything was different from what it had been when my father was buried."

"Just as you wish, of course, sir." The detective-inspector took out his notebook, wrote in it and handed it over to the young squire. "In that case, would you mind signing to say that you were invited to be present, but declined? It might save trouble later."

"Oh, well, all right. But, look here – Dame Beatrice threw out a hint a little while ago – what do you expect to find when you open the grave?"

"That some of your ancestors have been removed from it, sir."

"Some of my ancestors? Then you *do* know something! You're on to something! Why wasn't I told?"

"So far, there is nothing to tell you, sir. We are working on surmise. Do you still prefer not to be present at the opening of the vault?"

"If you put it like that, all right, I'll come. When will it be?"

"Tomorrow afternoon at half-past two, sir. We have arranged for the necessary apparatus to be forthcoming to raise the lid," said Callon.

The police, Dame Beatrice realised, had chosen a good time for the opening of the tomb. At that hour of the afternoon the men had gone back to work, the children were in school and the women, as Fenella had discovered on her first visit to the village, preferred to remain indoors behind closed front doors and drawn curtains. If one or two of the last were pulled aside as the crane, a small affair mounted on a lorry, came trundling down the main street, that was the only obvious sign of curiosity, and when they arrived at the lych-gate (the lorry having used the double gates opposite the south porch) Dame Beatrice and the police had the churchyard to themselves except for the vicar and the men in charge of the crane.

The tackle was fitted and with very little trouble the great stone lid was removed and placed on the grass. The detective-inspector, armed with a powerful torch, descended into the depths and began an inspection of the stone slabs which acted as shelves for the iron-sheeted dead. He remained down there for about a quarter of an hour while the crane-driver and his mates, outside the churchyard wall, took the opportunity of having a quiet smoke, the vicar talked about the church tower to Dame Beatrice, and the superintendent stood at the edge of the cavity in case his colleague needed assistance or wanted to give him information.

When Callon returned to the surface he said to Soames,

"Want to go down, sir? Five suits of armour are empty and have been tampered with, I should say, as the various parts have only been put together very carelessly, as though the tomb-robbers were in somewhat of a hurry, as I've no doubt they were."

"Fingerprints any good?"

"Not at this stage, sir. I'm pretty sure we wouldn't have any on the files to match up with them. Anyway, they'll keep. I didn't need to touch anything. My torch was sufficient."

"Anyway, the suits of armour were empty shells?"

"Five of them, sir. There was no sign of Shurrock and his wife and servants down there. No substitutions had been attempted, although that's what I'd rather suspected."

"That's something, anyway. Those skeletons were placed in the cellar of the pub before the Shurrocks left the place, that's very certain. The thing to find out is whether Sir Bathy's murder had any connection with the determination of some of the villagers to provide themselves with some more skeletons – or whether advantage was taken of the fact that the grave had been opened to receive his body."

Callon put the question to Dame Beatrice when she and the vicar joined them.

"The last point must not be lost sight of, as Sir Jeremy Bitton-Bittadon has already appreciated," she said. "But people with a fixed idea in their minds do not always see clearly. Still, unless the zodiac people wanted the skeletons, it is difficult to assess a motive for the murder of Sir Bathy. If we could show any reason for his death other than a determination to get the grave opened so that the skeletons could be abstracted to be used in further ritual buryings, I would be better able to refute Sir Jeremy's argument. I think the only thing to do is to pursue our enquiries in the hope that another motive for the murder will emerge."

"Anything more, sir?" asked one of the workmen, coming up to the group. "If not, we has Lady Bitton-Bittadon's order to close all down again."

"Right. Carry on," said the superintendent. The vicar, having made a vague offer of tea at the vicarage which, to his obvious relief, was refused, took himself off. The others watched while the lid of the sarcophagus was replaced and then Callon said,

"Well, all it boils down to (unless or until we find this other motive Dame Beatrice mentions) is that the zodiac people may have had deputies who pinched the skeletons while they themselves were otherwise engaged on Mayering Eve. They would hardly have dared to rob the grave during the daytime, and we can account for them during the whole of the evening and up to midnight. Of course there was plenty of time for operations to take place between midnight and dawn, though."

"I could bear to know what really happened to the Shurrocks and the others," said the superintendent. "The London end hasn't come up with anything concerning them, but my bet is that they're somehow concerned in all this."

"Well, at any rate, they were not murdered on Mayering Eve, so *that* does not account for their disappearance from the scene," said Dame Beatrice, "for my great-niece is a witness to the fact that the household was alive and at the inn up to and including the lunch-hour on Mayering Day."

"Do you have any special reason for saying 'on Mayering Day', Dame Beatrice?" asked Callon, as the three of them left by the lych-gate. "You have a way of choosing your words, I've noticed."

"Well, I feel we ought to keep an open mind about the Shurrocks, you know, Detective-Inspector."

"In what particular way, Dame Beatrice? As to their complicity, do you mean, over the removal of the skeletons? I'm not at all sure that it was a criminal offence in itself, you know, to remove them, unless Sir Jeremy wants to prosecute for trespass with damage. The grave was not on consecrated ground and the skeletons were ancient bones in the same sense, I take it, as bones dug up by archaeologists, but I'm not sure of my ground here, of course. We should have to get a lawyer on to it, if it came to the point."

"Of their complicity, in one sense, there can be no reasonable doubt," said Dame Beatrice. "I do not believe that the original skeletons could have been kept in the crypt of the old church (otherwise the cellar under the inn) without the Shurrocks' knowledge and consent. Whether the consent was given willingly or under duress is, of course, another matter. The important thing is that the Shurrocks must be found."

"It's a long shot if they've gone to London, ma'am, as I've mentioned," said the superintendent. "Still . . ." he glanced at Callon, "the net of the C.I.D. is pretty wide."

"If we find them and they decide to keep their mouths shut, we shan't be much forrarder," said Callon. "If they deny all knowledge of the skeletons in the crypt – these present ones or any others – it's going to be difficult to shake them. On Mrs Pardieu's evidence, retailed to us by Dame Beatrice, the crypt is under a part of the inn which was never used and which has its own door leading on to the street. We could never prove that they even knew of the existence of the crypt, much less that they'd ever been into it. Apart from that, they were comparative newcomers to the village – they had only had the pub for three years – and their knowledge of the Mayering ceremonies may have been anything but profound."

"You were good enough to say that I choose my words," said Dame Beatrice, "and you asked me a question to which I can give only a tentative answer. I deliberately chose to indicate that nobody murdered the Shurrocks on Mayering Eve, but I am not at all convinced that they are still alive at the present time."

"Have you anything to go on in saying so?"

"Nothing at all, unless the Shurrocks knew something about the death of Sir Bathy which would incriminate the murderer or murderers if it were communicated to the police."

"But Sir Bathy was murdered a week before Mayering Eve!"

"The Shurrocks had not outlived their usefulness by then, perhaps."

"And their pub was the meeting-place for the zodiacs," said the superintendent thoughtfully. "They only may have been fools, not criminals, of course."

"Did you go into the crypt on this last visit to the *More to Come*?" Dame Beatrice enquired.

"Oh, no. There was no point, so far as we could see. The skeletons don't interest us officially," said Callon.

CHAPTER THIRTEEN
A Little Nearer the Truth

"He looked at me, with an unearthly quiet in his face. 'Wait,' he said, 'I shall come back. . . . Wait and look.' "

Wilkie Collins – *The Woman in White*

"Come to think of it," said Callon, when they reached the police car which had picked up Dame Beatrice at the manor house and was to deposit her there before it returned with the two officers to Cridley, "I suppose we might have left the grave open for Sir Jeremy to return his ancestors to where they belong, if that's them in the cellar of the *More to Come*."

"Wouldn't have done to leave it open, with nobody about," said the superintendent. "No telling what the village kids might get up to when they're let out of school. A fine thing if one of them, skylarking round that hole, tumbled in and broke his neck. Besides, there's no evidence (except that of possibility) that the skeletons at the *More to Come are* Sir Jeremy's ancestors, Mr Callon. The laws of probability indicate that they are, but there's no actual proof."

"Exactly," agreed Dame Beatrice, getting into the car. "We shall do better to leave well alone, and the cadavers where they are, for the present. It will not interfere with your plans if I have a last talk with the people at the manor house, I trust?"

"A *last* talk? Are you leaving, then, ma'am?" enquired the superintendent.

"I have no further excuse for staying, unless my interviews produce better fruit than any I have managed to pluck so far. I cannot help feeling that, whether she is aware of it or not, Lady Bitton-Bittadon *must* know more than she has told me, but. . . ."

"Well, I've had a number of interviews with her myself, as you know," said Callon, "and her story doesn't vary. Summed up, what it amounts to, as you also know, (but it never hurts to recapitulate), is this: According to the medical evidence, Sir Bathy died at between ten o'clock and twelve midnight on April 25th. The sun set that day at about a quarter past eight, so the inference is that he was killed after dark. His wife says that he often went out for an evening walk. He was a man of simple tastes and of a gregarious nature, and she thinks this evening walk took him, more often than not, to the *More to Come*, for a drink and a game of dominoes, but with whom he played, and whether it was always with the same person, she has no idea.

"They always dined early, as neither of them cared for afternoon tea and Sir Bathy liked his lunch at half-past twelve. The couple occupied separate bedrooms and she was usually in bed by the time Sir Bathy came back from his walk, so she did not miss him on this, any more than on any other evening, and had no idea he was missing until he failed to turn up to breakfast on the following morning. The servants substantiate all this, and the butler had standing orders to lock up at half-past ten but to leave the side door unbolted. It has a Yale lock, but Sir Bathy had a key. The butler states that he always carried out his orders and never knew at what time Sir Bathy came in, as the side door leads directly into the gun-room and is nowhere near the servants' quarters.

"When Sir Bathy did not appear at breakfast, Lady Bitton-Bittadon, who always came down to the meal and never had it in her room, sent the butler upstairs to find out whether Sir Bathy was unwell. She was dismayed when the man came back and reported that Sir Bathy did not appear to have slept in the house that night. She ordered the chauffeur to drive to the *More to Come*, and told the rest of the male staff – the butler, two gardeners, a groom, a stable boy and the odd-job man – to search the grounds.

"The body was found by one of the gardeners about midway along the boundary wall which marks off the manor grounds from a public footpath. This man seems to have kept his head. He returned to the house, made his report and was ordered to tell the groom to ride for the doctor (the car having been sent to the village) while Lady Bitton-Bittadon telephoned the police. Sir Bathy, as we know, had not been killed in his own woods, but the body, we deduce, had been thrown over the low stone wall from the public footpath. He was not a particularly big or heavy man, so one person *could* have thrown the body over, but our opinion (which is in line with the medical evidence) is that at least two people were involved, since the body struck the trunk of a tree with sufficient force to cause post-mortem bruising. The actual cause of death was a stab-wound between the shoulders which penetrated the heart.

"We can find nobody in whose interest it would have been to kill him, either for gain, revenge, or any other motive. His marriage seems to have been satisfactory, his heir was wealthy beyond any need to be in a hurry to inherit the estate, Sir Bathy was a bit of a philanderer, but he does not appear to have made any enemies and he was not, so far as we have been able to find out, a blackmailer or in debt. Suicide is entirely ruled out, owing to the position of the wound, and accident seems so unlikely that we have disregarded it as a possibility. In fact," concluded Callon, "we simply don't know the answer, and I don't think we shall get any further until we find Shurrock and the rest of them."

"Do you assume, then, that Sir Bathy went to the *More to Come* that night? I understood that your enquiries along those lines had been without result," said Dame Beatrice.

"Yes, that's true, Dame Beatrice, but you know what people are like when they think there's trouble brewing. Nobody wants to know. We've gone through the pub's regulars with a small-tooth comb, but nobody ain't saying nothing, and there's nobody so mum as a rustic who's made up his mind not to talk, except maybe a schoolboy who's in trouble."

"I have never asked you for a personal opinion before, Detective-Inspector, but you are a man of experience in these matters, more so, if he will forgive the remark, than the superintendent, maybe. . . ."

"Lord, yes, ma'am," said the superintendent cheerfully. "I've never had a murder case before. Mostly it's motoring offences and petty larceny, with one case of malicious wounding and a couple of suicides."

"That being so, you will not take it amiss if I ask Mr Callon how he sums up Lady Bitton-Bittadon."

"I think she's told us all she knows, but perhaps not all she surmises," said Callon, "but, of course, surmises are not evidence, although I must say I wish she'd advance one or two. They might put us on the track, and we could do with it. It's true she's talked about the zodiac people, but I don't think she knows much about them."

"Have you anything particularly in mind?"

"Well, no, Dame Beatrice, I can't say I have. There's only one thing which seems to be just a bit out of line."

"Yes, that had struck me, too. You mean that she sent the groom on horseback for the doctor while she telephoned the police. One would have thought her reaction would have been to telephone for the doctor and leave the police until later."

"Ah, you noted that, too. It's clear to me that nobody knew at first – when the body was discovered, I mean – that Sir Bathy had been stabbed to death. Not only was there no trace of blood round about, but he was lying on his back, so that the wound was not visible as he lay there. There was nothing to be seen at first glance except the big post-mortem bruise down the side of his face. I said just now that the gardener who found him didn't panic. I can't believe he didn't touch him, though. It would have been a completely natural thing to do. However, he swears he simply realised that Sir Bathy was dead and so he tore back to the house without another thought except to report the matter."

"Whether he touched the body or not, the body was dead all right," said the superintendent, "and not a clue, so far, as to who did the job. Your own researches, ma'am," he added, turning towards Dame Beatrice, "seem to have been as no-good as our own, and that's a comfort, in a way. Do you think Lady Bitton-Bittadon is holding out on us?"

"Not consciously, perhaps, superintendent, but that is the farthest I feel able to go. There is a strangely unsatisfactory relationship between her and Sir Jeremy, and I feel that both are hiding something. Whether it is something connected with the murder, however, I have not yet discovered. I am inclined to think that in Sir Jeremy's case it is more of a purely personal matter than anything directly connected with his father's death. About the actual murder, the deed itself I mean, I doubt whether he has any hidden knowledge which would help us. Needless to say, both wife and son appear to have given all the co-operation they can, but with no result so far, and for the time being I am persuaded that your own researches at the *More to Come* and in the village are likely to be far more profitable than my own efforts at the manor house. It is the *motive* behind the murder which we still need to establish, and I no longer believe it concerns the zodiac people. I think I must consult Mr Pardieu, the schoolmaster, before I decide what to do next."

"You think he might know something he hasn't told you?" asked Callon. "But what could he know about Sir Bathy's death? You don't suspect *him*, do you?"

"He knows a great many things about which, so far, I have made no enquiry, Detective-Inspector. I refer to his wide knowledge of folk-lore."

"Oh, the Mayering," said the superintendent. "Yes, that might be an angle, I suppose. You're again of the opinion that the murder was done to get the grave opened, are you?"

"Well, it had that effect," said Dame Beatrice, "and five skeletons have been removed from the ancestral tomb and are now, so far as we know, in the cellar at the *More to Come*."

"So far as we know? But we *do* know, ma'am, unless your great-niece is under an hallucination."

"I think that is most unlikely. I rather wish you had seen them for yourself, but I have no doubt at all about their being there."

"Oh, well, that's all right, then, ma'am."

"It has not been established that they are the skeletons which were removed from the grave, though, superintendent, as I think we are all agreed."

"So you're going to leave me to the tender mercies of those policemen," said Lady Bitton-Bittadon. "I'm very sorry to hear it. I suppose there is no further news?" She spoke perfunctorily and her expression of regret did not ring true.

"I am afraid not. I wonder whether you would find it too tedious if I were to ask you to give me your account all over again?" said Dame Beatrice smoothly.

"If you think it will help."

"I may interrupt you from time to time with questions?"

"Well, you always have, up to now," said the tall, voluptuous woman, with a slight smile.

"You know," went on Dame Beatrice, "I have been surprised that never once have you asked me what caused the police to think that I ought to come here and interest myself in your affairs. You have offered me hospitality, borne with my curiosity and my questions, allowed me to talk to your servants without either yourself or your step-son being present. . . ."

"Oh, I thought you knew I'd had a letter from the Assistant Commissioner. And then, of course, you are one of *us*, and that makes such a difference when it's official business, especially of this most unpleasant kind. Again, of course, I consulted my lawyers when I received the official letter and they vouched for you, so I was delighted to invite you here and obtain what I hoped would be your support."

"I see. What is holding up the police enquiry is that, so far, we have been unable to establish where your husband went, and what he did, on the night of his death. The most searching enquiries in the village – and I assure you that the police have investigated the matter with their usual thoroughness – have failed to establish any connection with, for example, the *More to Come*. There is general agreement that he was, if not a frequent, at least a well-known visitor to the inn, but, so far, nobody can be found who is prepared to swear that he was there on the night of his death."

"We have discussed all this before. Are the police still thinking along the lines of a public house brawl? I assure you that my husband was the very last man to involve himself in anything so disgraceful. I have never known him the worse for drink. Indeed, that is an understatement. Except for the evidence of my own eyes at table, or the smell of spirits on his breath, I would never have known, during the whole of our married life, that he ever drank at all, and, drunk or sober, he was the last man in the world to pick a quarrel. Besides, owing to his station in life, none of the villagers, however inebriated they might be, would have dreamed of crossing or insulting him. He was genial to a fault, but there was always the invisible line between him and them."

"Yes," said Dame Beatrice, who believed only part of this statement. "I was not envisaging a brawl, but it would be most helpful if we could trace his movements that night."

"You mean, I know, that it might be of help to the police if they could establish exactly where he was killed."

"Well, a location might suggest a person, and a person might suggest a motive."

"I thought we had decided that the motive was to get the family vault opened so that tomb-robbers could obtain possession of skeletons for that macabre business of the burials on Pikeman's Hill. That certainly remains my own opinion. Some very strange practices obtain in the village, you know."

"That is the first time I have heard the hill named."

"Oh, I believe it was the scene of a battle during the Civil War. I don't think it is marked on the Ordnance map, except in Gothic lettering as an ancient monument."

"The people who might be able to tell us definitely whether Sir Bathy went to the inn that night are the very people whom the police are trying to trace, the previous lessee of the inn and his wife and servants."

"I can't think why the police did not question them before they left the place. My husband died more than five days before they left the inn to go on holiday."

"Leaving a message to say that they did not propose to return. That was a little strange, to say the least of it. But the police did question them, you know."

"You think they had guilty knowledge of my husband's death?"

"Oh, I would not be prepared to go so far as that, but, in a baffling case such as this one, the police are naturally interested in anything which strikes a false note."

"How do you mean – a false note?"

"My great-niece stayed there on Mayering Eve, you know. There was no suggestion then that the couple had any intention of giving up their tenancy."

"Well, they would hardly have confided in a stranger, especially a young woman."

"The lessee and his wife might not, but I have a feeling that the maidservant, who seems to have been a very simple country girl, would have let something slip. After all, there was her employment to be considered. I cannot believe that Shurrock and his wife took Sukie, Clytie and Bob with them when they went on holiday, (and certainly not if they never intended to return to the village), yet the police have combed the neighbourhood in vain for them. Sukie has no relatives in the district. She lived in at the *More to Come*, so I suppose it is possible that she went with the Shurrocks, particularly as it seems to be rumoured in the village that she was Shurrock's mistress, but Clytie, no doubt, would have preferred to remain in service in the village where she was known. According to police enquiries, Bob's friends take a lighter and more philosophical view, but even they admit that they would have expected the young man at least to have dropped a hint if he had made up his mind to leave the village and seek his fortune elsewhere."

"Oh, I don't know. Boys can be very inconsiderate. The first I knew of Jeremy's going off to India was when he announced it quite casually at breakfast one morning, a week before his departure. I was just as much surprised when he came home again. As for the young servant girl you mentioned, well, girls don't always confide in their parents, do they?"

"Clytie, I believe, is an orphan. Well, now, we have established that Sir Bathy left this house soon after dinner to go for his usual evening stroll. You have asserted (and this has been confirmed by your servants) that it *was* a stroll. . . ."

"By which you mean that he did not take the car . . ."

"That is what I mean."

"He was fond of walking, and it is not so very far from here to the *More to Come*."

"You still think that that is where he went, but we can find no evidence of it, as I say. If he did not go there, you can suggest nowhere else which might have been his objective? You have had no second thoughts about that?"

"None. There are half-a-dozen walks he might have taken or, of course, he need not have left the grounds at all."

"It is the first time you have suggested that."

"Is it? I don't know why that should be. Our park is not extensive, as such holdings go, but one could easily take an evening stroll in it without ever going outside the gates."

"That is true. Now it is established that this evening stroll took place on the Saturday."

"Yes, on the Saturday. His body – we found him on Sunday morning."

"Yes, you sent out a search party because Sir Bathy had not appeared at breakfast and it was clear that he had not spent the night in the house. Then you *sent* a man for the doctor but you *telephoned* the police. Did you realise at once that your husband had been murdered?"

For the first time since Dame Beatrice had met her, Lady Bitton-Bittadon flushed with annoyance, and her dislike of her questioner was more obvious than ever.

"Dame Beatrice," she said flatly, "I have been questioned by you and by the police until I am almost distracted. I deeply resent the implication I detect in your last remark. After all that I have been through at your hands, nothing has come out which will help in finding my husband's murderer, and I don't believe anything will. As to what I did or did not do when I had the shock of seeing my husband's body, that cannot, surely, have any significance now."

"You are right, I am sure, in saying so, but tell me, Lady Bitton-Bittadon, what you know of this organisation (if such it can be called) which dresses up its members as the signs of the zodiac."

"The signs of the zodiac? I know almost nothing about them. I have heard of such an organisation, of course, and, as you are aware, if I suspect anybody of causing my husband's death, it is they."

"May I ask the date of your husband's birth? – not in years, but the day and the month."

Lady Bitton-Bittadon looked surprised and, Dame Beatrice thought, perturbed.

"His birthday? It was on the twenty-third of April," she said. "But why do you ask?"

"Not out of mere curiosity, I assure you. When did your son arrive home from India?"

"Oh, Jeremy came back on the third of May. He was too late for his father's funeral, of course, but that could not be helped."

"Did that fact distress you?"

"I would rather have had him present, needless to say."

"Yes, of course. Had you any objection to having your husband's coffin carried around the springs from which the village takes its name?"

"I had no idea that such a thing was the custom, but I did not object." She appeared relieved by the change of subject.

"Who told you what the custom was?" asked Dame Beatrice.

"Two middle-aged women, quite respectable persons, who keep the village shop and post-office."

"Did they give any reason for the custom?"

"Not so far as I remember. They brought a very handsome wreath, which was by way of introduction, I suppose, and they particularly asked to see me personally in order that they might convey to me by word of mouth the sympathy of the village. After that they made their request. When I understood that a special vehicle was to be used for what they termed the well-wishing, I was inclined to refuse permission, but they brought with them a letter from the vicar who explained that it was an ancient local custom, so I gave way. Then when the well-wishing was over, the truck – it was nothing more, although it was garlanded – came back here, the coffin was transferred to the family hearse and the funeral took place in orthodox fashion."

"Well, not quite in orthodox fashion. There was no burial service, was there? I understand that your husband inherited the title and the estate from his brother, by the way," said Dame Beatrice.

"Yes. We have lived here for eight years, that is all. My husband's brother was a childless widower and so my husband was his heir."

"And was his body, too, subjected to this ancient ritual when he died? I suppose you were present at the funeral."

"Oh, the brother was buried abroad. He was killed, along with others, in an aeroplane crash in the Andes. I believe most of the bodies were unidentifiable and were buried out there in a communal grave."

"I see. So when was the last time the family tomb was opened?"

"Until my husband's death it has not been opened since – oh, I don't remember how long ago. Before the 1914 war, at any rate. The heir of that era was killed on the Somme and a later holder of the title died at Dunkirk, so far as is known. Neither of them was buried here. My husband's brother, Sir Gerard, inherited as a minor, I believe, and of course my husband had never imagined that he himself would inherit. When Sir Gerard's wife died we confidently expected that he would marry again and have a child of his own for his heir."

"By the way, when did you notify Sir Jeremy of his father's death?"

At this question Lady Bitton-Bittadon became agitated.

"I was far too much upset to notify anybody until after the inquest," she said. "I knew that Jeremy could not get home in time for the funeral. I sent to him on the Monday. Tell me, Dame Beatrice, have you gained anything from this conversation? You have asked one or two questions which you have not put to me before, and which, I am bound to say, seem hardly relevant to the matter in hand."

"Time will show whether I have gained anything from them. A chain is only as strong as its weakest link, and that the chain of which I am thinking possesses several weak links I am beginning to be convinced. More than that I cannot tell you at present, because that is all I know. I would not willingly keep you in the dark, but until I can single out the weak links to which I refer, there is nothing further I can say except to thank you for your hospitality."

"These weak links. . . ."

"Are voices, but whose voices I cannot possibly say. I am relying on somebody else to relate them to their owners."

"Do they belong to these zodiac people you mentioned?"

"I hope they do."

"And you know who these people are?"

"I do not, that is the trouble."

"But you think you know somebody who can identify them?"

"I may do."

"Well, it all seems very mysterious."

"So was your husband's death mysterious, Lady Bitton-Bittadon," said Dame Beatrice aloud. To herself she added, "And so is the fact that you have never once referred to Sir Jeremy as your stepson, nor he to you as anything but 'the lady mother'."

"Tell you anything more about my father's death? But I can't, Dame Beatrice. And what I've told you so far is only hearsay. I wasn't here; I wasn't even in England at the time. The first I knew of it was when we got back to base camp.

Then, of course, I took the first plane I could, but he had been buried days before I arrived," said the heir.

"Which day would it have been, then, when you received the news of your father's death?"

The young man looked at her as though he suspected that the question might be loaded.

"It was on the Tuesday, I suppose," he said. "I know they told me that the message had been at base camp for four days. They couldn't easily reach us from base, you see, and they didn't know, anyway, that the message was important. What does it matter? As you know now – as everybody has told you – I was too late for my father's funeral."

"What does it matter? It matters because it is extremely interesting. You received the news on the Tuesday. Your father was killed on the previous Saturday. You received the news of his death when you returned to your base, but the message had been there four days. I think the police might be interested in checking these dates, you know."

The young man stared at her.

"I don't see what you mean," he said.

"You do not? Your father was killed so late on the Saturday night that nobody except his murderer or murderers knew, until well into the Sunday morning, that he was dead. It is stated by her that your mother sent a message to you on the Monday which you appear to have received on the following day. I find that extremely interesting and, if you work it out, I think you will see why. You also may find it interesting. *I* should, if I were in your place."

Sir Jeremy still looked perplexed.

"I see what you mean, but it's impossible," he said.

"It appears to be a fact, if you received the message after it had lain at your base camp for four days. And if it is a fact, it *cannot* be impossible, because it actually happened. How do you account for it that a message reporting your father's death must have reached your base camp *before he was killed?*"

"I can't account for it. The chaps at base must have been mistaken."

"A strange mistake, surely? You see, Lady Bitton-Bittadon informs me that she despatched her message on the Monday. If she did, that cannot have been the message which had lain at the base camp for four days, could it? We can check, of course, but I do not think the second message ever reached you. I think you had left India before it was delivered. What we have to discover now is the person with second sight who sent the first one."

"But that must have been the murderer!"

"Not necessarily, but we may infer that it was somebody who knew that murder was premeditated."

Dame Beatrice was a very light sleeper. This was partly owing to her great age and partly because, in the course of her professional life, she had worked in institutions which housed homicidal lunatics. She was awakened that night by hearing someone outside her bedroom door. She had fastened it, and the fumbling at the handle ceased as soon as she asked, "Who's there?" She picked up one of the heavy metal candlesticks with which the guests at the ancient manor house were provided, went to the door and listened. She thought she could hear the sound of retreating footsteps, but she knew that her room was near the head of the stairs and that her visitor would be out of sight by the time she had unlocked and unbolted the door.

She said aloud, with an eldritch cackle, as she returned to bed,

"Was I to be victim, mother-confessor or merely the recipient of stale information, I wonder?"

CHAPTER FOURTEEN
Jack-in-the-Green

"You little Jack o'lent, have you been true to us?"
William Shakespeare – *The Merry Wives of Windsor*

"So there we have something which may or may not be helpful," said Dame Beatrice. "Lady Bitton-Bittadon remarked that Sir Jeremy went out to India almost without giving a moment's notice, a remark which did not surprise me, so casual are so many of our young people at the present day, and she also confessed that she was surprised when he came home again. That observation would not have interested me either, except for the curious and illuminating piece of evidence which I obtained, almost by chance, from the young man himself."

"We've checked," said Callon, "and he certainly came back by the route he claims he travelled. There is no doubt in our minds that he could not have been directly concerned in his father's death and, as we have already seen, except for the title, such as it is, he had nothing to gain from it, and, by reason of the death duties, financially he had quite a lot to lose. I really think we can rule him out."

"His lady mother?" said the superintendent. "Not that I think this was a woman's crime."

"She had nothing to gain, either, so far as we know," said Dame Beatrice. "There is no evidence of a quarrel or of any ill-feeling between her and Sir Bathy. Moreover, even if she had killed him, she could hardly have thrown him over that wall. We might know a great deal more if we could find out *where* he was killed."

"And where the murder weapon came from," said Callon. "We've been working on that, but a heavy knife of that kind could have come from any house in the village. According to the medical evidence it was probably just an old-fashioned but very broad-bladed carver. That's another thing, though, in Lady Bitton-Bittadon's favour, supposing we did suspect her (which we don't), and it's equally in the favour of her servants, supposing Sir Bathy had got across one of them. We've searched the manor house from cellar to rafters and there's not a trace of such a weapon, nor in the grounds, either. All the kitchen equipment is up to date and the staff all swear they've never seen at the manor a knife such as we've described. 'Must be a museum piece, such as my grandfather used to have,' one of them said. 'There's never been anything like that in *this* kitchen.' I believe him, because forensic gave a very clear description of the wound."

"We shall have to do a house to house enquiry, I suppose," said the superintendent. "Not that that will get us anywhere. Nobody is going to have seen, heard or known anything. If there was ever going to be an informer, he'd have come forward by now."

"Well," said Dame Beatrice, "the task which I allotted myself at the manor house is completed, so far as I am able to complete it, and the result appears disappointing."

"You have given us a pointer, at any rate," said Callon. "We will see what the ladies at the post office can tell us about the two messages which were sent to India. One thing puzzles me about the first one, though, if it was not sent by Lady Bitton-Bittadon. How did whoever it was know where to send it?"

"Sir Bathy, who appears to have frequented the *More to Come*, no doubt referred to it there, and there may have been a chiel among them taking notes," said Dame Beatrice. "I doubt whether you will receive much information at the village post-office. Where the first message was sent from we do not know, but I think we may take it for granted that it was not sent from Seven Wells. Whoever sent it was either the murderer or somebody who knew that the murder was planned."

"Well, that rather does away with one of my theories." said Callon. "I've been working on an idea that Sir Bathy's death was the result of a pub brawl, but what you mean is that his murder must have been premeditated. By telling you about that first message, Sir Jeremy has put the cat among the pigeons with a vengeance, hasn't he?"

"I think he let it out of the bag inadvertently and had not realised which way it would jump. He did his best to recoup by saying that the men at the base camp – it looks as though he did go mountaineering, a point about which, I must admit, I had some doubts – had made a mistake when they said that the message had been waiting for him for four days."

"There would have been a postmark," said Callon. "Well, at present we're doing our best to trace the Shurrocks and their servants. Mr Soames still thinks that, whether the murder was premeditated or not, Sir Bathy was killed at the pub."

"It's where he was known to spend his evenings," said the superintendent. "I think one of the zodiac lot did for him there. Then, when the landlord found he was dead, a gang of the chaps brought him home and heaved him over the wall. Stands to reason nobody is going to admit that he saw any part of it happen. He thinks he'd only be bringing suspicion on himself. It's the likeliest thing, and it could tie up with the Shurrocks and the others clearing out. After all, Sir Bathy may have gone along and hobnobbed with 'em, but he wasn't their class or one of their pals, and they knew it, and they didn't want to answer any questions."

"The Shurrocks did not leave until a considerable time later, though," said Callon. "They didn't leave until we'd turned them inside out, them and their servants, you know."

"May have got wind up later. The thing may have preyed on their minds," said the superintendent obstinately. "Or somebody may have started blackmailing them. You never know what's going to start people panicking. Shurrock or the boy (or that gipsy woman, come to that) may even have been the murderer."

"You told me you gave all five of them *and* the pub itself a fair old going-over, you know, sir," said Callon, "before I arrived on the scene, and before Mrs Pardieu stayed there the night her car broke down. My own view is that, wherever Sir Bathy was killed, it wasn't on those premises. What I'd like to do is to find a connection between five people who've disappeared from the pub, and five skeletons which have appeared in the cellar there."

"Well, we know where the skeletons came from," said the superintendent. "There's no earthly reason to connect them with the missing Shurrocks and the others."

"What we don't know are the identities of these zodiac people, but Dame Beatrice thinks she may be able to help us over that." Callon looked hopefully at her. "Whatever the truth about Sir Bathy's death, there's no doubt in my mind, following the story her great-niece has told her, that they're the jokers responsible for transferring those skeletons to the pub, and that's another reason for trying to identify them. Apart from the murder, they've got some explaining to do."

"Something adds up there, I admit, Mr Callon," put in the superintendent. "Somebody wanted to bring young Sir Jeremy home in time to attend his father's funeral, although that didn't quite work out, and it wasn't out of sympathy for the family, either. There's that May-Day ceremony of blessing the seven wells – those springs, you know, down past the old forge – and that, so I've heard, is the squire's job. The way I work it out is that somebody – whether he was the murderer or not – *knew* the old squire was going to be killed and thought the new squire ought to be summoned home to carry out the ceremony. Doesn't that seem to make sense?"

"Nothing makes sense," said Callon, "until we find the murder weapon and locate the spot where Sir Bathy was actually murdered. All the same, we ought to be able to trace the sender of that message to India, and when we've found him we'll be halfway home, I reckon, whether he's the murderer or not. Anyway, we're very much obliged for your help, Dame Beatrice."

"Such as it has been," said Dame Beatrice, with her crocodile leer. "Well, my curiosity suggests that I should take a room at the *More to Come*, so that is where you will find me until further notice." She did not mention that she had had an unknown night-visitor at the manor house.

"I'm quite sure the people there haven't a clue to give us," said Callon. "One thing, though. I expect Sir Jeremy will want his ancestors back. I'd like to take a look at them and at the cellar they're in, just to make absolutely certain we've missed nothing, and then I'd better give him the all-clear, I think. There's no possible way in which he can be implicated in his father's death unless, of course, he had him murdered by proxy, and that's an idea so fantastic that I think we can lose it. How would it be if we all went to the *More to Come* and looked it over again, just in case the super and I missed anything on our other visits? And then we can claim the skeletons and have them re-interred."

"An excellent plan," said Dame Beatrice. "I am sorry that my great-niece will not be there to welcome us. When do you propose that we go?"

"I want a clear field, so I propose, sir," said Callon to the superintendent, "to go there during the time of the evening dinner, when the staff, except for the chambermaid, will be on duty in the dining-room for the most part, and there won't be any inquisitive guests roaming around and wondering what we're up to."

"Good idea," said the superintendent and, Dame Beatrice concurring, the two policemen arrived at the inn at seven (Dame Beatrice having preceded them) and confronted an obviously ill-at-ease receptionist with the news that this was a formal visit.

"Oh, I don't know, I'm sure," she said in a flustered tone. "I must see what my husband has to say."

"Please go and get him."

"He is in the dining-room. He does the wines, you know."

"He would be most unwise to attempt to frustrate the police in the performance of their duties," said Callon, in his most official tones.

"She'll tip him off," said the superintendent, when she had left them.

"There's nothing to tip him off about at present," said Callon, "unless they've moved those skeletons, and that wouldn't be an illegal act, so far as I know."

The landlord did not keep them waiting.

"I've left the wife to look after things in there," he said, jerking his head towards the dining-room door. "What can I do for you *this* time?"

"We'd just like to take another look round, sir."

"I can't think what you expect to find. You gave the place a thorough going-over the other times you came, and you can't even prove that Sir Bathy spent the last evening of his life here, and, anyway, the wife and I and our staff weren't even in charge of the place when he was killed. Frankly, I'm getting a bit cheesed off. These visits from you chaps are not going to do my trade much good, you know."

"So far, unless you have told them (which I think unlikely), there would be no need for your guests to know who we are or why we are here, sir," said Callon urbanely, "so if we may just go ahead. . . ."

"Oh, well, of course, I can't stop you. You might take umbrage and then perhaps my licence wouldn't get renewed," said the innkeeper, affecting jocularity. "I suppose this doesn't mean you're really on the track of something?"

"Well, it might, and it might not," said Callon. "You might let us know when the dining-room is clear. We'd like to have another look at that, too. I'm hoping this will be our last visit, so we may as well get a complete picture and then the chances are that we won't need to trouble you again."

"I surely hope that's so."

"Have you many guests booked in here?"

"There's young Mr Pardieu from the school, who is keeping on the room his wife booked, although he only dines and doesn't stay the night. He tells me we can expect her back when she's finished the business which caused her to leave us in such a hurry. Then there's a couple of commercials and two people who are sharing a room without, I fancy – you can usually spot them when you've been in this job a few years – without being married, but that's no crime except in the view of their other partners, as you might say – and that's the lot, except for an elderly lady who clocked in about an hour and a half ago and who signed the register as Mrs Lestrange Bradley."

"And are all these guests at present in the dining-room? As you say, you don't want to start people wondering what we're doing on the premises."

"Very thoughtful of you, Inspector," said the landlord, with a heartiness as false as his previous jocularity had been. "Just help yourselves. The chambermaid has gone home – she lives out – so there'll be nobody about to get in your way. I'll go back and relieve my wife in the dining-room and she'll be here in the office if you need any help or information. I'll be as glad as you to see the business all cleared up and the guilty party found. I believe the late squire was greatly liked and respected."

"Well," said Callon, when the manager had gone and his wife had not come back to the reception desk, "there goes a smooth worker, if ever I saw one. Let's get cracking, sir, shall we? Dame Beatrice will have finished her dinner pretty soon, so if we start at the top of the house and work downwards, leaving the dining-room (which won't tell us any more than the rest of the house will) until the very last, she'll be able to join us by the time we're ready to take a look at the cellar."

Meanwhile, in the dining-room Dame Beatrice was sharing a table with Jack-in-the-Green.

"To what are we indebted?" he asked, when she had beckoned him over. "Did Fenella send you here? You know, of course, that she's decamped and gone to stay with her relatives in Douston until the end of term?"

"Oh, yes, I am aware of that. I think she is wise," Dame Beatrice replied. "Quite inadvertently, to begin with, she mixed herself up with those rather strange people who held a meeting here on the eve of May-Day, and then her own curiosity took her further. I do not think the people concerned would be very pleased if they knew the extent of her activities, and one is never sure of how much these secret societies – and I call this one of them – do contrive to find out about people they think they have reason to distrust. You know the company to which I refer, no doubt?"

"Oh, yes, of course I do, but they're not really a secret society, you know. It's just a lot of hooey got up by the late Sir Bathy's brother, the previous holder of the title."

"Really? How do you know that?"

"I know because he wanted to make me a founder member."

"But I understood that he died eight years ago."

"Killed in an air-crash in the Andes. I was a mere youth when I knew him, and in my first term as a schoolmaster at Saint Crispin's. He got to know that I was interested in folklore and suggested first of all that we should form a team of Morris men. I pointed out that there was no village tradition here of any such thing, but I said I was willing to introduce the idea to the boys, if he liked, and see whether there was any response. Modern public schools are always quite keen to embark on new out-of-school activities, you see, and this one could have been good fun and valuable exercise. He remarked, bellowing with laughter, that it would lead to excessive beer-drinking as, in his opinion, the exercises had the effect of producing an inordinate thirst, so I pointed out that the boys would only be permitted to perform on the school premises, and that didn't suit him at all. The whole point of Morris dancing, he alleged, was that the team should tour the neighbourhood.

"Well, I knew the headmaster wouldn't agree to that, and I didn't see myself, either, cavorting around the village and its environment with a team of lively boys, so we abandoned the project and then he came up with this other suggestion, which, of course, was what he'd really been thinking about all the time. I turned it down flat, telling him that it wasn't a folk thing at all, only a way for people who cast horoscopes to make money, and I wanted no part of it.

"Anyway, he went ahead with the idea and started it off at the vicarage fête, of all places. People were invited to write down their birthdays on a card with the promise that the lucky ones would receive a prize. There was a warning that the results would be checked against the vicarage register of births, so that nobody could win who had not given truthful information. As a packet of cigarettes or a bag of sweets was promised and, later – to do the old boy justice – awarded, to every *bona fide* competitor, he got a pretty good number of cards sent in and was able to choose his founder members from it. He wanted, of course, twelve people whose birthdays were at the right time of year."

"What was his object in forming the society?"

"He wanted to have a sort of council of elders who, with him at their head, could more or less rule the village, I think. The members were to snoop around and report upon drunks and ne'er-do-wells, men who ill-treated their wives or their children or their domestic pets, those who were in debt or had committed adultery or were suspected of communistic leanings – oh, so on and so forth. They were to be a sort of combination of vigilantes and secret police, in fact."

"Dear me! And what was the result?"

"What one would expect. A spate of anonymous letters, some beatings-up of his members, scurrilous letters put through his door, his car tyres slashed – you know what it's like nowadays. Even village people won't stand for that sort of tyranny. After all, they read the newspapers and listen to the radio and some of them have television sets. Besides, most of them don't even work on the estate, so he had no power over them there."

"Did he abandon his scheme, then, when he found that it did not work?"

"Well, he couldn't have done, if the members still hold meetings, could he? – and Fenella is a witness to the fact that they do. But now, apparently they deal with nothing but the skeletons, and nobody minds that. Anyway, I'd forgotten all about him and his dotty feudal ideas. He died only a year and two months after the scheme was inaugurated, and then Sir Bathy inherited."

"Was there anything suspicious about the death?"

"Of the previous old boy? Sir Gerard Bitton-Bittadon, you mean? Oh, no. There was no question of sabotage or a hijacking of the plane. It was perfectly straightforward and accidental. There was nobody to blame."

"And the late squire, Sir Bathy. Did he carry on the society?"

"He made it into a drinking club if he did. From all that I ever heard, he was a perfectly harmless man, but greatly addicted to the bottle and to fairly low company."

"Why was he murdered?"

"How should *I* know. It looks as though it was to get the mausoleum opened so that the zodiacs could get hold of some more skeletons, doesn't it?"

"You speak flippantly, I fear, but I have known of stranger reasons for murder. But, talking of the skeletons, were these ritual interments on the hill-fort also introduced by Sir Bathy's brother?"

"According to the vicar, who's got some old records, the ritual buryings must have been going on for hundreds of years. The zodiac gang took them over from the reluctant Guardians of the Well, that's all. The present holders of the office of Guardian were either superstitious or scared when they were elected, and turned all the old records over to the incumbent who held office before this one, and refused to be parties to the business of burying the cadavers."

"How did the village receive their objections?"

"I never heard of any repercussions. It must have suited somebody's book to have the ladies opt out and for the zodiac people to take over."

"How interesting," said Dame Beatrice. "Please go on. I feel that something interesting and important may emerge from what you are telling me."

"I don't think there is any more to say, because that's about all I know."

"Was the late Sir Bathy actually a member of the zodiac society, or did he merely encourage it to carry on its work?"

"I have no idea. I should think it more than likely he was a member. He was always at the *More to Come* and that, I suppose, was the zodiac headquarters because that's where the bones were kept."

"You do not know the date of his birthday?"

"Yes, certainly I do. The school always had a whole day's holiday on the squire's birthday. The Bitton-Bittadons were our benefactors in the days when they could afford it and the custom of honouring the patron has been kept up for decency's sake and because I think there would be a school riot if it were dropped."

"So Sir Bathy's birthday was. . . .?"

"March 23rd, almost at the end of the Easter term."

"But are you certain?"

"One doesn't make a mistake about a whole day's holiday."

"You could not possibly mean April 23rd?"

"Oh, no. It always came towards the end of the term unless (I suppose, but it hasn't happened in my time) Easter was incredibly early."

"Sir Bathy was born under Aries, then."

"Oh, was he? I wouldn't know. Does it make any difference?"

"Only that it explains – I should say, rather, that it *might* explain – why a youth of under twenty years of age has become one of the village elders since Sir Bathy's death. I suppose Lady Bitton-Bittadon is not one of the members? I know she claims little knowledge of them, but that proves nothing. What do you think?"

"I've no idea. Why do you ask about her being a member?"

"Only because Fenella mentioned that Pisces was a woman with a cultured voice, and I know of none other in the village."

"Oh, she couldn't be Pisces. We had a half-holiday for her in September. I can't imagine *her* frequenting the *More to Come*, anyway."

"No, there *is* that," agreed Dame Beatrice. She was wondering why the lady in question had made a mistake in giving the date of her husband's birth, and whether it was merely a slip of the tongue or a deliberate lie.

CHAPTER FIFTTEEN
Substitution

"Awful shape, what art thou? Speak!
Eternity. . . . Demand no direr name.
Descend, and follow me down the abyss."
Percy Bysshe Shelley – *Prometheus Unbound*

Dame Beatrice refused coffee and left the dining-room to find the superintendent and Callon waiting for her in the entrance hall.

"Thought you might like to be with us, ma'am, when we take a look at that cellar," said the superintendent. "This is the way."

The long corridor, with its ups and downs of short flights of inconsequent and inconvenient stairs took them to the door of the priest's room and so to the stone spiral which led to the trapdoor. The superintendent had a torch and lighted Dame Beatrice solicitously down the steps, warning her to be careful. The inspector followed. At the foot of the descent Dame Beatrice produced her own torch and the three climbed down the ladder and examined the floor of the crypt.

It was bare and it had been swept. There was no trace of even the most insignificant bone, let alone the five complete skeletons which Fenella had seen. The superintendent, after an astonished silence, said, "I suppose Mrs Pardieu couldn't have had a nightmare or something, ma'am, could she?"

"No," said Dame Beatrice. "If my great-niece declared that she found five skeletons down here, she did find them. Besides, we know that skeletons disappeared from the Bitton-Bittadon mausoleum."

"Somebody got an attack of conscience and put them back, perhaps," said Callon.

"It is more likely that somebody found out that they had been seen and so the zodiac people have hidden them somewhere else," said Dame Beatrice. "It is clear that they are regarded as ritual objects and history provides us with many examples of the lengths to which devotees will go in order to preserve such relics."

"But the sort of relics you refer to would have a religious connection, ma'am," objected the superintendent.

"These bones have the oldest religious connection of all," responded Dame Beatrice. "From what my great-niece has told me, it seems that the ceremony of burying them on the hill-top is a concession made to the gods of fertility." She cackled harshly and quoted solemnly,

"Crops for your blood,
Blood for our good."

Then she added, "Among certain savage tribes the blood was human. We may be thankful that in Seven Wells the victim is a cock and we may hope that it dies instantaneously. The villagers here seem to have inherited various traditions, but, of course, the ancestry of most traditions is mixed and the result, in the village of Seven Wells, as so often happens, is that superstitions and ritual observances, being also of mixed origin, have been altered and (if one may employ the term in default of a more exact one) humanised with the passing of time and the fusion of one culture with another. No doubt the swift slaughter of the cock antecedes the slow slaughter of a young man or girl, and the burial of the skeleton is a bowdlerised and merciful version of the live burial of a human being."

"Horrible," said Callon, "the things people used to get up to."

"I had dinner with Mr Pardieu," Dame Beatrice went on, "and, from what he has told me, it seems certain that Sir Bathy was a member of the zodiac society. His death may have been a ritual killing, although I do not think so. However, that is a factor which we have to bear in mind."

"I suppose Mr Pardieu isn't a member, too?" said Callon. "He's mixed up with all this folklore stuff, isn't he?"

"He told me one thing which interested me very much. He said that the predecessors of the Guardians of the Well were also expected to be the overseers of the interment ceremonies at the hill-fort, but that the two sisters who now hold office refused to be participants in these pagan goings-on, so some years ago the zodiac party accepted responsibility for the burying of the skeletons."

"I wonder the two women got away with their objections," said Callon, "if the village is as superstitious as we're led to believe."

"Their persons and property are probably sacrosanct," said Dame Beatrice. "I am inclined to think that they represent tree spirits, and how far back the worship of trees can be traced, I doubt whether anyone can say. I believe we should find, if we went back far enough, that originally it was not the seven springs here which were held to be sacred, but the ash-trees which grow on the banks of the stream whose waters feed them. I have a theory, too, that if there were no trees men would not have invented giants."

"Well," said the superintendent, "be that as it may, ma'am, what about these Bitton-Bittadon skeletons? Seems as though we've let them slip through our fingers, and no doubt Sir Jeremy and his 'lady mother', as he always calls her, will be expecting us to get them back. Not that it's our job to deal with the bones of the Bitton-Bittadon ancestors, but there it is."

"If the bones of his ancestors had anything to do with Sir Bathy's own death, I suppose it *is* our job, sir," said Callon. "Well, a word with the landlord here is indicated, I think. If anything – and that includes skeletons – has been removed unlawfully from his premises he ought to know something about it, and if they *haven't* been removed unlawfully he's got some explaining to do. Wittingly or unwittingly he's been a receiver of stolen goods and he's got to account for their appearance and also their disappearance, I reckon."

"Well, that part of the operation has nothing to do with me," said Dame Beatrice, "and you will be glad, no doubt, to dispense with my presence at the interview. I think I will take a short stroll and, if you have no need of me when I return, I shall then retire to my room with a book."

Her stroll took her in the direction of the church. She had had no previous intention of passing underneath the roof of the lych-gate and did so, in a sense, involuntarily, guided, no doubt, by a subconscious association of ideas. To her surprise, the tackle for raising the lid of the Bitton-Bittadon mausoleum was in position again and Sir Jeremy himself was directing operations. He raised his hat as Dame Beatrice came up and said:

"Thought I'd take a look at my last resting-place, don't you know. Didn't want a lot of pop-eyed villagers and their offspring getting interested, so I paid the workmen double overtime for leaving the job of raising the lid until the evening when, with any luck, everybody is indoors, even in lovely weather like this, watching the TV. As I've had a tip that the missing ancestors have been traced and may shortly be reinstated, I decided to open up in readiness for their return. My men have only just gone home."

"Do the police know that you have opened the catacomb?" asked Dame Beatrice, standing beside him and peering into the depths.

"I haven't said anything yet. Thought I'd go down and take a look round and make sure there's been no more vandalism. Care to join me?"

"By vandalism do you mean you suspect that some more of the skeletons may have been stolen?" asked Dame Beatrice, postponing her answer to his question.

"I was thinking more along the lines of rude inscriptions or people carving their names or obliterating the names and dates which are already there. The grave was open for some time when the skeletons were taken and these village yobs nowadays have no respect for anybody or anything. Why, in my great-grandfather's time, everybody would have stood still when he drove down the street and touched their hats or curtsied, but there's nothing of that kind now. 'We're as good as you are, or better,' is the slogan, 'and if you don't like it there's nothing you can do about it, so you'll have to lump it.' Of course the pendulum had to swing, but in my opinion it's swung a sight too far. All this egalitarianism is a bit tough on us grand old crusted Tories, you know."

"Have you come to any conclusions about your late father's association with the zodiac people?" asked Dame Beatrice, not committing herself to any political alliance.

"Oh, those lunatic yokels!" said Sir Jeremy impatiently. "I had a letter signed *Leo*, regretting that my father's place was already filled and my own birthday doesn't fit, anyway."

"Yes, your father's place has been filled, I think, by a mischievous anti-social youth who has taken – or had thrust upon him – the horns of the ram."

"A Jewish boy, do you mean? I didn't know we had any Jews in the village."

"I was merely referring to a youth who happens to have been born under the sign of Aries, and whose identity I wish to uncover."

"I may be able to help you there. As I expect you know by this time, it was my uncle who began all this zodiac nonsense. He took a great interest in such matters. In fact, although I've nothing much to go on, I always suspected him of being Pytho of the *Daily Bulletin*, and I know he used to draw horoscopes and sell them. It was commissioned work, of course, and it lost him a good many friends, I believe, because he used to badger people into letting him do one for them and then charging them the earth for it."

"In what way could you help me to identify this youthful Arian?"

"Oh, ah, yes, I was coming to that. My somewhat besotted father also got sold on this zodiac thing and he used to keep a list of all the villagers who were born under Aries, as he was, and send them a good luck card on their birthdays. There must be a list somewhere. How old is this yobbo you want to find?"

"Somewhere between seventeen and twenty, I imagine, and I have an idea that he is now the only Arian in the village, otherwise he seems hardly the best choice to fill your father's place."

"Well, shall we inspect my ancestors?"

They descended the steps.

"Opened it up again, ma'am?" said the superintendent. "But why would he want to do that?"

"To be in readiness to re-house his ancestors, it seems, and to take a look at his own future resting-place."

"A bit premature, surely? Did you tell him we've mislaid those skeletons?"

"No. I thought it better to allow him to hear officially from you that the skeletons are gone from the crypt."

"Oh, well, yes, you're right. But I still can't see why he wanted to be in such a hurry to open the grave. You don't think he's up to some hanky-panky, do you?"

"How do you mean, Superintendent?"

"Moved the skeletons himself in the first place, and restored them to the *sta-*

tus quo, ma'am, for some reason we don't yet fathom."

"Whether he himself removed them from the crypt I am unable to say, but I can bear witness to the fact that they have not been restored to their niches. I was careful to assure myself of that, as I, too, thought it somewhat strange that he should have had the mausoleum re-opened without a word to anyone."

"I suppose he's a right to do as he likes on his own land, so long as it's not against the law," said Callon. "And it *is* his own land; it doesn't count as part of the churchyard."

"So the grave is to remain open, presumably until the skeletons are restored to it," said Dame Beatrice, thoughtfully.

"Did he ask you any questions about them, ma'am?" asked the superintendent.

"None at all. We descended, examined the shelves, confirmed that there were still the five empty shells, and returned to the surface. You would not consider putting a guard on the lych-gate and keeping the open sarcophagus under observation, I suppose?"

"We've no reason to do that, ma'am. As Mr Callon has just pointed out, Sir Jeremy has a right to do as he pleases on his own property, and if he likes to take the risk of losing more of his ancestors, or of having village louts playing merry hell down there, that, as I see it, is his business. It's certainly none of ours."

"Oh, well," said Dame Beatrice, "maybe he knows that those who were responsible for the removal of the five skeletons will seize the opportunity to refill the empty spaces and make the tally complete."

"You don't think Sir Jeremy knows who the tomb-robbers are, and is in cahoots with them (perhaps with a promise of money) to get the skeletons put back?" said Callon, who, with a more perceptive ear than that of the superintendent, had detected something a little odd in the wording of Dame Beatrice's last remark.

Dame Beatrice shrugged her thin shoulders, deeming this a sufficient reply to the question. She asked, as the police officers prepared to leave the *More to Come*, to which she had returned after her meeting with Sir Jeremy:

"I suppose the new landlord and his wife still deny all knowledge of the use to which the crypt has been put?"

"No shaking them on that, ma'am," said the superintendent. "They deny, hook, line and sinker, that they've ever been down into it since they took over the pub. They admit they've been into the room which opens on to the street, but declare that they've never had any occasion to lift the trapdoor, because the pub has a perfectly good cellar at the car-park end of the building, running underneath the public bar. They even took us down there, to prove that there's no connection between the beer-cellar and what you call the crypt, and there certainly is none."

"It seems unlikely that they have never lifted the flap of the trapdoor to the crypt if they knew it was there. One would imagine that curiosity alone would have suggested such a natural procedure," observed Dame Beatrice.

"Oh, I've no doubt they *have* lifted the trapdoor," said Callon. "It would only be human nature, as you say, Dame Beatrice. I'm perfectly certain that the landlord and, probably, the barman have been down that ladder and had a look round the crypt. All the same, if they'd found any skeletons down there, I don't believe they'd have kept that discovery to themselves. We've had the landlord carefully vetted, and it seems that he has an excellent record with the brewers for acting as a *locum* when any of their managers or lessees go on holiday, and I'm informed by them that he was actually paid a retaining fee during the winter months so that he and his wife would always be available to fill any gaps caused by illness or holidays, for, as you know, to retain its licence a pub must stay open every day of the year. There is no evidence that the couple have ever before been nearer Seven Wells than one *locum* job they did in Cambridge a matter of six years ago. I can't see them monkeying about with dead men's bones or not reporting them if they found any."

"What about the considerable alterations to the inn?"

"It seems that the brewers have been contemplating opening up bedrooms and making the place residential for some time, and the Shurrocks never opposed it."

"Indeed? That scarcely corresponds with the other story we were told."

"No, it does not, but which story is the true one is anybody's guess. All the same, from talks which we've had – the super and I – with the villagers, it doesn't seem as though Shurrock was at all the sort of man to cut his stick in this abrupt sort of fashion, whatever the argument, if there *was* one. It seems clean out of character, and, in my experience, what's out of character can bear a bit of explaining."

"Undoubtedly," Dame Beatrice agreed. "Besides, even allowing that the landlord and his wife did resign their position abruptly and in anger, what has happened to the servants? Where are Sukie, Clytie and the lad named Bob? I decline to believe that nothing but loyalty to Mr and Mrs Shurrock impelled them to relinquish their employment in as summary a fashion as the circumstances seem to suggest."

"I know, ma'am, and I've been pursuing enquiries," said the superintendent. "None of the three of them was exactly what you might term a local boy or girl. Sukie was a gippo and (between ourselves, although I dare say it's common knowledge in the village) was picked up by Shurrock about a year ago to be his fancy woman. Bob was a rolling stone and was taken on only six months or so ago, having been in a variety of odd jobs, none of them offering a permanency, ever since he left school in Essex a matter of five years ago. The school doesn't give him much of a build-up, either. As for the girl, Clytie, she came from an orphanage and has no known relatives."

"You mean that they may have thrown in their lot with the Shurrocks and gone off with them? I still find that hard to believe."

"Well, no doubt they'd found an anchorage with the Shurrocks, ma'am."

"I could easily believe that of the two women, but I am not nearly so certain that it is true of Bob. A rolling stone usually finds it almost impossible to settle down for long at a time, or to make permanent attachments. You appear to have made very thorough enquiries, though, Superintendent."

"Oh, we do our homework, ma'am, you know. It's what we're paid for. Nothing spectacular; just the constant dropping that wears away the stone, that's what most police-work is like."

"The next move," said Callon, "is to the post-office to interview those two women and find out what they can tell us – if anything – about the message which was sent to India to announce Sir Bathy's death before he was actually murdered, but that will wait until the morning. There is no need to worry the good ladies by calling there tonight. The shop will be shut and by this time they may even have gone to bed. We'll say good night to you, then, Dame Beatrice and we'll meet you at the post-office at ten tomorrow morning, if that will be a convenient time for you. We'd like to have you with us when we talk to the two ladies. For one thing, you'll be able to give them the psychological once-over and, for another, you'll inspire confidence and so, in front of you, they may speak more freely than they might to the two of us. Maiden ladies of that age in a place like this are apt to be suspicious of men, I'm afraid, and terrified, anyway, of being mixed up with the police."

Dame Beatrice promised to meet the two police officers at the appointed time, saw them off from the inn and then went up to the room which she had taken over, as it happened, from Fenella, although she did not know this when it was allotted to her. She went to the window and studied the contours of the hill-fort. The time was a quarter to nine and the sun was beginning to set, but the sky was clear and the hill stood out, bold, black and menacing, against the greenish heavens.

It was a thought-provoking scene and a thought-provoking hour, and the more she thought, as she stood at the window, the more extraordinary it seemed to her that the communal grave of the Bitton-Bittadons should have been opened yet again.

Ever since she had first met them she had not been predisposed in favour of the new baronet or of Lady Bitton-Bittadon. For one thing, their mutual antagonism was embarrassing, and not only because it made meal-times almost unbearable. She felt that it was a disguise for other emotions and might be a cloak for a very different kind of relationship from the one they were attempting to display.

Apart from this, she was deeply suspicious of the meekness with which Lady Bitton-Bittadon had accepted the surprising (surely?) determination of the police to introduce a psychiatrist into the manor house ménage. If there had been nothing to conceal, would not Lady Bitton-Bittadon have regarded the presence of the psychiatric adviser to the Home Office as an affront and a most undesirable encumbrance? Had Lady Bitton-Bittadon so much to fear from the police that she was ready to allow them to ride rough-shod over her rather than offend them or appear to want to interfere in their plans for discovering her husband's murderer? Her invitation and her welcome had been too effusive to be genuine, Dame Beatrice felt.

Cogitating thus, while the evening darkened and the hill-fort became nothing more than a silhouette against the evening sky, Dame Beatrice decided that a visit to the open tomb might resolve some of her doubts. On each of the occasions on which it had been left open during the night, something mysterious had happened, and with the disappearance of the skeletons from the crypt it was possible, she thought, that some measure of history might repeat itself.

She put on a coat, transferred her torch to one of the pockets and returned to the church. The lych-gate, she discovered, was locked, but a perambulation around the outside of the churchyard brought her to a small iron gate which opened on to a narrow path so overgrown with grass and weeds that in the fast-fading light it was almost indistinguishable. Dame Beatrice pushed the gate open with some difficulty and made her way to what proved to be the north side of the church.

The north door had no porch in which she could take shelter and remain hidden, and this was a disadvantage, as from the doorway she could just obtain a glimpse of the crane and its appurtenances, but fortunately there was a tall marble angel presiding over a grave near at hand. She took up a position behind it and shone her torch on to her watch. There was nothing to suggest that the tomb of the Bitton-Bittadons would be visited again that night, but, as there was no doubt that advantage had been taken of its previous opening, she decided to wait and hope.

She had no intention of confronting any visitors who might turn up, but she thought that she might be able to obtain a sight of anybody who came, so that she could give the police a description of him. Whether Callon and the superintendent would think fit to act upon any information which she had to offer was their own affair and she was content to leave it at that.

She had not long to wait, but, even so, she was glad of her warm coat, for the late evening was turning chilly. There was the sound of a motor-vehicle drawing up in the quiet road, followed by the slam of a car door and deep-toned, male voices. Then there came the rattling of the lych-gate, but apparently the newcomers were not surprised to find it locked, for they retreated in good order and soon were approaching the mausoleum by the path which Dame Beatrice herself had used.

The newcomers appeared to have no intention of using lights which might have advertised their presence in the churchyard, but advanced as looming, dark shapes, (an army of them, it at first appeared until Dame Beatrice, sorting them out, thought she could count four). All of them were disguised with what appeared to be outrageous, enormous hoods of extravagant make and shape.

"The signs of the zodiac, or some of them," she said to herself, "but I wonder which, and why the rest of them are not here?"

The four (they were all men, she was certain) were bearing burdens, two men to each object, which was wrapped and swathed about with what appeared to be a sheet. They laid these down close to the open grave and returned by the way they had come. They repeated this excursion, and then two of them began to carry the sheeted objects down the steps to the mausoleum, while the other two returned to bring along another white-wrapped figure.

The two who were climbing down with the first burden were experiencing difficulty because of the darkness. Dame Beatrice heard some hoarse cursing and then one voice said,

"No help for it, Brother. Whatever 'e says, us'll have to show a light. Might break our bloody neck, else." They heaved their recalcitrant burden up on to the grass again and one of them remained with it while the other disappeared towards the gate. Dame Beatrice, whose ears were acute, could hear some low-toned argument going on, and then a figure swinging a stable-lantern appeared. He set the lantern down and, as he stooped, the light caught his crest and that of his companion and, from what Fenella had told her, she had no difficulty in recognising them as Leo and Taurus. The lion and the bull masks were terrifying, especially in the dramatic light of the lantern, and not less so were those of the other two when they arrived with a fifth burden and laid it beside the others. The lantern this time showed the masks of Pisces and Scorpio.

The task of getting the sheeted objects into the grave proceeded in silence except for grunts and an exclamation at one point from Taurus.

"God! What a . . . stench!" he said. Then one of the extraordinary quartette picked up the lantern, the four bizarre figures stole out of the churchyard, and Dame Beatrice heard the sounds of an engine which gradually died away in the distance.

CHAPTER SIXTEEN
Friendless Bodies

"Woods cut again do grow,
But doth the rose and daisy, winter done;
But we, once dead, no more do see the sun."

William Drummond – *Spring Bereaved*

"Before we enter the post-office," said Dame Beatrice, when she met the police officers at ten on the following morning, "I have something to report." She gave them an account of the previous evening's happenings and added, "Needless to say, when I was certain that the men and their lorry had gone, I descended into the mausoleum – I had a torch – and inspected it. The previously empty suits of armour from which the skeletons had been removed were occupied."

"You mean they'd replaced the skeletons, Dame Beatrice?" asked Callon.

"No, that is not what I am about to convey to you, Detective-Inspector." She turned to the superintendent. "Each iron shell was indeed tenanted, but not by a skeleton. Three of them contained bodies fairly recently dead. The other two held bundles of stones and straw. Of course, you will need to have the bodies identified, but the strong probability is that they are those of the Shurrocks and one of their three servants. From a cursory inspection I should plump for the pot-boy. Well, shall we go into the shop and find out what the Guardians of the Well can tell us about the message to India which was sent off several days too soon?"

"Just a minute," said Callon. "These four people you saw last night. As I understand it, it seems that, from what Mrs Pardieu told you, the twelve signs of the zodiac include several women."

"They include three women, to be precise, Inspector; these are Pisces (according to my great-niece), Virgo and the female half of Gemini. The bearers, however, were men, and from my great-niece's description of the signs of the zodiac I venture to suggest that they represented Leo, Taurus, Scorpio *and Pisces*. I was intrigued by the last – undoubtedly a man and a tall one – because my great-niece seemed to think that the representative of Pisces was a woman. However, there is a probable explanation with which I have no need to trouble you at present, as none of these people, so far, has been *positively* identified."

"You spotted four of the zodiac people? Well, that lets out Sir Jeremy, at any rate," said the superintendent, in a tone of relief. "Can't say I was looking forward to nicking a local landowner for murder."

"Murder hasn't been proved yet," said Callon. "We must have the bodies medically examined before we can state the cause of death, although there doesn't seem much doubt about what has happened. I think, sir, we ought to go along to the churchyard right away. These two women in the post-office will keep. Their evidence, if any, will do just as well tomorrow as today, but the sooner we get those bodies above ground and in the hands of a pathologist, the better."

"Just so," agreed the superintendent. "Does Dame Beatrice propose to come along?"

"There is no need for me to accompany you," said Dame Beatrice. "Two persons are sufficient for the task in hand. I have a fancy to inspect the local folk-museum, which, so far, I have not visited. By the way, Superintendent, I was very much interested in your reference to Sir Jeremy just now. Is he still on your list of suspects for the murder of his father?"

"Well," replied the superintendent cautiously, "he is and he isn't, as you might say, ma'am. We haven't exactly crossed him off, and when you mentioned a tall man who seems to have taken the place of Pisces, who ought to be a woman, I must admit it put ideas into my head. All the same, if Sir Jeremy was in India, he couldn't have been here that Saturday night murdering his father, could he?"

"Not if he was in India," said Dame Beatrice. "How would it be if I made enquiry about those messages at the post-office while you are paying your visit to the mausoleum? I can put off my inspection of the museum until this afternoon. I also want another word with Lady Bitton-Bittadon. It has occurred to me that there is a question I ought to ask her."

"Yes," said Callon, who appeared to read her mind, "all things considered, I think there is a question which might well be asked her at this juncture."

"Ah," said Dame Beatrice; "so the superintendent's leap in the dark has given you, as well as myself, something to think about. We have never established beyond doubt that Sir Jeremy ever *went* to India, have we? It seems unreasonable to question it, but, now that we appear to have done so, it will be as well to leave no stone unturned, no avenue unexplored, as my secretary would say."

"We did check that he was on the plane he said he came home by, ma'am, but it's only fair to the gentleman to place him in the clear," said the superintendent stolidly.

The police officers parted from her. Her first move, as soon as they had gone, was to make certain that the coast was clear and then to traverse the long corridor and descend the spiral staircase to the crypt. After her last night's adventure she was not at all surprised when, by the light of her torch, she saw that the five skeletons had been replaced and were neatly and decently laid out on the stamped-earth floor again. The police moves had evidently been known, and it had been assumed that they would not be repeated.

She tried the big door which led out to the street, for the bolts were not shot home, and found that it opened easily. The skeletons, therefore, it seemed fairly certain, had been carried in by that way. The bearers had not risked bringing them through the house itself. Either they dared not – and, if this had been so, it eliminated the landlord from complicity – or they realised that nobody from the village except themselves would think of climbing down into the crypt, even if curiosity caused somebody to open the street door into what were the remains of the early church.

She returned to her room, having made certain that the coast was clear, put on her outdoor clothes and made her way to the post-office. Here she purchased stamps from one of the sisters and notepaper and envelopes from the other. She was apparently about to pay for her purchases when a thought appeared to strike her.

"Oh, dear!" she said. "How stupid of me! I ought to have bought airmail paper and envelopes. I wonder whether you would be good enough to allow me to make the exchange?"

"Why, of course. I haven't rung up yet," said the shopkeeper sister. Dame Beatrice made the exchange from the rack of assorted stationery and then said,

"I expect I've purchased the wrong stamps, too. Can I use these for a letter to India? Such a long way off, isn't it? But I suppose, in these days, now that the world has become so small because of air travel, people often send letters by airmail to relatives abroad."

"Not in this village," said the post-office sister.

"Really? How unusual. Most of the people I know seem to have at least one relative in Africa or the Middle East or India, or even in Europe, where I believe it is cheaper to live because of taxation."

"England should be good enough for English people," said the shopkeeper sister. "I consider it very unpatriotic to live abroad just to save a little money."

"I am sure you are right. Besides, I do not see how they can save very much if food, as we are told, and even clothing, is so much dearer abroad than it is here. I suppose, when you spoke of the village, you were not including Lady Bitton-Bittadon? I paid her a short visit a few days ago and met her son, who had come back from India. He had been climbing mountains out there – the Himalayas, I suppose. Yes, I will take these rather patriotic envelopes and this writing tablet of very thin paper, and perhaps you will tell me about the stamps when I have written my letters and have come back to post them."

She turned as though to leave the shop, but before she reached the door the shopkeeper sister asked,

"Did you really stay with Lady Bitton-Bittadon? We were invited to one of her garden parties last summer, but, of course, we did not go into the house. I suppose Sir Jeremy brought back some trophies with him – a tiger-skin, perhaps, or elephant's tusks?"

"I hardly think so. He said nothing of his experiences, either, but I expect he told his parents – Sir Bathy was alive when he went, of course – all about them in his letters home."

"Oh, he wrote no letters, so far as we know," said the post-office sister. "Naturally we should have noticed them if he had. I suppose –" she hesitated for a moment – "I suppose he got on well with his parents?"

"Sons usually get on with their *mothers*, I believe," said Dame Beatrice, angling for a *riposte* which did not come.

"It seems strange that they never wrote to one another all the time he was away," said the post-office sister. "We should have known if there had been any mail. Of course, men don't write family letters and *she* was only his stepmother."

"Now, Marty, that is no business of ours," said the shopkeeper sister. Then she spoilt this righteous admonition by adding: "It does seem unusual, all the same, but, of course, as this lady says, his father was alive then, and perhaps forbade correspondence between him and his stepmother. There were always rumours that Sir Bathy and Mr Jeremy did not get on too well, and all because of her. She was a great many years younger than Sir Bathy, I believe."

"Oh, really?" said Dame Beatrice. "Well, of course, fathers and sons do not always see one another's point of view. All the same, it seems a very Victorian attitude to have taken, if Sir Bathy really forbade any correspondence, but, as I did not know him, it is not for me to judge. As a matter of fact, it was because of his death that I felt I ought to visit Lady Bitton-Bittadon in the first place."

"You know her well, then?"

"Oh, very well indeed," said Dame Beatrice, who felt that, all things considered, this was rapidly becoming the case, if all her suspicions were justified. "Well, I must get back and write my letters, or they will never get posted, will they?"

"I believe you are now staying at the inn instead of the manor," said the post-office sister.

"The *More to Come*. A most unusual name, is it not?" said Dame Beatrice agreeably.

"It's an unusual public house, too, from what one hears," said the shopkeeper sister. "Of course, we never indulge in village gossip, but one can't help gleaning a little information here and there. People have very little to occupy their minds in a place like this, and that means it takes very little to set tongues wagging."

"I have heard a few rumours myself," said Dame Beatrice. "It seems that the former occupants left the inn in rather a hurry. Did they leave owing money, or something of that sort, I wonder?"

"Oh, is that the rumour which is going the rounds? *We* heard that the brewers had dismissed the Shurrocks for incompetence, and for allowing betting to go on on the premises, but one can't believe all that one hears. So they owed money, did they? I expect Shurrock over-spent on that gipsy woman. By all accounts she was a very bold piece," said the post-office sister. "I can't think why his wife allowed her to stay in the place, if all the rumours about her and Shurrock were true."

"I believe she had the reputation of being a good cook," said Dame Beatrice.

"Yes, but she had this other kind of reputation as well," said the shopkeeper sister, "if one can believe all one hears, and it's well known there's no smoke without fire, but the less said about *that* the better. This is a most respectable village except on Mayering Eve, and the things that go on then are hallowed by custom, I suppose."

Dame Beatrice returned to the *More to Come* and while she waited for the police officers to join her she wrote a couple of letters to friends abroad, thinking that another visit to the post-office in order to make the promised but unnecessary enquiries about stamps might result in further fruitful conversation with the sisters.

Time passed. She finished her letters, put them aside, had her lunch, and still the superintendent and the inspector failed to arrive. After lunch she retired to her room and read. Three o'clock came, and she still had been sent no summons. She remembered her proposed visit to the folk-museum, but decided not to undertake it until she had met the two officers again, for an idea, which gradually appeared less wild than when she had first conceived it, had now taken shape in her mind. If she were right, it might or might not assist the police; if she were wrong, there would be no harm done."

She settled again to her reading, content to wait, since she guessed what was delaying Callon and the superintendent. She was not mistaken. At just after four o'clock there was a polite tap on the door.

"Somebody to see you, madam. In the hall."

Dame Beatrice descended the main staircase. A young plainclothes man was there. She had never seen him before, but she recognised him for what he was.

"Dame Beatrice Lestrange Bradley?"

"Yes."

"Would you be good enough to accompany me to Cridley, madam? I can give you a lift there and back."

"I have my own car, Mr. . . . ."

"Detective-Constable Carter, madam. Just as you wish about the car."

"I will use yours, then." Installed in the front seat beside the detective-constable – 'it looks better, madam, as this is probably known for a police car, and we usually put suspects on the *back* seat' – Dame Beatrice asked, "Have they disinterred the bodies?"

"Yes, madam. They are now in the mortuary at Cridley, awaiting identification. The super said I was to apologise on his behalf for keeping you waiting so long, but when he and Detective-Inspector Callon got to the churchyard the grave was closed down again and the lifting gear had been dismantled and taken away. They had to make arrangements to have it all opened up again, and that took time, and then they had to bring the bodies out again as well."

It was thirty miles to Cridley and the police car covered them in forty minutes. At the police station Dame Beatrice found Callon and the superintendent with the Chief Constable.

"We're obliged to you, Dame Beatrice," said the latter, "for bringing this frightful business to our notice. Identification is going to be difficult enough as it is, but if much more time had passed before the bodies were discovered, it would have been well-nigh impossible to say whose they are. There isn't so much as a rag of clothing among the three of them. The bodies had been inserted starkers into those suits of armour. Whoever closed the grave again must have removed those sheets you saw. Of course, they're not really suits of armour. They consist of a breastplace and leg and arm pieces – half-pieces, so to speak, because they are just shells placed over the limbs – and laid over the faces were masks in the shape of a helmet with vizor. Just a family conceit, as it were, I suppose."

" 'Sheathed in his iron panoply.' Yes, I see," said Dame Beatrice. "Identification should not be too difficult, however, if two of the bodies are those of Mr and Mrs Shurrock, for one assumes that, at some time or other, they had consulted a dental surgeon."

"Yes, maybe that's the line we'll take," agreed Callon, "if we can't find any quicker way. Trouble is that the Shurrocks and the gipsy were comparative strangers in the place. I mean, in a village, nobody reckons to take much stock in people who've only been there three years. Still, the brewers will be able to put us on the track, no doubt, because they'll know where Shurrock came from."

"To begin with, your police surgeon – or I myself, come to that – can determine such matters as the sex, stature and probable age of the bodies, and could also estimate the general colouring of skin, eyes and hair, unless – particularly with regard to the eyes – decomposition is sufficiently advanced to change the original colour of the iris."

"Well, we'll get on to it, ma'am," said the superintendent. "There's little doubt in any of our minds, I take it, as to who two of these people are, but we've got to have proof to give the coroner. It don't do to be airy-fairy about the identity of persons who've met with a violent death."

"I only hope it was a quick one," said Dame Beatrice, "and I wish we knew how and where the deaths took place. I imagine we know the means. . . ."

"A good old clonk on the base of the skull," said Callon, "seems to have been the method employed, and I think I see what you mean, Dame Beatrice. To lay out one person would have been easy enough, but to account for three, and all in the same way, would have taken some planning, wouldn't it?"

"If all were killed at the same time, but the medical evidence will establish that, no doubt."

CHAPTER SEVENTEEN
Recapitulation

"And were this world all devils o'er
And watching to devour us,
We lay it not to heart so sore;
Not they can overpower us."
Martin Luther – *A Safe Stronghold*

trans. Thomas Carlyle

"Well, now," said Dame Beatrice, who had taken herself off to Douston Hall to meet her great-niece, "as soon as our dear Nicholas arrives I think we will begin at the beginning of this bizarre affair, include the middle and (if I have read the runes a-right) proceed to the end."

"Proceed!" mimicked Fenella, whose spirits had risen appreciably since she had heard that Nicholas was to be summoned to the conference. "Anybody can tell that you've been working with policemen!"

"And very good, intelligent policemen, too," said Dame Beatrice serenely.

"Because they've kept off your neck and given you a free hand?"

"Yes, if you care to put it that way. They also have paid careful and courteous attention to what they must have regarded in the beginning as my wild theories and are now gracious enough to concede that I was on the right lines almost from the beginning."

"*Almost?*" said Fenella cheekily.

"Only the Pope, and, at that, only, I believe, in his official capacity, is infallible," said Dame Beatrice, benignly disregarding Fenella's impudence. "But I wish to check my findings. After that, I think we may expect two immediate arrests."

"Two? But I thought. . . ."

"Ah, but that is exactly what you did not do, dear child. What is more, I am not asking you to think, even now. It is your memory, not your intelligence, which I wish to invoke. But nothing can be concluded until Nicholas gets here, because there will be gaps in your narrative which he will be prepared to fill in. At least, I hope he will. However, we shall begin and we will find out how far we can get before we need him."

"Fire away. I suppose it will be question and answer, won't it? You think so poorly of my intelligence that you'd better lay down some guidelines."

"The method I shall use is that practised in courts of law and in B.B.C. interviews, dear child. It is not a question of intelligence, but of economy and clarity. May we begin?"

"I'm on the *qui vive*. Is this *viva voce* going to be embarrassing and intimidating?"

"I hope not. Now, then: what, in the very first place, made you decide to take the turning to Seven Wells?"

"Nicholas says it was Fate. I think it was merely a whim. The point was, you see, that I was much later, at that point, than I expected to be. I spent far too much time at Romsey Abbey, and then I was held up in Evebury, so that, by the time I got to this turning which said *Seven Wells 7*. I was not only thirty miles from Cridley, where I had planned to get some lunch, but desperately hungry. I knew there was nothing much between Evebury and Cridley except one or two horrible road-houses with open-air swimming pools and incessant pop-music, so that signpost to Seven Wells seemed a positive invitation to have a ploughman's lunch at the village pub, and I rather thankfully accepted it."

"Why do you think your car broke down?"

"I think somebody tampered with it."

"Who?"

"Oh, well, when I found I couldn't get it to start, I asked some frightful lout to direct me to the post-office. He boasted that he and some mates had put the public telephone out of order, so I thought it wouldn't have been past him to damage my car."

"Nicholas told you, at your first meeting with him, that he had seen you lunching at the *More to Come*, I believe?"

"Good heavens, darling! You don't think *Nicholas* put my car out of action?"

"I cannot produce any evidence of it, other than to point out that the damage (if one can describe it as such) was subtly dealt to the car, and hardly accords with what I imagine hooligans would have done to it. Moreover, whereas nobody would have queried what a gentlemanly and self-possessed young man was doing tinkering with a car, (which, it could have been assumed, was his own), I think somebody at the inn – I am looking particularly at Bob, the young pot-boy or whatever he was – would have given warning to the landlord if your young vandal had been seen touching it, you know."

"I certainly never thought of Nicholas," said Fenella, wrestling with this new idea. "I have always thought that if it wasn't that little whistling yob, (who afterwards, I'm perfectly certain, was Aries), it was the landlord himself who put my car out of action."

"That would have been most unlikely. He did not want or need a lodger at the inn that night. How much he knew about the zodiac people and their macabre employments one cannot say, and unfortunately he is no longer here to inform us, but I am sure that the last thing he and his wife would have wanted was a lively and restless stranger at the inn that night. They gave you a bed as far removed from any scene of zodiac activity as they could. . . ."

"But that's just what they didn't do, darling. They gave me a room directly over the spot where the zodiacs really went to town to begin their job with their skeletons."

"Having warned you, in a way which was calculated to deter any virtuous young woman from indulging her curiosity, that she must bar her door against Mayering Eve intruders, do not forget."

"Oh – 'Maiden virtue rudely strumpeted' – yes, I suppose they did rather labour the point with the slots on the inside of the door and that dirty great bar of teak. And then, when I'd gate-crashed the lounge while the zodiacs were holding their meeting, I ran into Mrs Shurrock and she was anything but pleased with me. What was the connection between the zodiacs and the people at the inn, that the Shurrocks and the boy Bob had to be murdered? Did the zodiacs think the Shurrocks knew something about the death of Sir Bathy? I can't really believe they did, you know."

"Oh, the Shurrocks and at least one of their servants almost certainly did know something about the death of Sir Bathy, so that may well be the reason why they had to be eliminated."

"Well, that would explain *their* deaths, but it wouldn't explain Sir Bathy's murder, would it? We're still completely in the dark about that."

"Oh, I think Sir Bathy was murdered because of something *he* knew."

"About the zodiacs?"

"Oh, no, not so far as I know. But I think I hear the voice of the turtle in the passage, and – yes, indeed! – here he is."

"I wish they'd stuck the word 'dove' after 'turtle' in that particular passage," said Fenella, as her husband entered the room. "It sounds so odd to talk about turtles in a love poem."

"Yes," said Nicholas. "The Scots put it much better." He kissed Dame Beatrice's yellow claw and then embraced his wife. "Ma bonnie wee croodlin' doo," he continued, illustrating his contention.

"Well, that's all about turtles," said Fenella, extricating herself and giving him a push in the chest. "What's all this I hear about you putting my car out of action the first time I went to Seven Wells?"

Nicholas looked reproachfully at Dame Beatrice.

" '*Et tu, Brute?*' " he said sorrowfully. He turned back to his wife. "Use your imagination, my angel," he urged her. "There was I at a small table in the saloon bar getting outside a modest demi-litre of wallop, and there were you fortifying yourself with ambrosia and nectar. I *had* to get to know you before you vanished beyond my ken."

"*Well!*"

"I'd watched you from the moment you came in through the back door and went to the bar to chat up the landlord. What were you talking about just now, by the way, before *turtles* introduced themselves into the discussion? I caught the tail end of it as I came in."

"Great-aunt was leading me up the garden, I think," said Fenella.

"She's a great kidder. But why have I been summoned hither? I've got to get back to take prep., by the way."

"We were having a résumé of the chapter of events which led up to your marriage with Fenella and the murders of the Shurrocks and one of their servants," replied Dame Beatrice.

"You don't think there was any connection, I hope?" Nicholas's choice of words made these sound frivolous, but his eyes were steady and looked seriously into hers.

"No, no, of course not. I was merely answering your question as succinctly as appeared to be appropriate," said Dame Beatrice. "I am sorry we suffered an intrusion of turtles and the Song of Solomon, but it was entirely gratuitous and had little or nothing to do with the subject under discussion."

"Which was?"

"So you *did* wreck my car, you abominable leper!" said Fenella, before Dame Beatrice had time to answer the question. "Well, you jolly well owe me five pounds and the price of a night's lodging."

"I merely broke eggs to make omelettes, and jolly fine omelettes they've turned out to be. But we'll discuss that later. Meanwhile, pray silence for your chairman. What *was* the subject under discussion, great-aunt-by-marriage? – or should I be able to guess?"

"Oh, I expect you can guess. I imagine that, once you knew that Fenella was obliged to remain for the night at Seven Wells, you dogged her footsteps to the best of your ability during her enforced stay in the village."

"Only wishing that my ability was even greater, yes, of course I did. I followed her up the road on Mayering Eve to warn her against her ruin at the hands of mafficking yokels, and, having a free day because the school had been given a whole holiday, I jumped out on her as Jack-in-the-Green and found that she was bound for Douston Hall. Incidentally, I subsidised Shurrock to make sure he kept her at the pub that night. Before I could formulate any future plans – not very hopeful ones, anyway, because she had told me she was going to her wedding – *you* came into the picture and, from then on, all was well. Such is my simple story."

"Yes," said Dame Beatrice. "Well, now, this is a time for frankness and non-concealment. Please tell me all you know about the late Sir Bathy Bitton-Bittadon, his wives, his son, the zodiac people, the May-Day revels and anything else which it occurs to you may have a place within these contexts."

"You say his wives?" They seated themselves. "I don't know where to begin."

"The beginning doesn't make a bad start," said Fenella.

"Well, of course Lady Bitton-Bittadon is the second wife. She couldn't have a son as old as Jeremy," said Nicholas. "The beginning, I suppose, was my appointment as a junior master as St Crispin's. It was my second job, so I soon knew the ropes and I found the headmaster and most of my colleagues very decent and easy to get along with. In fact, there was, and is, nobody really disagreeable, not even the headmaster's wife or the boys. I settled in and began to enjoy myself, especially as the senior English master soon took me aside and told me that as the drama had no meaning for him except printed and enclosed within the covers of a book, I was to take over the choice and production of the school play. I chose *Macbeth*, a favourite, naturally, with the boys, and set myself (just for fun) to read up witchcraft. From that it was a case of gravitation to folklore, I suppose, and I also began to think that something of our very own might give the parents and friends a bit of a rest from Shakespeare and Dekker and so forth, and I sat down to plan it out.

"We put on a hybrid sort of show with lots of bucolic dances and Elizabethan songs and things, and after it was over I thought I'd try to do the thing properly and form a folk-lore society as an extra-mural activity – all the boys are required to opt for one, and I must say that, with a lively and enterprising staff, they are given plenty of choice and scope. . . ."

"Where is this getting us?" asked Fenella.

"To the signs of the zodiac, I hope," said Dame Beatrice.

"Yes, well, I wish he'd get to the point. We don't want him rushing back to take prep. before he gets to the interesting part."

"I'm coming to it right away," said Nicholas. "It seemed only civil to acquaint the Old Man with the project, and to my astonishment he was dead against. He began by stalling a bit – I'd already found out that he hated to discourage us, especially the younger men on the staff – so he sold me a load of guff about treading on the senior masters' corns by enticing boys away from such solemn pursuits as the archaeological society and the musical appreciation group.

"Of course I said I'd no intention of stealing anybody's young disciples and would limit my appeal to first-year and second-year boys who were still at the stage of experimenting with different hobbies. Then he came clean. His objection, he said, was that I might annoy Sir Bathy Bitton-Bittadon, the chairman of the governors, who had formed a band of some kind – or, rather, had inherited one from his elder brother. Well, I already knew all about that, of course, as I think I told you."

"But the zodiacs aren't a folklore group," objected Fenella.

"I know they're not, but apparently the headmaster was mortally afraid of offending Sir Bathy. He couldn't tell me much about the old boy's sinister gang, but he said, in a peculiar sort of way, that *birthdays* came into it, and asked me whether I'd read a thing by M. R. James called *Lost Hearts*. He left me so fogged that I thought I'd find out more about these zodiac people, and I began by questioning, in a cautious, roundabout kind of way, one or two of the senior English and history chaps who'd been on the staff since the Flood."

"And got nowhere," said Fenella.

"Well, I got only part of the way, it's true, but it was enough to send me sneaking into the village next Mayering Eve and following the crowd to the hill, where I saw what you've told me *you* saw – namely, the bonfire, the wide grave and the skeleton, complete with slaughtered cockerel and the rest of it. After that, I contented myself with my own researches into folklore and with bringing it, here and there, into the school plays.

"All the same, although I'd been told enough about the zodiacs to realise that they were only a society formed by Sir Bathy's brother and inherited by Sir B., I couldn't believe that the brother had invented the Mayering Eve ceremonies, so I shopped around, as it were, and found out that the traditional burial went back into the Dark Ages and was a version of the Persephone legend, that the skeletons were taken from the cellar of the *More to Come*, and that the pub was also the centre of the zodiac cult. I had just begun to add two and two together when Fenella appeared upon the scene, with the result which you know."

"And your addition sum? What did that amount to?" asked Dame Beatrice.

"That the *More to Come* was running short of skeletons and that the zodiac society might have been formed for a very unpleasing sort of purpose. It looks as though events have proved me right."

"A society of thugs? How perfectly horrible!" said Fenella. "No wonder you didn't want me to wander about alone on Mayering Eve."

"What did you propose to do about your suspicions," asked Dame Beatrice, "if they turned out to be well-founded?"

"I don't know. I suppose I had some idea that when the murders began to happen, as it seemed logical to suppose they would, I'd go to the police, but at the back of my mind I rather expected, I think, that the police, using their own methods, would come to my conclusions and that I'd be able to lie doggo. What completely threw me, of course, was that Sir Bathy himself was the first person who was murdered. That simply made nonsense of my theory until. . . ."

"Yes, until the bodies of three of the five tenants of the *More to Come* were found in the Bitton-Bittadon grave," said Dame Beatrice. "That certainly gives your theory some validity."

"It doesn't explain who killed, or would have wanted to kill, Sir Bathy, though, and, anyway, without a leader, I doubt very much whether the villagers, from what I know of them, would set to work to kill anybody, let alone the landlord of their local pub. Shurrock and his missus hadn't been there all that long, but they were very well liked and thought of, and I can't see the villagers, zodiac society members or not, setting about murdering them, you know."

"It is interesting that you should say that. I am of the same opinion."

"You don't think the zodiacs murdered the people at the pub? Then who did?" demanded Fenella.

"We seem to have led ourselves to the conclusion that it must have been the person or persons who murdered Sir Bathy," said Dame Beatrice.

"Well, yes, that makes sense, I suppose, if the zodiacs are in the clear," said Nicholas.

"They are grave-robbers, of course, but I do not think they are grave-fillers, except that they did restore three bodies and two dummies to the Bitton-Bittadon tomb."

"Then *who*?"

"Yes, indeed – who? Perhaps I should tell you my own story and then we can compare notes and sum up. Before we do so, however, I think Fenella might have something to say. She looks as though she had."

"It's about just before that time I met you and George on the hill near the manor house," said Fenella. "You know – when Sir Jeremy dropped out of the tree and nearly frightened me to death. Well, I don't know whether I told you, but, before that happened, I met a man at the seven springs, to which I'd paid another visit. He was one of the village people by his appearance and speech, and when he said, 'Good evening' I suddenly told him I was wondering where the Shurrocks had gone. At that he turned most unfriendly and more or less told me to mind my own business. Well, I thought I recognised his voice, and something about the baleful look he gave me made me certain I'd met him before. Suddenly I realised who he was. He was Leo of the zodiac people. That's another reason why I'm glad I've left Seven Wells. I'm scared of that man. Besides, it did mean that I was in a position to recognise two of the zodiac circle, this man and that horrible boy who, I'm sure, was Aries."

"It might or might not be a help to know that you would recognise them again," said Dame Beatrice. "We shall see. For the moment, however, I would like to concentrate on Sir Jeremy."

"Yes, what on earth was he doing falling out of trees?" asked Nicholas.

"He didn't fall. He dropped," said Fenella.

"Like a ripe apple. Yes, but why choose you for Sir Isaac Newton?"

"I think he wanted to frighten me."

"But I thought you told me he asked you not to say you had seen him?"

"He did say that. I thought at the time that he must be a madman and that the manor house was a private nursing-home for the insane."

"He was climbing trees because he was either looking for something or spying, I think," said Dame Beatrice.

"Spying? But on whom?"

"I could not say, unless it was upon his step-mother, Lady Bitton-Bittadon."

"What makes you think that?"

"It is not thinking, but only wishful thinking, and that, as we ought to know, is not true thinking at all."

"And by that time you had already become a guest at the manor house?" asked Fenella.

"More of an encumbrance than a guest, by that time, I fear. In other words, although she was very charming to me outwardly, I sometimes think she must have toyed with a little wishful thinking herself."

"Such as arsenic in your soup?" said Nicholas.

"Well, I have always wondered about the identity of a night visitor I had, but who could not get into my room," Dame Beatrice conceded. "As I have pointed out, it was entirely at Lady Bitton-Bittadon's invitation that I stayed at the manor house, but I often found myself in a somewhat embarrassing position there, for my hostess and her stepson appeared to live in a state of armed neutrality which at times erupted into a war of nerves, and which did not deceive me. Far from being inimical to one another, I think it was quite the reverse."

"Did you find out whether Sir Jeremy ever went to India?" asked Fenella. "I've often wondered whether he ever did, or whether he was trying to give himself some sort of alibi."

"You regard him as a possible patricide?"

"It sounds horrible when you use that word."

"I did speak with the two women at the post-office. It appears that no correspondence passed between Seven Wells and India, but that proves nothing. If Sir Bathy or his wife knew that, very shortly after reaching Karachi, or wherever it was, Sir Jeremy would be out of touch with his mail, they may well not have troubled to write. Equally, we do not know for certain the terms which obtained between the father and son, although my own view, for what it is worth, is that Lady Bitton-Bittadon was a bone of contention between them. Another explanation could be that another post-office was used. The police are still trying to find out whether this might have been the case, but that sort of enquiry takes time."

"What is your own impression?" asked Nicholas.

"Oh, I think he went to India. My doubt is whether he went mountaineering there. I have some reason to think that he had been sent news of his father's death before Sir Bathy was murdered. There is no doubt that he got back almost in time for the funeral."

"What!" exclaimed Fenella.

"But what has that to do with mountaineering?" asked Nicholas.

"I am not certain yet," Dame Beatrice replied, "but time will tell us all that we want to know, I think."

"I wish you'd tell me all *I* want to know," said Fenella.

"I will tell you what I can, child."

"Well, one thing still puzzles me. How do you come to be mixed up in all this at all?"

"I thought you knew that I had received an official communication from Assistant Commissioner Robert Gavin."

"Yes, but why should he have communicated with you? I mean, at that time, surely only one murder had been committed? I mean, so far as anybody knew, the Shurrocks and the others with them were alive and well. Why should the police have called in a psychiatrist to help solve a simple village murder?"

"Because I asked them to do so," Dame Beatrice calmly replied. "The letter I received from Robert Gavin was in answer to one which he had received from me as soon as I heard of your adventures at the *More to Come*."

"Well, really!"

"I happened to have read a short paragraph in the press reporting Sir Bathy's death. I filed it, as I usually do, and then I must confess that I thought no more about it until you said that you had stayed a night in the same village because your car had broken down. I thought, even then, that somebody had made himself responsible for the damage to the vehicle, but I did not know, until a few minutes ago, that Nicholas was the culprit. However, I do not believe you had told me at that time the circumstances under which you first met him."

"I must get back to take prep.," said Nicholas. "So, if it hadn't been for me, you would never have concerned yourself with the case at all!"

"And now," said Dame Beatrice, when the young man had gone, "There is something else you may be able to tell me, my dear Fenella. Again it depends upon your memory."

"Oh, dear! Most unreliable, I'm afraid."

"It has not appeared to be unreliable so far. This is what I want to know, and to answer me you must cast your mind back to Mayering Eve when you broke in upon the meeting of the zodiac people."

"Oh, I can remember *that*, all right. In fact, I shall never forget it. I don't believe I've ever felt so unwanted and unpopular in my life. When I die, the signs of the zodiac will be found engraved on my heart."

"Really? Well, now, how much can you recall of what you heard?"

"Most of it, if not all. They were so extraordinary, and so unexpected, you know, those masked and gowned figures with their comic head-dresses, and they were rather frightening, too."

"Yes, I can well imagine that. Now please take your time, because your answers will be very important. First of all, can you remember which of the characters spoke and, roughly, what they said?"

"Oh, yes, I'm sure I can remember which of them spoke."

"So you can also remember which of them did *not* speak."

"Well, that follows, doesn't it? Scorpio spoke first. He put on the electric light and denounced me as an interloper."

"*He*? You are certain it was a man's voice?"

"Oh, yes, positively a man's voice, and thick with local accent. I'm all the more certain, because I remember that the next person who spoke was just as definitely a woman and, what's more, a 'lidy'."

"The only cultured person there, I imagine. Do you think you would recognise the voice again if you heard it?"

"Well, I wouldn't like to bet on that. You know how it is with women of that class. You can't go by accent, because they all have the same one!"

"What did she say?"

"She said: 'She's broken the magic number. She makes us thirteen.' (Meaning me, of course)."

"How extremely strange!"

"Why do you say that, great-aunt?"

"Because you did not make them thirteen; you made them fourteen. There are twelve signs of the zodiac, it is true, but one of them is Gemini, so that twelve signs were represented but, actually, there were thirteen persons in the room before you entered it."

"Is that important?"

"Psychologically it is of the most extreme importance, I hope. It supplies me with an arrow which may well bring down my quarry."

"How do you mean?"

"I mean that the speaker, Pisces, knew that one of the company was missing. . . ."

"Sir Bathy, I suppose you mean, but surely, by that time, they all knew that. He'd been dead for nearly a week."

"Ah, but the significant thing is that Pisces had forgotten for the moment that another Aries had been substituted, and that leads me to a further conclusion."

"I see – or, rather, I don't. Shall I go on?"

"No, thank you, child. There is no need for you to tax your memory further. I have found out what I wanted to know. Three more persons have been murdered. They are two males and one female, and I no longer believe that two of them are the Shurrocks. Besides, at their burial, Pisces had changed from a woman into a man. Is not that significant?"

CHAPTER EIGHTEEN
Fresh Evidence

"Two obvious conclusions presented themselves to my mind, after hearing it.
In the first place, I saw darkly what the nature of the conspiracy had been;
how chances had been watched, and how circumstances had been handled. . .
."

Wilkie Collins – *The Woman in White*

"It's Detective-Inspector Callon on the telephone, Adela," said Hubert, some days later. "He wants to talk to you."

"Could you come over to Cridley again, Dame Beatrice," said Callon, "and bring Mrs Pardieu with you? We've got some news which may surprise you. Those three bodies which the zodiacs put in the tomb have been identified, and they're not the ones we thought they were."

"I'll come this afternoon," said Dame Beatrice, "Meanwhile, something which somebody said some time ago has given me a notion which you might care to consider between now and when we meet. You remember that when you were asking about kitchen knives and so forth at the manor house (and, I imagine, in your house-to-house enquiries in the village), somebody remarked that the description you gave of the murder weapon was reminiscent of a museum piece?"

"Yes, indeed, ma'am."

"Well, there is a folk museum in the village, you know. It might just be worth while to pay it a visit, I think. Oh, and while you are looking at *knives*, you might also think about policemen's truncheons. I am told by my great-niece that she saw several when she was there. Heavy ancient ones."

"Policemen's truncheons?"

"And then find out from the forensic experts whether a heavy, old-fashioned truncheon could have been used to kill the three people you mention. As they are not the people we assumed they might be, I take it that they are Clytie, Bob and the youth whose name I do not know, but whom we may call Aries."

"What makes you think of *him*, Dame Beatrice? He had nothing to do with the people at the *More to Come*."

"I will tell you what I think, and why I think it, when I see you. I should be with you by four, if not sooner."

"Callon said, when they met in the superintendent's office:

"So the news isn't really a surprise to you, Dame Beatrice. By the way, we took your tip and had a look round that museum at Seven Wells, and I think your hint may be going to pay off. We found the knife, of course, with which Sir Bathy was killed, but even though it came from the museum it's going to be difficult to find out who purloined it and whether, whoever took it is the actual murderer. Oh, and we got the curator chap on the go, and he says the heaviest of the truncheons is missing."

When Soames emerged from his office at the Cridley headquarters and greetings had been exchanged, the superintendent said:

"We've other visitors, ma'am, so perhaps Mrs Pardieu will identify them for us and then you may like to hear their story." The sergeant who was in attendance opened the door to an inner room and invited the occupants to come out. "Now, Mrs Pardieu," the superintendent went on, turning to Fenella, "I believe you can identify these persons."

"Why, of course," said Fenella. "How do you do, Mrs Shurrock? Mr Shurrock? And this is Sukie, Superintendent. I'm afraid I don't know her other name."

"Lee," said the gipsy, scowling, "same like the rest of my tribe."

"Our London people found them," said Callon. "Now let's hear the story all over again, Shurrock. I'm sure Dame Beatrice will be interested."

"I shan't alter it for her benefit or yours," said the landlord. "I've done nothing wrong, and neither have the others. We did skip, but it was only to save ourselves, or so we thought."

"Do you know who murdered Sir Bathy?" asked Dame Beatrice, looking directly at the gipsy. "You knew more about him than anyone else did, I think."

"So I was his fancy. So what?" said Sukie belligerently. "Anything wrong in that?"

"Ah," said Shurrock, his face clearing to its habitual expression of good humour, "folks put it about as Sukie was *my* light o'love, and we never contradicted it, wishing to do Sir Bathy a favour. Kept his secret well, we did, and not many evenings as he didn't spend down at the *More to Come*."

"Nothing wrong in it," said Sukie. "He wanted company, that's all. Couldn't get it at home, not the sort of company he fancied, so had it with me after he'd had his drop of beer down in the bar."

"Very natural," said Dame Beatrice. "When did you find out that he had been killed?"

"Same night as it happened," said Mrs Shurrock, speaking for the first time. "Officially Jem and I never knew how he spent his evenings once he'd left the saloon, which he did around half-past nine, although we did know he didn't go straight home. That son of his had took his wife, you see?"

"Officially you didn't know what he did. Actually, you knew perfectly well that he was with Mrs Lee?"

"Let's say we guessed, then."

"I used to let him out by the big door in the room over the old cellar as used to be part of the old church," said Sukie. "Eleven o'clock on the dot I used to let him out, so he wouldn't be spotted leaving the place after hours by way of the bar."

"So that Saturday night," said Shurrock, taking up the tale, "Sukie didn't come back, like she always did, to wash up glasses and clear away ash-trays, like usual, so I was just saying to the wife. . . ."

"When she came in and told us Sir Bathy was lying out there in the road with a knife in his back," said Mrs Shurrock. Dame Beatrice looked at the gipsy, who nodded, her black eyes expressionless.

"Well, of course, I went along to see," said Shurrock, "and there he laid, not half-a-dozen yards from the big door where Sukie had let him out. So I says, 'Well,' I says, 'us can't leave him there. Get my house a bad name, and the police, and all', I says. 'Best put him where he belong.' But the wife says, 'Not just yet. Drag him inside again till you know all's quiet and he's done bleeding.' So Sukie and me, we drag the poor old fellow in through the big door again and then, round about one, when we think all's quiet, I get out the car and we dump him in the back and take him to his home. Worst part was having to carry him the last bit of the way and chuck him over the wall. Then Sukie starts in to bellow, because we hear him hit a tree, but I shut her up and drive her back to the *More to Come* and at first light we have a good scout round for any traces, but there don't seem to be nothing on the road where us found him because he'd been stabbed in the back and there wasn't much blood, anyway, I don't reckon, on account the knife was still in the wound, and he'd fell on his face, poor old sod, and what blood there was had soaked into his clothes, I reckon. There wasn't nothing on our floor. Then I looked at the car and sponged it over where we'd crammed him on to the back seat, but there wasn't no mess, so far as I could see, and that, honest, is all we done, and that's as much as I know."

"Did you come to any conclusion as to the identity of the murderer?" asked Dame Beatrice.

"The wife and me, us talked it over and decided one of Sukie's relations had laid for him, that's all, though Sukie, her said not, being she'd left her own folks for good and all. Wasn't our business, anyway. All we thought of was getting him off our ground and on to his own. Wasn't as if we could do anything for him. He was as dead as the dodo when we found him."

"What made you think of going outside to see what had happened, Mrs Lee?" asked Dame Beatrice. "It wasn't your usual practice, was it?"

"No," replied the gipsy, "but it was Saturday night and when I got back to my room I looked for the usual little present he give me and it wasn't there, so I thought I'd slip out after him in case, the next week, he swore he *had* left it. Well, it was moonlight – that's how whoever stabbed him could see just where to put that knife, I reckon. . . ."

"But what a fearful risk to take!" exclaimed Fenella. "Anybody who happened to be about could have seen it done!"

"Nobody about in Seven Wells our end of the village that time of night," explained Shurrock. "We're on the outskirts and to get back to the manor he was walking *away* from all the cottages, you see, taking his way round the village instead of through it. Just a precaution, like. Exceptin' for the manor house itself, there's nothing that side of the village but Pikeman Hill, and them that's buried up there won't tell no tales!"

"Did you never suspect anyone in the village of murdering Sir Bathy?" asked Dame Beatrice.

"These here," replied Shurrock, jerking his head towards the police officers, "asked me that. What I thought at the time was one of Sukie's lot had taken a jealous fit, like I just told you, and didn't like her being friendly in that sort of way with a *gorgio*."

"No," said the gipsy, shaking her head, "I lost my man when I was twenty. Only four years we were married and then he got ill and he died. I went *gorgio* myself after that, and took service and never knew my own people no more. It wasn't a *Romani* killed Sir Bathy, that I know, but I don't know who it was, unless it was his son."

"It was common knowledge they never got on after Mr Jeremy left college," said Mrs Shurrock, "but it couldn't have been Mr Jeremy, if he was in India at the time, as we heard."

"He *was* in India at the time," said Callon. "That much we've established beyond doubt. But this isn't the end of the story, Dame Beatrice."

"No, of course it is not," she replied. "What caused your flight from the *More to Come* and your resignation of your position as landlord, Mr Shurrock?"

"I got scared, and the wife and Sukie was even more frit than me. We had an anonymous letter. That was the first thing. Somebody knew what we'd done with Sir B's body."

"The murderer, most likely," said Dame Beatrice." Did you not think of that?"

"But you didn't keep the letter," said Callon, "and that's a pity, you know."

"Keep a letter like that? Of course us didn't. It was dynamite! Us put it behind the fire and decided to quit. Us couldn't leave straight away, but we was in a lather to go, and our holiday was due, anyway, so that made a good enough excuse to get away. Wrote my resignation as soon as we got to London, but didn't post it from where we was staying, of course, because of the postmark. I don't know how you rumbled us. We laid low enough."

"Oh, we have our methods," said Callon. "It seems to me that you quit pretty easily, though. I should have thought a man of your type would have stuck it out and chanced his arm and dared the writer of the letter to do his worst."

"Not with Bob and Clytie going missing," said Shurrock grimly. "When they didn't show up on the morning we'd planned to pack up we decided they were the ones who'd writ the letter and, that being so, that Sukie and me had been properly rumbled and most likely laid ourself open to black-mail, if nothing worse – not as the letter mentioned money."

"There is nothing much worse than blackmail," said Dame Beatrice. "Where did you think Bob and Clytie had gone?"

"We didn't wait to ask," answered Shurrock. "Quite enough for us when Clytie didn't come down to breakfast – she lived in, you see – and Bob didn't turn up for work."

"Was there any known connection between them, apart from the fact that both were employed at the inn?"

"Oh, yes, there was," said Fenella eagerly, as Shurrock began shaking his head. "They were engaged to be married, I think. I know there was an understanding."

"First *I've* heard of it," said Mrs Shurrock sharply. "I'd have warned Clytie against, had I known. Bob wasn't much of a catch, and I didn't like some of his friends."

"I think they fixed it up just before Mayering Eve," explained Fenella, "from something Clytie said."

"Nothing was ever said to me. Of course, when neither of them turned up to work – that would have been soon after you left us to go to Douston, Miss – Mrs Pardieu – we knew they must be in it together. Well, I mean, that's what we thought at the time. Now, of course, poor things, they're both dead," said Mrs Shurrock, in a gentler tone, "so it don't look as though it could have been them."

"And the third dead youth is the one whom Fenella knows as Aries," said Dame Beatrice, "is he not?"

"He's been identified as Edwin Bartle Pitsey," said the superintendent. "Turns out to have been a mate of Bob's, although Clytie didn't fancy him, or so Mrs Lee here has told us."

"I should think not!" said Fenella. "Of all the . . ." She stopped and bit her lip, realising that the objectionable youth was dead.

"We're left with the conclusion," said Callon, "that the zodiac people are implicated up to the hilt. The trouble now is going to be how to get them identified as individuals."

"Well, I know Leo by sight," said Fenella. "I met him one day when he wasn't Leo, and I'm sure I'd recognise him again."

"Perhaps, Shurrock, *you'd* care to give us a few names," suggested the superintendent. "You're facing a charge, you and Mrs Lee, you know, so any information you give us now may help you."

Shurrock shook his head.

"Can't be done, Super," he said. "They all come to the pub incognito, and, so far as I'm concerned, that's the way they'll stay."

"How often did the zodiac members meet?" asked Dame Beatrice.

"Once a month, of course. They'd have to, wouldn't they, being what they was. Twelve months in the year, so twelve meetin's is what I make it. But which *day* of the month they picked on, and who they was, I never concerned myself with. They turned up, they had their drinks and they went, but where they went, and who they were, I haven't a notion and don't want to have."

"I find that difficult to accept," said Dame Beatrice. "I think you know perfectly well who they were. Tell me, for instance, who took Sir Bathy's place as Aries."

"I dunno nothing about it, I tell you," said the ex-landlord obstinately.

"Very well. Then I'll tell *you*. He was this murdered young man named Pitsey. Now you tell us who was Leo."

"You've got me, haven't you? But if you know it all, you don't need to hear it from me. Still, to oblige you, Leo is Bert Sawmills."

"Thanks," said Callon, writing it down. "We'll have a chat with him. Where does he hang out?"

Unwillingly, but seeing no help for it, Shurrock gave the address.

"He's no murderer, though," he said defiantly. "He's a surly sort of devil, but I've never known him so much as raise his fist to anybody."

"Now we want the names of Taurus and Scorpio," said the superintendent.

"I don't know 'em, and that's the truth. I don't know none of the others, I'm tellin' you. I only know about Bert Sawmills because he was the leader of the gang under Sir Bathy and used to make all the arrangements with me for use of my lounge and havin' snacks and beer sent up, with a drop of gin or sherry for the ladies."

"Ah, yes, the ladies," said Dame Beatrice. "Pisces was a changeling on occasion, I think."

"I dunno what you mean," said Shurrock.

"Oh, Jem, don't fight about what you don't have to," urged his wife. "It can't hurt to tell 'em as the real Pisces was Sir Jeremy, as both of us knows. But what is meant by him being a changeling – well, I thought that was something to do with the fairies, and I don't reckon as Sir Jeremy would have any truck with *them*."

"It is not in your power, then, to confirm that, on Mayering Eve, Lady Bitton-Bittadon attended the zodiac meeting in the character of Pisces? And that she carried what turned out to be a lethal weapon in her fish-hat?"

"I don't know why you keep harpin' on about *her*. *She* wouldn't drink at a pub, not a lady like her," growled Shurrock.

"But she made one of the gathering in the lounge on Mayering Eve, did she not?" persisted Dame Beatrice.

"I tell you I don't know. If she did, she never come into the bar. She must have sneaked upstairs without me seeing her."

"That means," said Fenella, "that she must have gone into the *More to Come* by way of that big door to the old church."

"How could her? 'Twas always kept bolted 'ceptin' when I let Sir Bathy out," said Sukie.

"But all the zodiac people knew about it," said Fenella, "because. . . ." She met her great-aunt's compelling eye and did not finish the sentence.

"Come, now, Shurrock," said the superintendent, "it's no use you holding out on us. Do yourself a bit of good, man, and tell us what we want to know."

"I can't," said Shurrock doggedly. "I can't do nothing to help. I've lost my living and seems I've lost my liberty, and nothing won't bring them things back." He turned to Fenella. "A bad day it was for me when *you* first stepped into the *More to Come*," he said. "I suppose it was *you* as thought you'd spotted her ladyship up there in the lounge. I knew you meant trouble soon as I saw you, and I wish to the Lord I'd never tooken Mr Pardieu's money to keep you the night."

"I have never met Lady Bitton-Bittadon," said Fenella, "and it isn't my fault you're in trouble. I'd help you if I could, and I don't see why on earth you won't help yourself."

"But you *have* met Lady Bitton-Bittadon in a manner of speaking," said Callon. "That is, if Dame Beatrice is right, and she was Pisces."

"It is the merest guess that she was Pisces that night," admitted Dame Beatrice, "but when you mentioned her voice, Fenella, and that her headdress was in the form of a salmon, it occurred to me that the body of such a large fish could easily have concealed the policeman's truncheon which I think she purloined from the museum at the same time as she took the knife with which her husband was stabbed to death. An enquiry will readily establish when, and how often, Lady Bitton-Bittadon visited the folk museum, will it not?"

"You mean she's a murderess!" exclaimed Mrs Shurrock. "Then, Jem, we've got nothing to lose by telling what we know." She turned to Callon. "She *did* come here that night. She took Sir Jeremy's place by a special agreement with the others – or so she told me when she give me money to let her upstairs on the quiet with nobody knowing. I told Jem, of course, but nobody else knew – not Bob or Clytie or Sukie, I mean. Sir Jeremy *was* Pisces, only he was in India."

"So Sir Jeremy was a member of the band," said Dame Beatrice. "Our jig-saw puzzle begins to fall into place."

"I haven't charged you," said the superintendent to Shurrock, "and I'm willing to forget this little conversation if matters are settled to our satisfaction. I'll forget that you and Mrs Lee threw Sir Bathy over the wall; I'll forget how obstinate you've been about answering questions – *only*. . . ." he paused and looked straight at the ex-landlord. . . . "if I do, you'll have to answer one more question and answer it straight."

"Answer it to your liking, I suppose you mean," said Shurrock. "Well, that I don't promise to do, but go ahead."

"Where could the bodies of young Pitsey and two others – Clytie and Bob, I'm very sorry to say – where could they have been hidden away before they were put into the Bitton-Bittadon tomb?"

"Bob and poor little Clytie? – don't cry, Liz, my old dear! Well, I'll tell you. You know them tumble-down cottages opposite the *More to Come*? That would have been the handiest place, I reckon. Nobody go in there 'cepting maybe an old tramp, and us don't get many of that sort through the village. Nothing for 'em, you see. Nobody wouldn't think of lookin' in there. Been falling down for donkey's years, I reckon."

"But what about children playing hide-and-seek or cops and robbers?" suggested Fenella. Shurrock shrugged his shoulders. "Search *me*," he said. "Don't suppose they thought about that."

"I imagine young Pitsey was killed on Mayering Eve, after the bonfire-burial," said Dame Beatrice.

"He was killed before the other two, the doctor thinks," said Callon, "but the post-mortem will confirm it."

"But wouldn't he have been missed?" asked Fenella.

"He was a real bad lot, by all accounts," said the superintendent. "I reckon them as missed him were glad of it. Anyway, no enquiries came our way, so far as I know. What about Bob and Clytie, though? Did you really think they were going to blackmail you when you received that anonymous letter?"

"Didn't know what to think," said Shurrock. "Just set on getting away, and taking Sukie with us, her being a party to you know what, and that letter naming her as well as me."

"You mentioned that the knife had been left in Sir Bathy's body," said Dame Beatrice.

"Didn't think *we* was going to leave our prints on it, did you? Far as I know, it was still in the body when us chucked him over the wall."

"But it wasn't in the body when he was found," said the superintendent, "and it *was* returned to the museum." It looks as though whoever returned it took the policeman's truncheon and hasn't dared to put that back."

CHAPTER NINETEEN
The Lady Mother

"It is not that Lord Lindsay's heir
Tonight at Roslin leads the ball,
But that my lady mother there
Sits lonely in her castle hall."

Sir Walter Scott – *Rosabelle*

"Well, our immediate course seems clear," said Dame Beatrice, when the Shurrocks had been dismissed.

"We can't make an arrest on present evidence, ma'am," said the superintendent.

"We may be able to produce a little more. I think we must make sure that we know what happened about the knife with which Sir Bathy was killed."

"We made every enquiry about that, and the whole neighbourhood was searched," said Callon. "We impounded all the knives in the museum collection, at your suggestion, Dame Beatrice, so it was up to the forensic people to identify the one that was the murder weapon, and they haven't any doubt, as you know. Trouble is as there's no way of finding out who took it."

"Yes, we have to establish who returned it to the museum and who removed the ancient truncheon."

"The last person to ask for the key, barring yourself, ma'am, was Lady Bitton-Bittadon, and one of the truncheons is still missing," said the superintendent. "If she took it, she hasn't put it back. I shall obtain a search warrant and give the manor house another going-over, but I don't suppose we shall find it there, so the search for it may be a long one. Still, if we can pin the murder of Sir Bathy on his lady we shall get a conviction all right. All the same, I can't believe she bludgeoned two boys and that poor little Clytie. A truncheon isn't a woman's weapon and I can't see Lady Bitton-Bittadon using it."

"I think there is very little doubt she used it on the youth Pitsey, and it could have been used *on her behalf* to kill the other two, Superintendent."

"By whom, ma'am? Not by her stepson."

"Why not?"

150

"They're at daggers drawn. You said so yourself, if you remember, and what an uncomfortable house it seemed."

"Because a play was being acted there, and by actors who were on edge in case, in front of a stranger, they should fluff their lines. Far from Lady Bitton-Bittadon and Sir Jeremy being at daggers drawn, my impression is that they were carrying on a passionate and illicit love-affair. If we accept that as a starting-point, we shall go a long way towards understanding what has happened."

"How do you mean? The two of them plotted to put Sir Bathy out of the way?"

"Not the two of them. I do not believe that Sir Jeremy was as much at odds with his father as Lady Bitton-Bittadon would have us believe. I feel sure that his journey to India was genuinely undertaken and that Sir Bathy Bitton-Bittadon urged it. He probably told his son that certain conduct was causing malicious gossip and that it would be as well if he and his stepmother separated for a while. Sir Jeremy may even have wished to go. After all, there is a considerable difference in age between him and his stepmother, and he may already have become slightly tired of a woman who, although of gratifying beauty, is on the verge of middle age while he himself still ranks as a young man. Well, knowing that Sir Bathy had got rid of Jeremy temporarily, I think that Lady Bitton-Bittadon, now that he knew the truth, set to work to get rid of her husband permanently. I think she followed him one night – or possibly for several nights, so that she was sure of what his movements would be – and stabbed him when he left the *More to Come*. She had known for months, I think, that he kept a woman at the public house, and also who she was. Therefore (so her calculations probably went) if Sir Bathy was found stabbed and lying in the road outside the inn, the inference would be that Sukie, the gipsy, had killed him. Unfortunately, the whole thing had been seen, I think, by the lad Pitsey, who must have been with a girl in one of those ruinous cottages opposite the inn. Of course Lady Bitton-Bittadon had no idea of this at the time, and actually her first and possibly worst mistake was to anticipate the murder in a letter to Sir Jeremy in a frenzied bid to have him home again."

"Yes, but why did she write it?" asked Callon. "It seems incredible that any-body could be so foolish. When did you begin to suspect Lady Bitton-Bittadon, Dame Beatrice? Did you think of her from the very beginning?"

"No. My first suspicions were of Sir Jeremy himself. I wondered whether he had ever been to India at all, and it was in the hope of proving or disproving this that I agreed to go to the manor house. Then you, Fenella, mentioned that one of the zodiac people spoke in an educated voice, was a woman, and had made a curious slip of the tongue."

"You mean she'd forgotten that Sir Bathy wasn't there at the meeting?"

"No. She would not have forgotten that. I think she had not counted *herself*.

People sometimes do not, you know. It told me two things: first, that she was in a state of anxiety and, second, that she was not accustomed to making one of that particular company."

"Why did she join them?"

"I think she wanted to be in close touch with an anonymous blackmailer who (she probably guessed) was one of the zodiac people. It would not have been long before the uncouth, destructive, stupid youth Pitsey gave himself away to a woman of her intelligence. I can forgive her *his* death, but not for the murders of Bob and Clytie, whom she got Sir Jeremy to kill, I believe. Of course she was trying to guard against those things which are better (in a murderer's own interests) left alone. Once the murder scene appeared to have shifted from the *More to Come* to the manor house – it must have been a terrible shock to her when the body was discovered in the grounds – she decided that somebody had actually been a witness to the stabbing."

"Which, it seems, somebody had," said Fenella, "and the first anonymous letter she had from Pitsey proved it."

"Yes, as it happened, but if she had kept her head she need only have seen it as an attempt at blackmail which was almost certain to fail if it came to—"

"A show-down between a yobbo like Pitsey and the lady of the manor. Well, I still don't know whether we'd be justified in making an arrest," said the superintendent, "especially as there's the question of the other murders still hanging in the air. We shall have a job to pin those on Sir Jeremy."

"I agree. There is also the anonymous letter which was sent to Shurrock at the *More to Come*."

"Who sent it? You think it was the lad Pitsey, don't you?"

"Yes, the lad Pitsey. He had witnessed the murder of Sir Bathy, and had seen the subsequent reactions of Sukie and Shurrock. He blackmailed Lady Bitton-Bittadon. . . ."

"But the worm, meaning her ladyship, turned. It seems likely enough, when you begin to think about it, I suppose."

"Yes. She brought the truncheon to the zodiac meeting and used it after the ceremony on the hilltop in lieu of paying the blackmail money, I think. No doubt she and young Pitsey, who were both at the zodiac meeting, had an arrangement to meet in one of those ruined cottages when the ritual burial was over and the young people were chasing one another all over the hillside so that she could pay him the money."

"But she must have taken somebody else's place in the zodiac meeting," said Fenella, "mustn't she, not Sir Jeremy's. I mean, when Sir Jeremy went to India I don't think they would have left his place empty."

"If you make enquiries, I think you will find that Sukie had been made a member of the band by Sir Bathy when his son went to India. But when Sir Bathy was killed, Sukie was probably willing enough to yield her place in return for a small sum of money, never realising that Lady Bitton-Bittadon was Sir Bathy's killer."

"But wouldn't Leo and the others have objected? He, in particular, seemed a very tough character," said Fenella, "and Lady Bitton-Bittadon wasn't born un-der Pisces, anyway. She had a birthday in September. Nick's school had a half-holiday for it every year."

"I doubt whether they were aware of the substitution. It was only for that one meeting, I feel sure," said Dame Beatrice.

"But the voice! Wouldn't *that* have given her away?"

"I doubt whether they had ever heard Sukie, as Pisces, utter. She never came into the bar, but always remained in the kitchen. Also, you must remember, they had serious business in front of them that night – business which you yourself interrupted."

"You mean how they were to provide themselves with more skeletons."

"Exactly. And Lady Bitton-Bittadon did not speak until you had entered the room and distracted everyone's thoughts. Well, Superintendent, I think my next move is to visit the manor house again."

"Not alone, Dame Beatrice. I have to get a search-warrant, but Mr Callon, I am sure, will wish to go with you if your intention is to confront Lady Bitton-Bittadon with your findings."

"I think it right to give her the chance to refute them."

"Or to force a confession from her," said Callon, with a slight smile. "Well, I shall certainly be in the offing, Dame Beatrice. If her ladyship has committed two murders and instigated two others – Sir Jeremy, you say, killed the girl Clytie and the lad Bob. . . ."

"I imagine so. Pitsey and Bob were friends, and Clytie was involved through Bob, who was her fiancé. No doubt Pitsey had informed Lady Bitton-Bittadon that he was not the only person who was aware of what she had done, and she prevailed upon Sir Jeremy to silence the other two for her sake."

Arrived at the manor house, Dame Beatrice did not beat about the bush, al-though Lady Bitton-Bittadon received her with what struck Dame Beatrice as relief.

"I've been expecting you," she said. "Is there any news?"

"On the contrary," said Dame Beatrice, "I have come to you for information and before I put my questions I should wish to make it clear that I neither expect nor desire you to answer them if you consider that they border on the personal. They are about your son and his visit to India."

"Jeremy is not my son. He is the son of his father by his first wife. I thought you understood that."

"I did understand it, of course. You do not seem old enough to have a son of Sir Jeremy's age."

"I am forty-one. Jeremy is thirty."

"As he is not your son, my questions may not surprise or wound you."

"Wound me? Nothing in connection with that young man could upset me emotionally in any way. What do you want to know."

"You did not write to him while he was in India?"

"Only at the very end. He had to know about his father's death."

"And he did not write to you, or communicate with you in any way?"

"Certainly not. I did not expect or wish it. It was a relief when he took himself off. We had nothing in common and I think he always resented me. Stepmothers tread an uneasy, thankless path, Dame Beatrice. If I had known Jeremy when he was a very young child, it might have been different, but he was twenty years old when I married his father and from the very beginning he was antagonistic to me."

"How soon after his mother's death did you marry his father?"

"Oh, she died when Jeremy was fourteen, just the age when a boy begins to get sentimental about his mother and to think of her as a woman, if you know what I mean. When I married it was not too difficult, because Jeremy was at college and spent the vacation travelling or with reading-parties. It was only after he left college that I realised how difficult it was all going to be."

"How did he get on with his father?"

"Not at all well at that stage. I knew this hurt Bathy very much, because, apparently, up to the time of our marriage, Bathy and Jeremy seem to have been on particularly friendly terms. Jeremy never forgave his father for marrying again. Goodness knows we both did our best to placate him, but he wouldn't come round and I think the situation soured on him, and year by year the relationship between him and his father deteriorated. I could watch it happening. It was dreadful."

"I suppose – and this is the crux of the matter – I suppose Sir Jeremy did go to India?"

"Go to India? Why, of course he did!"

"You have no proof of it, though, have you?"

"But all his kit! All the money he was given for travel and special equipment! Besides, his father went with him to the airport to see him off. What are you saying?"

"I am not saying anything. I am merely enquiring. Did his father hear from him while he was away?"

"No, he didn't, but, as I told you, relations between them had become more and more strained as time went on. Jeremy was annoyed that his father even wanted to go with him to the airport to see him off, but he needed the car to get himself and his belongings to the airport, and that meant that his father had to go with him to bring back the car. That is how it came about that Bathy saw him off. He would not have expected to hear from him, although I know he went to some trouble to find out whether the plane had landed safely. After that, the next

I knew was that, in answer to my letter, Jeremy came home but was, unfortunately, too late for the funeral."

"Where is he now?"

"In London, I believe. He left here some days ago and I have no address. But what makes you think he may not have gone to India after all?"

"He seems to have received notification of your husband's death before Sir Bathy actually died."

"From the murderer? That seems incredible. Besides, it does not prove that Jeremy was not in India at the time. And who told you that Jeremy had received this extraordinary notification? It could not have been Jeremy himself."

"Why do you say that? No doubt, whatever their relationship was, and however much it had deteriorated, Sir Jeremy must have taken some interest in his father's death, particularly as it was a violent one."

"Oh, perhaps. I mean, I suppose so."

"Why does Sir Jeremy climb trees?"

"Climb trees?"

"And drop out of them on the wrong side of the wall, thus alarming young women who may be taking a quiet stroll up the hill?"

"As though I would have any idea! I believe his mother was considered eccentric, if that is anything to go by."

"Sir Jeremy appears to have behaved very strangely, it seems to me. He goes to India and is there when his father is murdered; he learns of his father's death before it actually takes place; he then finds out that the body was discovered in the grounds here, but that the knife with which he was stabbed is missing. I wonder how he knew the knife was missing, and why he thought it important that it should be found. By the way, did Sir Jeremy often visit his uncle here?"

"As a boy I believe he came here to school and boarded with his uncle and joined his father for the holidays," said Lady Bitton-Bittadon, looking relieved by the change of subject.

"And his uncle was interested, I believe, in the local folklore."

"I don't know to what extent, but I believe he founded a kind of secret society in the village. Bathy was invited to join it when we came to live here." There was no doubt now that for Lady Bitton-Bittadon the tension was eased.

"Indeed? I believe I heard something of the kind. That would be the zodiac people, no doubt."

"I suppose so, if that is what they call themselves."

"And *did* Sir Bathy join them?"

"I have no idea. He spent a good deal of his time at the *More to Come*, which I believe was a kind of headquarters, but I think he went there only to drink in a convivial, neighbourly sort of way with the villagers. He was a very gregarious man, but had little use for the sort of people one might have expected him to like. I believe he dropped out of things when his first wife died. I could hardly ever persuade him to meet people of our own standing."

"I see. Do you know whether Sir Jeremy was ever invited to join the zodiac society?"

"I really have no idea. He would have been too young, I think, when he used to live here with his uncle, and I'm afraid I know nothing of his interests nowadays."

"All the same, I expect the society does accept young men."

"Why do you say that?"

"It would seem reasonable that they should, if only because a tradition, if it is to be carried on, depends upon the training of the young in order that they may grow up to take the places of the old, otherwise the tradition would die out."

"If this zodiac society, as you call it, is supposed to be secret, how do you come to know anything about it?"

"Perhaps you can guess the answer to that question."

"No, I cannot, I'm afraid, unless one of the members has taken you into his confidence."

"And you think that would be unlikely?"

"Well, you are a stranger in the place, are you not? And the village does not much care for strangers, especially strangers who work with the police. I believe there has been some talk about your activities already. I hope you have not set the villagers against you. You know what these rural communities can be like."

"Perhaps the one in which I live is different from this one."

"In what way?"

"More agreeable and less prejudiced, let us say."

"You are fortunate. And now, Dame Beatrice, let us put our cards on the table. All these questions about Jeremy and his going to India are leading up to something. What is it?"

"I was wondering whether you thought he might have killed his father," said Dame Beatrice, with the devastating frankness which sometimes conceals a lie, as, in this case, it did.

"Jeremy? Good heavens! You can't be serious!"

"Well, *somebody* murdered Sir Bathy, and it is common knowledge, based on statistics, that the likeliest suspects are the members of the murdered person's own family."

"But the motive! What possible motive could Jeremy have had? I grant you that he is anathema to me, but – a *murderer*? The idea is ludicrous! What could he possibly have to gain? The title, such as it is, means nothing to him, or the estate either. He is rolling in money and although, since our marriage, he did not get on with his father, their relationship had certainly not soured to the extent which you suggest."

"I am relieved to hear you say so."

"You did not seriously suspect him, did you?"

"One was inclined to look at the matter from all angles. Did you know that your husband's family tomb has again been desecrated?"

"By these vandals?"

"By the zodiac people – or so we are inclined to think. Alien bodies were placed on the shelves of the vault in place of the skeltons which had been removed."

"Really? What an extraordinary thing!"

"Now that the inquest on them is over, they will lie in the churchyard again, but in another and a consecrated spot."

"Consecrated? – Oh, yes, of course! I see what you mean. The Bitton-Bittadon tomb is not part of the churchyard, is it? But where did the bodies come from?"

"I had hoped that you might have read the report of the inquest, because I was going to put the same question to you."

"But why should I know anything about them?"

"I can hardly say. They certainly seem to be no concern of yours. They have been identified as those of a youth named Pitsey, and the young man and girl who were in service at the *More to come*."

"But I thought – I mean, aren't the innkeeper and his people supposed to be on holiday or something?"

"The two young people I have mentioned are certainly not on holiday, unless one regards death itself as a holiday. It may be, for some people, of course. Suicides appear to be under that impression, if to be on holiday means (in the popular phrase) to get away from it all."

"But I don't understand. Do you really mean to tell me that these three people have been murdered, just as poor Bathy was?"

"Well, not precisely as Sir Bathy was. He was stabbed to death; these three had been struck on the head. Did you not read the report of the inquest?"

"I never read the papers."

"Oh, I thought you might have been particularly interested in these deaths."

"Why so? Villagers' brawls do not concern me."

"Why did you not return the truncheon to the folk museum, I wonder?"

"Return the. . . . What on earth do you mean?"

"Well," said Dame Beatrice in a reasonable tone, "you returned the knife. Is that when you collected the truncheon? I suppose young Pitsey had begun to blackmail you. I do not blame you in the least for relieving yourself of such a menace. Blackmail is a peculiarly detestable crime. But it was cruel and unnecessary to kill the other two young things."

"I didn't kill them! I have never killed anybody! What an utterly ridiculous idea!"

"Then why was Pitsey murdered, and where is the truncheon? Do you realise that the police are applying for a search-warrant and already have a representative on these premises?"

"Oh, have they?" said Lady Bitton-Bittadon. "How interesting! As for the truncheon, I suppose Jeremy may know where it is. I believe he borrowed it, but he's gone to London. In any case, he only took it for a fancy dress party in Town."

"Why did you notify him of his father's death before it happened?"

"Oh, you keep harping on that, do you? How should *I* know that his father was going to be killed? Answer me *that*, if you dare."

"And why did he go to India?"

"Ask yourself, and tell yourself the answer."

"Very well. I think he had grown tired of you."

"*What!*" The woman facing Dame Beatrice suddenly shed the veneer of half-amusement, half-boredom with which she had treated the interview so far. "Never! Never! If he was tired of me, why did he come flying back from India? Why did he kill for my sake? Why did he shut the mouths of those idiotic villagers by letting them have their wretched skeletons so that we could get rid of those three horrible young bodies? Why . . ."

"I think we'll have all the answers down at the station," said Callon, coming into the room. He caught Lady Bitton-Bittadon as she fainted. "She's a lost soul," he said.

"Nobody is that," said Dame Beatrice, "and we've still to *prove* she killed Sir Bathy, you know, and also young Pitsey, who was blackmailing her."

"She's given Sir Jeremy away, though. We'll get 'em both, I think, ma'am, thanks to you."

THE END

About the Rue Morgue Press

"Rue Morgue Press is the old-mystery lover's best friend, reprinting high quality books from the 1930s and '40s."
— *Ellery Queen's Mystery Magazine*

Since 1997, the Rue Morgue Press has reprinted scores of traditional mysteries, the kind of books that were the hallmark of the Golden Age of detective fiction. Authors reprinted or to be reprinted by the Rue Morgue include Catherine Aird, Delano Ames, H. C. Bailey, Morris Bishop, Nicholas Blake, Dorothy Bowers, Pamela Branch, Joanna Cannan, John Dickson Carr, Glyn Carr, Torrey Chanslor, Clyde B. Clason, Joan Coggin, Manning Coles, Lucy Cores, Frances Crane, Norbert Davis, Elizabeth Dean, Carter Dickson, Eilis Dillon, Michael Gilbert, Constance & Gwenyth Little, Marlys Millhiser, Gladys Mitchell, Patricia Moyes, James Norman, Stuart Palmer, Craig Rice, Kelley Roos, Charlotte Murray Russell, Maureen Sarsfield, Margaret Scherf, Juanita Sheridan and Colin Watson..

To suggest titles or to receive a catalog of Rue Morgue Press books write 87 Lone Tree Lane, Lyons, CO 80540, telephone 800-699-6214, or check out our website, www.ruemorguepress.com, which lists complete descriptions of all of our titles, along with lengthy biographies of our writers.